Waiting For You

Cora Rose

Credits

Editor: Angela O'Connell
Cover: Ari Basulto

To my editor Angela O'Connell. You always tell me the things that are hard to hear, but end up making my story better. The parrot was for you.

Preface

I set this aside so many times, but they just wouldn't be quiet. So here you go. I hope you enjoy their story.

Chapter One

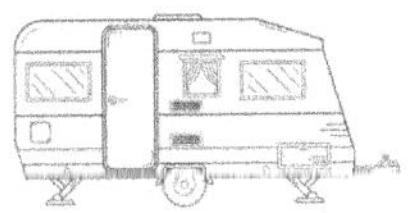

Grey

"Hey, Grey," a voice says right next to me, and I jolt, knocking my head against the trailer's outside compartment I'm packing. Goddammit, that hurts. If I keep this up, I'm going to have a concussion. This isn't the first time I've knocked my head while loading this camper up—or smashed my fingers in cabinets. I glance down at my black and blue thumbnail in frustration.

What's next? My toes? My legs? My balls?

The things I do just to get to spend a little time with my kid.

"Shit, Quinn," I mutter, rubbing the back of my head while taking in my son's best friend. He's leaning against the side of the trailer, some of his dark brown hair slipping from his ponytail and falling against his shoulders, his dusky green eyes meeting mine. He has a slight flush on his cheeks, made more evident by his pale skin, and if I look really closely, I can see a smattering of freckles just across the bridge of his nose. The nose that has some kind of piercing in the front. Septum piercing, I think it's called. Looks like it was painful. I don't think I could manage having a needle pushed through my skin. I don't even have any tattoos.

But then again, Quinn is young—free and adventurous—so unlike me.

He probably doesn't scream at the sight of needles.

I'm a screamer.

I glance down at his faded blue jeans and gray t-shirt, his clothes smudged with clay. His hands are white around the knuckles. Ah, so he must have been working in the art studio again. I know that in the fall he's planning to go to college and major in art. Quinn is a sculptor.

I've never seen his pieces, but Joshua, my son, says he's really talented. When he talks to me, that is. Which is rare. Right now we communicate via text. Usually, it's me texting Joshua and him ignoring me.

Sometimes I go out into the backyard and try to telepathically communicate with him. Try to send up good vibes. Usually when I've been drinking.

Doesn't work too well. Probably my ex blocking them with her negativity.

Go away, good vibes. We like misery and anger here.

"Where's Josh?" I ask, my eyes scanning the distance, waiting to see my son stride up. He and I are supposed to be leaving on a trip in a few hours, and he should be here any minute. Quinn and Joshua are connected at the hip. Well, at least I think they still are. Now that Joshua has a girlfriend, he comes around even less, and I wonder if it's also affected his relationship with his best friend.

I haven't seen Quinn much lately, actually. So maybe it has.

Quinn fiddles with the silver hoop earrings in his left ear and shifts on his feet.

"Um, Josh is with Hailey."

I put my hands on my hips and sigh. I'm not surprised. Since they started dating a few months ago, Hailey has consumed my son's time. Young love and all that. I'm surprised he even agreed to go on this trip with me in the first place. I glance at Quinn again, and he looks uneasy, like he has a secret, something he wants to say but can't quite bring himself to.

Oh. *Oh shit.*

"What's that look for?" I ask, suddenly feeling so old. And tired.

Quinn stands up straight and takes a step toward me, the scent of him traveling across the space between us.

Clay and earth and pine.

"He's not coming, Grey."

My eyebrows meet and my heart stutters in my chest. I mean, Joshua and I aren't that close—we never were, despite my best attempts—because Karen and I were young when we had him, and I was so far in the closet that I didn't think I'd ever come out. But I eventually gathered the courage, and after years of trying to make it work between us, we realized we were just two kids struggling with being teenage parents. While I loved her, I wasn't in love with her. I could never be. How it ended between us years ago seems to have only made her angrier.

She's always so mad at me.

In the end, I was forced to walk away, and Joshua was raised primarily by his mother. Out of spite, she made sure I got very limited time with him.

Very little as in maybe once a month. I tried fighting, but she had the time, funds, and determination to stop me. So after years of losing, I just decided it was best to roll over and accept it.

But this was supposed to be *our* trip, our time to reconnect before he goes off to college in a few weeks in a different state. So very far away.

I pull my phone out and glance down at the message sitting there.

JOSHUA:

Sorry, Dad. Not going to be able to make it.

Well, at least there's an apology. Still, my heart cracks and sinks. I had our trip through the UP—the upper peninsula of Michigan—all planned out. I know no seventeen-year-old wants to spend time alone with their parent, but I even bought a travel guide to make sure this would be fun and exciting. I didn't want to disappoint him, didn't want him resenting the few moments he spent with me.

But it was all for nothing.

This trailer I rented and my truck with a full tank of gas

are going to be hauling my sorry ass around the UP—without him.

I'm going to spend the next two weeks alone—with my regrets.

Maybe I should get a dog so I'm not so lonely. We could have adventures. We'd be like *Turner and Hooch,* only doesn't the dog die in the end?

Maybe not then. I'd cry like a baby. Maybe I'll get a tortoise. Those live for ages.

"He wants to spend his last few weeks with Hailey," Quinn says, sounding apologetic.

He has nothing to apologize for. This is not his fault. He's just a kid.

"It's fine," I say, closing the compartment and eyeing my son's best friend, the guy who made an appearance when my son didn't. But Quinn often seems to do that—showing up unexpectedly.

This isn't the first time he's come by my place without Joshua.

I think he feels sorry for me. I don't blame him. I'm just a little bit pathetic.

"It's fine," I say again, swallowing roughly. "No biggie."

Quinn takes a step toward me, those lips of his pulled between his teeth.

"It is, Grey. It's a shitty thing for Josh to do..."

I shove my hands in my pockets and roll back on my heels, feeling my eyes sting. How does this guy get me so well when he's so much younger? He's always looked so intently at me, like he's peering into my soul...like he knows things about me that maybe I don't even know about myself.

"Look, what if...what if I go with you?"

My eyes snap to his, and he holds up his hands, shrugging. Like, no big deal, I'll just tag along on your two-week trip. "I have nothing else to do. It'll be fun."

"Shit, Quinn. I can't just tote you around Michigan without your parents knowing. You're still a minor."

He scoffs. "I'm nineteen."

"Yeah, but still...your parents. What would they think?"

I'm thirty-three years old, for fuck's sake. Yes, I'm an adult and capable of taking care of him along the way, but I'm a gay man. What would people think if they saw me gallivanting around with a kid half my age? Living and sleeping in close quarters? It would border on Creepsville. And no one likes Creepsville.

"You've met my parents, right?" He huffs a laugh, and when I only raise my eyebrow, he pulls his phone out and then dials a number. I listen to the ringing on speakerphone, and then a minute later his father answers.

"Heyo. What's up, son," his dad says, sounding...preoccupied.

"Hey, Pops, can I go on a trip with Joshua's dad through the UP for two weeks?"

"Why are you asking me? You can make those decisions. You're an adult."

"Eh, he wanted to be sure it was fine..." Quinn says, his eyes meeting mine and a smirk pulling those red lips up.

"Well, no need to ask me. You do what you want. Just make sure you two have fun."

Well, shit. I knew Quinn was independent, but I didn't realize that the reason for that was because his parents gave him free rein. He's always been...mature. More mature than Joshua, that's for sure. I always wondered how the two of them became friends...and then stayed friends. Quinn always seemed to be the one picking up the pieces.

And now here he was, picking up mine.

"Cool, Dad. I'll keep in touch."

"Sounds good, bud."

Quinn hangs up, shoves his phone into his pocket, and then shuffles on his feet.

"See?"

I run a hand across the back of my neck, not quite sure what to do. I mean, really. What the hell do I do?

Quinn tugs on his earrings again. "We could swing by my parents' and I can grab some shit."

I glance at him, and he smiles softly at me. My heart flutters in my chest. Stupid coffee, making me all jittery.

"Are you...are you sure? You want to spend two weeks...with *me*?"

Because my own son doesn't even want to do this. Why the hell would Quinn? I barely know this guy. Don't teenagers want to spend time with their own kind? I'm like a dinosaur compared to him.

But Quinn isn't bothered. No, he just shrugs again, like it's no big deal, and then takes another step toward me.

"Yeah, Grey. I think I'd really fucking like that."

* * *

"So, you two are going to the UP," his mom states as Quinn walks to his room to pack, leaving me to chat with this woman who seems completely unconcerned that her son is going on a trip with me.

I mean, not to parent-shame, but I'm pretty sure I wouldn't be comfortable with Joshua going on a trip with an older man for two weeks. Especially one I didn't really know all that well. Not that Joshua would listen to me. And not that Karen would either. She'd probably let him go just to spite me.

"Yeah, if that's alright with you?"

"Quinn can make his own decisions. He's always been an old soul like that."

I let out a huff because yeah, I've noticed that about him. Two years ago, when Joshua had blown me off on my birthday to go to a party, Quinn had shown up at my place with a pizza and two cupcakes.

"Why are you here and not with Josh?" I'd asked.

"Meh, I'd rather sit here with you."

We ate that pizza on the front porch because I was too afraid to let him inside. Of what that might look like to the outside world.

But that moment in time wasn't anything but a lonely old guy and his kid's best friend taking pity on him. The two of us watched the sunset and sat in companionable silence until he left.

It had made the abandonment I felt from Joshua a little easier.

And yet still, I worried for weeks about his parents coming after me or accusing me of something, despite doing nothing wrong. But they never brought it up. I wonder if Quinn ever told them.

Probably not. It seems like he's free-range and has been for quite some time.

It also seems like his parents have no issue with Quinn going camping with me for two weeks.

Shit, they know I'm gay, right?

"I'm sorry. I heard about what happened with Kevin," his mom, Catherine, says.

I shift on my feet, feeling awkward because how the hell does she know that? It's a small town, but it's not *that* small.

"Quinn told us. Said you were pretty upset about the breakup."

Well, yes, I was. For a few days. And then I realized I didn't miss Kevin all that much. I more so missed the *idea* of him. He filled the empty spaces of my life easily, but the truth is, I'd never loved him.

And to be honest, the sex was subpar. Passable, but not really enjoyable.

"I'm fine," I say, not quite sure what to say to her.

"Well, Quinn talks about you all the time," she goes on. "Really looks up to you."

Huh. I don't see why. I glance down at my worn work boots and my faded, loose jeans. I rub at my black t-shirt with some lingering script lining the front. Well, I could probably dress nicer, but I don't really care much to change. And I'm decent-looking, I guess, with dark-brown hair shaved close to my head and stubble lining my jaw. My work as a delivery driver has me moving often and lifting heavy things so I've always been in shape, but as an entire package, I sure as shit don't think I'm anything to aspire to.

Shit, I never even went to college. In fact, if there was

ever a bad decision to be made out there, I'm pretty sure I've made it.

"Mama, really," Quinn says, moving into the hallway, his hands clasping a duffle bag, a pillow, and a sleeping bag. "Stop telling him my secrets."

His mom laughs and pulls him into a hug, kissing his temple.

"Well, that's no fun."

Quinn pulls away and I reach out, grabbing his duffle bag, and then I can't help but ask once more. Just to be sure.

"You're sure it's fine?" I ask, needing reassurance.

"One hundred percent," his mom says, and Quinn eyes me quietly.

"Well, you two have fun. Send me pictures if you remember."

"Yeah, I will," Quinn replies as the two of us are making our way outside, the humid breeze hitting me almost immediately.

"Josh is an idiot," Quinn says when we reach the truck.

I look over at him and shake my head. "No, he's just young and trying to live his life. Plus, his mom tells him a lot of not-so-good and very untrue things about me. I don't blame him for the way he thinks," I say, and Quinn rubs at his chest.

"Yeah, well, he's missing out. I'm just sayin'," he replies as I toss his things into the back seat of the cab and then walk around and slide into the driver's side.

As soon as the engine rumbles on, I turn to look at my son's best friend and my heart thumps awkwardly in my chest.

"Ready?" I ask, wanting to give him a final out, just in case.

"Hell, yeah, Grey. I'm fucking ready."

I eye him, those high cheekbones, those red lips, those dark lashes, and then force my gaze back to the road.

Yeah, okay, here we fucking go.

Chapter Two

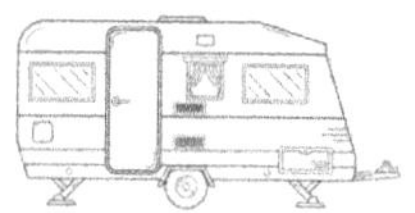

Grey

As soon as we hit the highway, Quinn is fiddling with the truck's stereo system, connecting his phone via Bluetooth, and minutes later, soft music floats through the speakers.

"You like this kind of stuff?" he asks, peering over at me, his phone spinning in his hands. Those knuckles of his are still caked with clay, and I wonder if it's just permanent. Like, no matter how much he washes, he can never remove his art from his skin.

It's a part of him.

"It's cool."

"I know you like country. I can pull up a playlist if you want," he says, and I shake my head.

"Nope, this works. Really."

He spins his phone some more and then leans back,

reaching for his duffle bag. His shirt rides up, showing a fraction of his waist and a tattoo there.

"You have tattoos?" I blurt.

"Yeah, designed them myself a couple years ago," he says as he rustles around in his bag and then sits back in his seat, a sketchpad in his lap and a pencil in his hand. I wonder if his parents knowingly let him get those too. Did they go with him? Probably. I bet they signed the waivers themselves. He didn't even have to forge them.

"I'll show you when we have a chance."

"Oh, that's okay, I don't need to see them," I say, and Quinn taps the pencil on his sketchbook.

"Nah, I'd like to show you."

I swallow and nod. Yeah, cool. It doesn't need to be weird. I'm making it weird. I have a way of doing that. Probably one of the many reasons Joshua has avoided me over the years. I embarrass him. I know it.

Speaking of, I glance down at my phone and see the texts I sent Joshua after Quinn invited himself on this trip.

I mean, they're friends first. I'd never want to make things worse between us. Or between them.

ME:

> Quinn is going to come with me since you can't make it. Is that okay?

JOSHUA:

> Yeah, you guys have fun.

ME:

I'll let you know where we are if you
and Hailey want to come and
hang out.

JOSHUA:

Sounds good, Dad.

And that was that. He hasn't texted me since. Probably too consumed with his girlfriend.

Young love, I guess. I never really had that. I spent most of my teens and twenties fighting with Karen, and then there were some casual hookups after we broke up. And then came Kevin.

I've been unimpressed with my dating history thus far, and I don't think it's looking up anytime soon.

Maybe I'll meet a hot older man on this trip and find a few seconds of satisfaction in a truck-stop bathroom.

Here's hoping.

"Can I sketch you?" Quinn asks, breaking me out of my thoughts.

I glance over at him, feeling a little...shocked, I guess. I mean, why the fuck would he want to sketch me? I run a hand across my buzzed head and shrug.

"Um, sure, I guess."

"Full disclosure, I've sketched you before. You're my muse."

My heart stops beating at that little tidbit.

"What? Why?"

"Dunno," he says, biting down on the end of the charcoal

pencil and flipping his sketchbook open. "Just saw you, and bam...inspiration hit."

I don't know what to say about that. That's weird, right? And a little inappropriate.

Is that why he's always watched me so intently over the years? Was he memorizing me to...draw me?

I glance over at him and see his bottom lip pulled between his teeth, his head cocked slightly toward his lap, and his hand moving over the paper. Long slashes of black on crisp white paper.

Shit. A muse? Me?

How did I manage that?

He has to be mistaken, but then again, he seems laser-focused, his eyes flitting from me to the paper and back again.

And what do I really know about art? Shit all, is what.

Maybe he can teach you something new.

"You ah...do you want to stop and grab a snack?" I ask, shifting in my seat. I don't know how to be a muse or what to do while someone draws me.

It's making me nervous. They need a how-to book for this shit or something.

The scratching of the pencil stops, and Quinn eyes me. "We just got on the road."

"Yeah, well..." I squirm a little. "Just wasn't sure if you were hungry."

He lets out a low chuckle, and I tighten my grip on the steering wheel. "You don't need to be nervous, Grey. You're perfection."

"Shit," I mutter, because what the fuck is that? What the hell does that mean? He can't say stuff like that to me.

I should turn this truck around and drive him home.

"Quinn, you can't say stuff like that."

He shrugs and goes back to sketching, and I squirm in my seat a little more, feeling jittery and...confused.

I'm a muse now, and he thinks I'm perfect. I don't think I've ever been either of those things.

"I need coffee," I say thirty minutes later when I can't stand it anymore. I need something in my mouth and in my hands.

Now, that sounds dirty.

There goes my mind—off the rails.

I pull off the highway a few minutes later and park on the street, shutting off the ignition and hopping out of the truck.

I'll grab some snacks, a shitload to keep me occupied, and something to drink. Hopefully, they have those extra-large cups that are the size of my forearm.

"Hey," Quinn says, jogging up next to me, his cheeks flushed slightly. "Wait up. I had to grab my wallet."

"I got it," I say, and he shakes his head.

"No, you're not my sugar daddy," he replies, and I just flush from head to toe.

Oh my god.

"Quinn," I warn, using my best dad voice, which isn't much of one, to be honest. I never really had to use it all that much.

"Sorry," he says with a small laugh. "I couldn't help myself. You're much older than me and now you're offering to buy me shit. You have to admit, it tracks."

I peek over at him and my lips twitch. "Fuck off."

He nudges me with his arm and then leaves it there, our

skin brushing as we walk. His is much smoother than mine. For just a moment, I wonder if his entire body is like that, before discarding it.

Hell no. Not going there.

Even if he is...pretty. Like a young Johnny Depp. I would have crushed so hard on him if he was around when I was a teen. Hell, if he'd been around back then, maybe Karen and I never would have messed around.

But then there'd be no Joshua.

I might have fucked up with her, but I don't regret it one bit. I'd do it all over again just to have Joshua, to be his dad.

I open the door to the convenience store for Quinn, and he strides through, those long legs eating up the linoleum floor as he moves straight to the candy aisle.

I wrench my eyes away from him and make my way toward the coffee. I groan in near relief when I see the selection. Thank god for caffeine. Now I can be anxious *and* have a palpitating heart at the same time.

Win-win.

After I've filled up an extra-large coffee cup, I move to the food aisle to pick out a few snacks, something that will keep my fingers and mouth busy for the next few hours as we chug upstate to the Mackinac Bridge and over to St. Ignace.

When we're back in the truck, Quinn buckles in and leans back, popping open a bag of M&Ms.

"Want some?" he asks as I pull us back onto the highway.

"Nope, got my own stuff," I say, sipping on my coffee.

Quinn sighs, resting his head back against the headrest. More of his hair has fallen out of its elastic and I wonder why he even bothers to pull it back.

It would look good splayed over his shoulders.

In an objective way, not a creepy way.

For fuck's sake.

"So, what's the plan once we get to St. Ignace?"

"We can set up camp, detach the trailer, and drive around? Grab dinner?"

Quinn tosses some more M&Ms in his mouth. "Sounds good..." he says, glancing out at the passing scenery. "You have an itinerary? Joshua mentioned something about it."

He did? Shit, I didn't think he was listening when I'd rattled that info off.

"Yeah, I bought a book. It's on my phone."

He reaches for it, holding it in his palm. "Passcode?"

I give it to him, because really, what do I have to hide?

Nothing, that's what.

"Just like that?" he asks. "You're not worried I'll find filthy pictures on here, secret drug deals, something not for my eyes?"

"Nope," I say as he chuckles, swiping around on my phone.

"It's in the Kindle app," I tell him, and Quinn peeks over at me.

"Yeah, I figured. I'm just snooping."

"Yeah, well, snoop away. Nothing exciting."

"Huh, well, how disappointing. No naked pictures, but you do have Grindr on here."

Oh shit, I forgot about that. Kind of embarrassing that I kept it, actually. "Hasn't been used in a long while."

"Any reason why?" he asks. And honestly, what am I doing talking to him about this shit? He's nineteen, for fuck's sake. Although most of the time, he doesn't act his age, which is a little...disconcerting.

"Quinn, that's not something I'd share with you."

"Why not?" he asks, looking genuinely confused. Like he has older men tell him secrets all the time.

Fuck, maybe he does. I don't really know much about Quinn.

"You're Joshua's best friend. And you're young."

"So?"

"So..." I run a hand over my head and then plop it right back down on the steering wheel. "So, it feels weird."

"We can be friends, Grey," he replies. "And I'm bi, so I get it."

I freeze, like full-on turn into a statue. I don't even think I could move if I tried. Because since when is Quinn bisexual? Why didn't I know this?

"How long have you known?" I mutter.

"Since..." he wets his mouth. "Well, since always."

Well, shit, for some reason that changes things. Why does that change things?

"So, I'm just saying that a guy like you.... You'd get a lot of hits. I'd message you."

"Oh, shut up," I mutter, feeling my cheeks turn red. "Stop it. You can't say stuff like that."

"Why? It's true," he replies with a wide smile. "You're hot. Like...really hot."

I choke a little and turn my focus back to the road before I swerve off of it.

"Stop teasing me."

"No teasing here. Cross my heart and hope to die. You're like..."

"Do *not* finish that sentence," I snap, trying to regain my composure and Quinn laughs lowly. "Just draw some more things or something. I...I need to focus on driving."

And not focus on the fact that I'm on a two-week road trip with my son's best friend who happens to look like a young Johnny Depp and is bisexual *and* thinks I'm hot!

Holy fuck.

See. *See!*

I never met a bad decision I didn't like.

Most of the time those bad decisions happen upon me without warning. Like right now. I never mean for these things to happen, they just do.

"Chill, Grey. I'm not going to like, hit on you," he says and then flips his sketch pad open. "But I may ogle you from a distance. You're my muse, after all."

He snorts a small laugh and I reach over and nudge him, my hand pressing against his shoulder.

"Knock it off, brat."

His bottom lip is pulled between his teeth and he peeks over at me.

Fuck, fuck. Look at him.

Don't fucking look at him.

"Kevin was an idiot," he says softly.

I avert my eyes.

"You need to find someone who will appreciate you."

I keep my gaze on the road. I will not look at him right now. Will not.

"Yeah, I know that."

We're silent once more, the only sounds the scratch of his pencil on paper and the soft music floating through the speakers.

When we approach Mackinac Bridge, one of the longest in the world and one that spans the space between the Upper and Lower Peninsulas of Michigan, Quinn shuts his notebook and sits up a little straighter.

"So fucking cool," he says, smiling over at me. "Joshua is so missing out."

My heart warms at that and I bob my head. "Yeah, he is. But I don't blame him. Don't hold it against him."

"Nah, I mean, I get it. Hailey is cool, but I'm kind of glad he bailed."

What the hell does that mean? I want to ask, but the words get stuck in my throat as I drive the five miles across the bridge. And when we pass over to the other side, I position my phone so I can see the directions to the campground.

"So, I thought we'd stay in St. Ignace for a few days and then head on over to Tahquamenon Falls."

"Yeah, I like that idea," he says.

Well, that was easy. But then again, things with Quinn are always easy. He never really makes a fuss and seems to just go with the flow. He's always been able to calm my son's teenage tantrums, the mild-mannered voice of reason. Things always seem better when Quinn is around.

When we finally pull into the state campground, I pay the fee and find our space, backing the camper into the spot. Then Quinn hops out and helps me level it.

God, he's helpful. We're almost like a team.

A rumble of thunder and a flash of light in the distance

signals an oncoming storm. The weather in Michigan changes as quickly as the tides, but still, the thought of rain has me rushing to get everything done before we head out to explore.

Michigan summers have long-drawn-out days with the sun setting around ten in the evening, so we have hours before we need to be back and in bed.

In bed.

We're going to share a small space, just the two of us. He's spent the night with Joshua a few times over the past four years, but they were so few and far between that I honestly don't remember them.

I wonder if he brought pajamas. God, I hope so.

Shit, I didn't consider any of this when I agreed to him coming on this trip with me. I never think things through.

"Want to do Castle Rock and then dinner?" I manage to ask, pulling the truck onto the main road and heading toward our destination.

Quinn nods. "Yeah, Grey. I'll do anything you have planned. I'm just along for the ride."

But I mean, the guy has to have opinions, right? Or maybe he really doesn't care.

"I'd like you to look up things you'd be interested in doing and tell me what you'd like to see. This trip isn't just about me."

He eyes me and then nods. "Yeah, okay. Sounds good."

He fiddles with the radio until we finally pull up to Castle Rock, a scenic point that you have to climb up to really experience. But once you're up there, you can see twenty miles across Lake Huron.

Or so I've been told.

I park the truck and turn it off, turning to face Quinn.

"Alright, you ready to climb?" I ask, and Quinn nods, hopping out of the truck. He pulls his phone out of his pocket and moves toward me.

"First, can we get a picture? To document our time here," he adds. "I want to create an album when we're done."

I can't say no, can I? I move toward him and his arm snakes around my back, those long fingers curling around my waist, and he shifts closer. Impossibly close. A few soft strands of his hair tickle my neck as he leans into me.

His bright green eyes meet mine and something flickers in the depths, something I can't quite decipher. He's much more complicated than I thought. His fingers flex against my side and a tingle of desire snakes up my spine.

Oh, this is not good. Not fucking good.

It's been too long since I've gotten off. I'm just acting horny now.

Quinn holds his phone out. "Smile for the picture, yeah?" he says and then turns his head.

Instinctively, my hand travels along his back, wrapping itself around him, and landing on his hip. I didn't need to do it, but I did. And as soon as my fingers curl around his side, he lets out a small moan as he snaps the picture.

It's low and almost indistinct, but it's there.

Immediately, my entire body perks up. And by "body", I mean my dick. My sad, lonely, untouched dick. It needs a friend, it seems.

"Oh, fuck," Quinn mutters. "I'm sorry, fuck, that's embarrassing."

No, what's embarrassing is I still haven't let go of him. I

seem to be holding on to him tighter. And he's not moving away from me either.

He turns slightly, the front of his torso shifting against mine.

I swallow roughly, just tilting my chin down to look at him. He's not that much shorter than me, maybe a few inches, but when he lifts his chin slightly, his lips are right there.

I've never looked at his mouth like this before...not with any real intent. But in this moment, it's all I can see.

"Quinn," I murmur softly. He blinks at me, his free hand settling gently on my stomach and I lose my breath. I can feel the heat of him through our clothes and my entire body zings with pleasure.

He's not even touching my skin and I'm already close to passing out. I can't even imagine what it would be like if he touched my skin. What it would be like if he slipped those clay-caked hands across my torso, up to my neck, to my mouth...

My son's best friend. *Nineteen.* Fuck, this is so wrong.

I'm immediately snapped out of my trance.

"We should go," I swallow harshly, and step away from him—very reluctantly.

Quinn lets his arms fall away from me and he turns to the side, adjusting himself indiscreetly.

Oh my god.

Was he hard? From just me holding him like that?

I'm going to Hell. The ground should just open up and swallow me whole.

Quinn could swallow me whole too...

I shake my head and run a hand down my face, forcing

my feet forward, needing some distance. Because if my thoughts are going there.... They cannot go there.

"Hey, wait up," Quinn says, jogging to my side as we start the climb up the stairs. I can't look at him, that was so.... My thoughts were so far from where they should be.

Thunder rumbles once more in the distance and I pick up my pace.

"Hey, it's not a big deal," he says as we begin trudging up the stairs to the lookout.

"Whatever that was...that can't happen again," I say, trying to sound authoritative but end up just sounding like I'm asking a question.

He sighs, nodding. "Yeah, totally. Never again."

Why don't I believe him? And why does that sound sarcastic?

We move in silence, his soft pants beside me, our arms brushing occasionally as we climb. And each time, *each time*, something indescribable zips through me.

I need to get a grip, like a major one. Because there is no way, *no way*, that I am messing around with Quinn Quillen on this trip.

My son would kill me.

Chapter Three

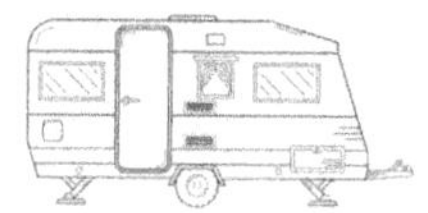

Quinn

God, look at those legs. The way his thigh muscles bunch and flex as he moves up the stairs, *ngh*.

And that ass. That tight, round ass. I want to slide my dick inside of it.

I am horny as fuck just looking at him walk. The next two weeks are going to be pure torture living in a small, enclosed space with him. Seeing him, breathing him in.

Just being near him.

He's been my fantasy for *years*.

His strong legs, broad shoulders, and scruffy, masculine face.

He's been my jackoff fodder since I realized I was bisexual. The moment I laid eyes on him, that was it. I have always wanted Greyson Hart fiercely and now I'm alone with him.

Alone.

And I'm finally nineteen.

The things we could do now that I'm of age.

"Right up here," he says, his breath coming out in little puffs.

Shit, those sounds. I adjust myself again, my hard dick not going down. Not at all. Because I know things about Grey, things I shouldn't...things that I really have no right to.

The night after they broke up, Kevin came into the pub where I bus tables and drunkenly spilled some little facts about Grey, and...well, they've only managed to make me hornier for him.

We come to a stop on the small lookout, and I press against Grey once more, craving the feel of him against me, of that hair on his arm slightly abrading my own.

He's hairier than me. Manly. I've seen him once with his shirt off and almost busted a nut in my jeans.

I want to run my fingers through it, want to bury my face in it, want to inhale him.

I am so far gone, it's not even funny.

Grey shifts next to me, and I clench my hands into fists, not wanting to scare him away. Placing my hand on his stomach moments ago was otherworldly.

I want to do it again, just reach under the fabric and run my hand along his skin, but I need to give him time. Let him come to terms with the fact this is happening.

He and I.

Or maybe, I just need to take it. Fuck waiting. Fuck wasting any more time.

"What do you think?" he asks, turning those amber-brown eyes on me, and I just stare at him, taking him in.

Fuck. He is so damn hot. I want to sink to my knees right now and mouth at his crotch like an animal.

Maybe he'd like that, public sex up here where everyone can see. I want to find out. I want to know what Grey likes and then I want to do every single thing with him.

I swallow and turn my head to look over Lake Huron. It's really gorgeous. It's like looking over the ocean, you can't even see where it begins and ends.

Kind of like my obsession with Grey.

If he'd let me, I'd give him everything. He'd know how absolutely perfect he is.

"Guess that's all there is to it," he says, shifting against me again, and my entire body tenses in anticipation.

"Yep," I say and then turn to look at him.

He meets my gaze and his Adam's apple bobs. Ngh, I want to suck on it.

"We can go, if you want," he says quietly. "There's really not much else to do once we've seen it."

Hm. Well, what I want is to lean up and taste him.

But instead, I just roll my lips between my teeth and shrug, turning my focus forward again, toward the horizon.

"Whatever you want, Grey."

He huffs and shoves his hands into the pockets of his jeans.

I want to stick my hands in there too, want to link my fingers with his. Those big, strong, capable hands. I want them on me.

"Guess we can go and eat, if you're hungry."

"Yeah, sounds good," I say as we begin our walk back

down, making sure to keep my body as close to his as he'll let me.

It's almost like a game I'm playing right now. I have to tread carefully or else I could lose it all. But then again, careful is overrated.

Why not just barrel in and take it? Apologize later. Not sure which way to turn with this one.

I need to give it some thought.

"Figure we could just drive into town and find a place. Unless you want to look online and find something," Grey says.

"Let's just be spontaneous," I say, my hand brushing against his.

He glances down at where our bodies connect and then takes a step away from me.

Fuck, just hold my hand, Grey. I've been waiting four years for this. For you. But he doesn't link his fingers with mine.

It seems if I want this to move in the right direction, I need to make it happen.

I've always been a self-starter. I had to be with parents like mine.

We make it back to the truck, and I slide inside, buckling in as Grey pulls onto the road leading into town.

The clouds are gathering overhead, signaling that, yeah, a storm is coming. I tap my hands against my thighs, trying to distract myself. Because all I want right now is to lean over the console and press my lips to his neck, to lick my way across his jaw and straddle those thick legs.

I want to sink to my knees and swallow him down my throat.

But I can't do that yet, so I just turn my gaze out the window and give myself a talking-to.

No sudden movements, Quinn, or you might scare him off.

Or maybe sudden is the way to go. Just scare him into acceptance.

This is your life now, Grey.

If there's one thing I know about Grey, it's that he's loyal to those he loves. He's loyal to his son, despite Joshua's mom trying to make him seem like he's never been. I know the things that Grey has done for him. I know the sacrifices he's made. That he's still making.

Doing *anything* with me could put his relationship with his son in jeopardy. So, I just need to convince him that I'm worth it—that I'm a chance worth taking.

That I'd be as loyal to him as he'd be to me.

I wouldn't be like any of the guys that came before me.

I would be different. *We* would be different.

"What about this place?" Grey asks, his voice breaking through my thoughts. I look at the little corner restaurant and shrug.

"Yeah, sounds good," I say, and Grey runs a hand over his head.

"You can tell me if it doesn't sound good."

Doesn't he see? I don't care where we eat. I just want to be near him.

"Yeah, this looks good. I'm really not picky."

He eyes me and then parks his truck on the side of the road, and as we walk inside the restaurant, I wonder what people think when they see us together. Friends? Father and son? Lovers?

I don't really care what anyone else thinks, to be honest, but I know that Grey does. He carries the weight of the world on his shoulders.

If only he had someone to help him carry it.

Me.

I'm young still, but I'd carry it.

We're led by the hostess to a booth, and our knees knock as we get situated. He tries to move away, but I tangle my legs with his, not allowing him to escape so quickly.

His eyes flash, but I divert my gaze to the menu like this is no big thing. Like I do this all the time.

Don't make this a big thing, Grey.

He sighs and then shifts a little, his legs sliding against mine and I bite back a moan.

God, if I ever fuck him, I'll come so fast it will be embarrassing. I'll have to pray I last an entire minute. Maybe thirty seconds would be more feasible. Okay, let's be real, ten seconds is how it's going to go down.

"What are you going to get?" he asks, and I shrug.

"A burger, fries, and a milkshake," I say, and he bobs his head.

"Yeah, sounds good. Think I'll do that too. Minus the milkshake. I'm getting old, can't eat shit like that like I used to."

I set my menu down and watch him. He's fiddling with the sugar packets and I just gaze longingly at his thick fingers.

I want them wrapped around my cock...want them in my hair as I fuck into him.

"You can have some of mine," I tell him. "We can share."

He meets my gaze and nods. "Yeah. Sure. If you can't drink it all..."

Really, I just want to watch those lips wrapped around my straw, sucking.

I shift in my seat and bite back another groan. Yep, I need to get off. Sometime very soon, or else I'm going to come from just watching him eat. God, these hormones flowing through me are making me irrational. But it's always been like this with him. He's my horny kryptonite. Who needs Superman when you can have Grey fucking Hart.

We order and when the food is brought over, I devour it. When I'm done, I take long sips of my milkshake before nudging it toward Grey.

"Go on," I say and then watch as his puffy, sexy lips wrap around the straw.

And then he moans.

It's a low whine and the sound shoots straight to my cock. I press the heel of my hand down against it.

Holy hell. Holy fucking hell!

"God, this is so good," he mutters, taking another long sip, and I just watch him, entranced.

Does he know what he does to me? How can he not know? I'm so totally obvious. I have been for years.

Maybe I should show him, show him how I feel. Just feed my cock between those lips and watch him swallow.

"You can have the rest," I manage to say, clearing my throat, and he shakes his head.

"Shouldn't."

"You so should," I choke out, and he flushes. "Those sounds you make while you're sucking..."

His cheeks darken, and I force out a laugh. I'm toeing the line. I want to cross it entirely. Just take a big step over and settle down, build a house on the land, and die there.

I want to be buried in Grey. Literally.

"Just been a while," he mutters.

Been a while for what? A milkshake? Or whatever else my filthy mind is conjuring up? Because I can help him with both.

I would be a willing participant. I'd make him drink milkshakes while I suck his dick.

The waitress brings the check, and I pull out my wallet, but Grey's hand covers mine, stopping me.

Oh my hell.

He squeezes lightly and then pulls away. "I've got it."

"I don't mind splitting things..."

"I know, but I budgeted for this, for two people. For Josh and me, so let me pay. You save your money for other things."

But I don't want to save my money for other things, like I'm a kid. I want him to know that I can pay my way, that I'm his equal, not some child he needs to take care of.

"I want to split it," I say stubbornly, and he eyes me, sighing heavily.

"Alright," he replies, and then we set our credit cards down and the waitress swipes them up a few minutes later.

And then we're on our way back to the trailer, thunder and lightning right overhead.

"No escaping it now."

No, no there's not.

"And it's already humid enough, so that will be fun," I say, and Grey grumbles something under his breath.

We make it back to the trailer just as the rain starts to pour from the sky and we jog inside, our clothes damp.

"Shit," he chuckles. "Fucking Michigan."

"I know," I reply, pulling my shirt over my head, and tossing it onto a chair.

Grey's eyes snap to my chest and then fall away, his body turning from me.

Don't turn away, Grey. Look. Look at what you can have.

He shuffles around, moving to the back of the trailer and grabbing his shower caddy.

"Yeah. Um, I'm gonna go shower," he mutters and then heads out into the rain.

I just watch him go, taking deep breaths, my chest aching.

Well, that didn't go as planned. Fuck.

But I'm not a quitter.

So, I grab my shower stuff and follow him.

Chapter Four

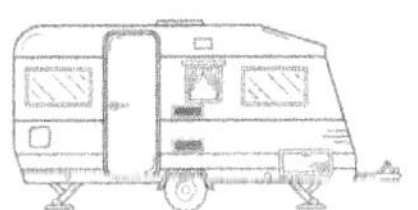

Grey

Rain pelts me as I jog toward the showers, my towel getting wet in the process. Don't really need a shower now, do I? I can just stand here in the downpour, rinse off, and get struck by lightning.

It's all that I deserve after the thoughts that just filtered through my head, seeing Quinn shirtless. I really liked what I saw.

Shit.

I make it to the little building in no time and skid on the wet tile floor before reaching out and steadying myself against the counter. Would be just my luck to fall and break my back. It's probably warranted at this point.

I glance around and realize the place is empty. It's just me and my thoughts.

Great. I can overthink now, really get into it with myself,

and talk myself down from this precarious ledge I've put myself on with Quinn.

But then suddenly, the door opens behind me and Quinn steps in.

Oh fuckity fuck.

He's still shirtless, his chest wet and dripping from the rain, his pink nipples pebbling.

My eyes shift down to where his pants are slung low on his hips, his tattoos poking out, his happy trail leading from his tight stomach to...

I wrench my eyes away and move toward the shower closest to me, pulling the curtain open and then quickly sliding it shut. I will not think filthy thoughts about my son's best friend. I will *not*.

I mean, I already did...but I will stop. I will not keep thinking about him. I have some self-control.

I think.

With shaking hands, I turn on the water and undress, my half-hard cock growing to full mast from just my boxers sliding across them. It's been far too long since I've had a good lay. Much, much too long. I step under the spray, my hands resting on the wall in front of me as I bend my head down, letting the warm water run across my shoulders and down my back.

My thoughts are a mess, and my brain is muddled. I don't know what that was with Quinn back there, or why he's constantly touching me, but it's doing things to me.

Maybe it's because he said he was bisexual. Or maybe it's the fact that he said I was perfection.

I'm his muse.

My cock lengthens and I squeeze it roughly.

Get a grip.

I hear another shower turn on, and I know that Quinn is naked somewhere nearby.

All that smooth, pale skin, wet and gleaming.

I squeeze my eyes shut and get to washing. It's quick and methodical. And when I step out a few minutes later, clad only in athletic shorts, I see Quinn wrenching the shower curtain open, his hair tangled and soaked, water dripping down his shoulders and chest.

And he's completely naked, his towel in his hand.

Our eyes meet and I feel my cheeks flush.

Fuck, he's hung. Even half-hard, it's still long and thick and uncut, the plump head peeking out from the foreskin.

Jesus, that image is forever burned in my brain.

I quickly turn my gaze away from him with a muttered apology, pushing my way back out into the storm.

"Grey!" he calls out, but I don't stop. Nope. I just keep on going.

If I stop, I may stay. And if I stay, I may do something I can't take back.

* * *

The trailer door is opened a while later, and I hear Quinn moving around. I lay in the back, under my sleeping bag, trying not to think about his dick.

Do not think about it.

"Grey," Quinn's voice is soft and concerned.

"Back here," I reply and sit up, pretending like I was

doing something, anything other than having these inappropriate thoughts.

"Hey," he says, leaning up against the wall, clad only in tight green boxer briefs. I can see the outline of his abs in the dim lighting.

I don't blame him for dressing like this. It's humid in here, the storm outside only making the air thicker. And here I am, sweating under my sleeping bag, trying to hide.

"Aren't you dying under there?" he asks, quirking an eyebrow at me.

I shrug like it's nothing, when it absolutely is. I'm going to pass out from heat stroke.

"Come on, get out from under there.... Let's open some windows and just chill."

I eye him warily but he just smiles softly at me, so I slowly peel the sleeping bag back, revealing the fact that I'm still shirtless and only in my athletic shorts. Quinn's breath hitches, his gaze heavy on me. I know I'm not much to look at. Not like him.

You're perfection.

My hand freezes, and Quinn's suddenly moving back to the other side of the trailer.

"Come on, Grey," he begins, clearing his throat. "You saw my tattoo earlier. Let me show you closer. Nothing else to do at the moment."

Well, that's not going to help the direction of my thoughts, but my body still slides out of my sleeping bag and follows him through the kitchen to the small table that's now folded out into a bed.

Because I'm not a coward and I can behave like an adult in this situation.

I am an adult.

I stop in front of Quinn, and he bites down on his bottom lip, his hair still damp from the shower. And I can smell him, that body wash he uses lingering between us.

"So, uh, whatcha got?" I manage to say, my voice rough.

"Let me show you," he replies, his lip popping out, wet and swollen.

I swallow and look away, only for my gaze to be riveted by his hand as it slides across his abs to the waist of his boxers.

He tugs them down a few inches and my entire body flames.

"These are sparrows," he explains, and my eyes snap to the black and grey birds flying across his hip bones.

"Why sparrows?" I ask.

"They represent loyalty. And commitment."

"Those are good traits."

"They are. I'm loyal, Grey. And committed."

I nod. "To what exactly?"

His hand leaves the waistband of his boxers and one of his fingers slowly trails a path across the back of my hand.

My nipples harden, my skin lighting up. Every inch of me is aware of him in this moment.

"You shouldn't have to ask," he whispers.

Our eyes meet in a clash of browns and greens and my breath stutters out of me.

"You're young, commitments change. We change," I say, and Quinn shakes his head, his throat bobbing.

"I don't. I'm steadfast."

He doesn't know what he's talking about. There is no way he can know what that word means.

I pull away, the electric current moving between us snuffed out, and Quinn lets out a disappointed huff.

"I should go to bed," I mutter, and he nods, his boxers still impossibly low on his waist, his abs clenching and flexing with each breath. He stands in the shadows, but still, he's so...

He's so stunning. Bright. Alive.

Someone will be so lucky to have him. One day.

"Night, Grey," he says, his voice following me to the back bedroom, and I send up a small wave before flopping down on the sleeping bag.

I stare at the ceiling, listening to the rain falling from the sky above until it lulls me to sleep.

Chapter Five

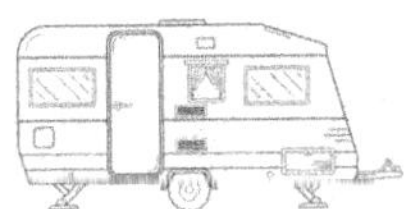

Grey

I wake with a start. The sound of someone rustling around in the trailer, the clatter of cabinets opening and closing echoing through the small space.

Quinn. He's here. With me. Alone.

I sit up, rubbing at my eyes, letting my vision focus before I stand up and make my way out to him.

He's on his tiptoes, peering up into the cabinets, his shorts slung so low on his waist that I can make out his ass crack. When he sees me, his eyes widen and rake down my chest.

I run a hand over it and feel the scratch of hair there.

Shit, I should probably put a shirt on. But it's humid and the fabric will only stick to me.

And maybe I like his eyes on me. Just a little.

"Morning," I say, averting my eyes.

"Hey, was just looking for some coffee."

"Ah, um, here, let me," I say, moving up behind him. My arm brushes against his, my chest pressed against his back. I reach up above him, feeling my body rub against his and he lets out a low groan. I glance down and see his fingertips curling into the countertop.

Oh fuck. I linger a little too long, taking my time pulling down the French press. I age a little with how long it takes. I'm now thirty-four.

"The grounds are up here too," I say lowly, still up against him, and Quinn trembles.

I reach up again and pull the tin out, setting it down on the counter where Quinn's hands are still clenched, knuckles white. I can feel him breathe, his ribs expanding with each inhale.

With great reluctance, I step away from him and move to his side.

"You know how to work one of these?" I ask, and he shakes his head, his hand moving up to fiddle with the earrings in his ear. I can see a slight tremble of his fingers and I wonder for a moment if I made him uncomfortable. Was I too close for too long?

God, I need to keep my distance.

Or, maybe he liked it.

Oh fuck, maybe he did.

That's almost worse.

"Why don't you teach me," he says, his gaze meeting mine.

I run a hand across my stubbled jaw and nod.

"Sure," I reply, showing him how to boil the water and how to measure out the grounds.

Quinn is staring with rapt attention like he always does when I explain things to him. Even the most mundane things seem to cause a spark to ignite in those dark depths.

It makes me feel a bit like a king, to be honest. No one ever listens that intently to me.

"Now you compress it," I say, and he reaches out at the same time as I do and our hands brush.

Sparks, electricity shoots up my arm, and I quickly pull my hand away, clearing my throat.

"Compress it," I say roughly, and he does, those long fingers pressing down, separating the grounds from the water.

And we both stare at it, like it's some kind of novel science experiment.

When it's done, I reach up and grab two mugs from the cupboard and hand him one. After pouring us each a cup, I gesture to the fridge.

"Vanilla creamer is in the fridge," I say, and he bobs his head.

"Cool."

Needing a little space, I take my coffee to the back bedroom, pulling the curtain shut to give myself some privacy, and lean against the wall.

I need to get dressed and put some distance between us. Whatever that was back there wasn't normal. Or maybe it is normal and I've just never experienced it before.

I don't fucking know. All I know is that I'm running out of the will to resist it.

My eyes snap open and then I'm moving with a purpose.

Pulling a shirt on quickly, I take my coffee and move toward the trailer door.

Quinn sits up straight when I walk past him.

"Heading outside," I mutter and push the door open, a warm breeze hitting my skin.

I hear Quinn following behind me and then feel his presence beside me. God, I wanted space, but fuck, it's nice to have someone close. Someone who seems to *want* to be close to me at all times. I haven't had that in...well, I've never had that.

"I love the smell of petrichor," he says, his shoulder brushing against mine.

"Me too."

Silence, just the sound of the wind rustling the trees. I feel calm, my heart rate slowing as I just take it in. For the first time, I'm with someone who isn't making me talk, who isn't upset with my reticence—who isn't prattling on and on about something, trying to fill the silence.

Looking back, I realize Quinn has always been this way, comfortable in the quiet. The few times we were alone, he would just sit with me, never forcing me to say a word. And whenever I did speak, he'd listen so attentively, as if he hung on every word.

I suddenly realize that I'm glad I'm not on this trip alone. I'm glad Quinn wriggled his way into joining...even if my mind is conjuring up filthy things it shouldn't.

"Did you sleep well?" I ask, and Quinn steps a little closer to me.

"Yeah, but I think I'd sleep better next to someone. I've always hated sleeping alone."

I eye him, sipping at my coffee, the bitter, warm liquid moving down my dry throat.

"I get that," I reply. It's been so long since I've held someone or had someone hold me. Things with Kevin were over long ago, our sex life petering out months before we broke up, but he was never overly affectionate to begin with.

"If you ever want to just...you know, sleep in the same bed, I would be cool with that," he says with a shrug. "It's no big deal."

"Don't think that's a good idea," I reply. The beds in the trailer are small. For the two of us to fit on one, we'd need to practically be on top of each other.

"Yeah, well, don't write me off so fast, Grey. Just think about it," he replies and then turns his gaze forward, and I just stare at him. For a little too long. His hair is pulled back in a messy, low ponytail again, the end short and frayed. His cheeks are a little rosy from sleep, a crease cutting down the middle of one from his pillow.

My eyes slide down to his bare chest, and I feel that stirring inside of me again. My cock twitches between my legs, and I force my gaze away. I cannot. I really can't.

But maybe you can.

"Heya!" a voice calls out and my head swivels toward the sound. Fuck, that voice, I know it from somewhere. Where do I know that voice from?

"Who's that?" Quinn asks, leaning further into me. And for some reason, my hand moves to his side, my fingers curling into his bare hip.

He lets out a stuttered breath and presses fully against me.

"Greyson Hart!" a deep voice booms. "Is that you?"

"Oh, you're shitting me," I mutter, seeing a familiar face

in the distance. I mean, seriously, what are the goddamn chances?

This stuff only happens to me, I swear it.

A loud squawk has me flinching. I forgot about the dreaded parrot.

For fuck's sake.

"Who's that?" Quinn asks, looking up at me. I should let go of him because right now, the way he's pressed up against me makes it seem like we're a couple, but still, I hold on. "And is that a parrot?"

"That's Robert," I mutter.

"Do you know him?"

"Yeah," I reply.

"Like...know him or *know* him."

I arch an eyebrow at him in confusion, and he lets out a small laugh. "God, have you fucked him, Grey?"

Well, technically, he fucked me, not that I'd ever tell Quinn that.

"None of your business," I reply, and he rolls his eyes. That one movement is so like Joshua that I let go of him and step away. What the fuck was I thinking, holding on to him like that?

"As I live and breathe. It's been a hot minute," Robert says, approaching us and letting out a long whistle. He looks just as good as he did years ago. He still has a muscular torso that fills out the t-shirt he's wearing well, and thick, hairy legs that I used to obsess over. On his right shoulder is an African Grey parrot, Tattletale, who lives up to his name.

Little shit.

"So, this is your type?" Quinn huffs, his eyes roving over

Robert. "Do you usually like men with birds? I can get a fucking bird."

I ignore his murmurs and take in the man standing before me. He's grown a beard since we last saw each other and it looks good on him, making him look more rugged than when we were together. I've always liked rugged men.

When I say I have a type, I have a type. And Quinn is not my type.

Which is why he and I make no sense.

"Nice to see you, Grey," Robert says, coming to a stop in front of me.

Tattletale eyes me with his beady pupils. Birds are smart fuckers. I bet he remembers me. Oh god, I hope he doesn't repeat anything I said during sex all those years ago. Should have kept my mouth shut while I was getting fucked, but damn, it's hard for me to be quiet.

I get really, really loud.

I nod, trying not to make eye contact with Tattletale, but doing a horrible job. He's watching me.

"Yeah, Robert. Nice to see you too. How have you been?" I ask, forcing my eyes to remain on his.

"Good, really good." He shifts on his feet and then smirks at me. "You look really good too. Been working out?"

I mean, no. If anything, I've gained a little cushion around my middle since we were together, but I don't say that.

"Bet that bird shits on your shirt, huh?" Quinn says and a laugh snorts out of me. Because it so does.

Robert's eyes swivel to Quinn, and Quinn stands a little taller.

"Who's this?" he asks. "Your son's friend? He here?"

It bugs me that he remembers things about Joshua. When we were fucking, we didn't talk much about our personal lives. I must have mentioned that I had a son at some point.

Makes me uncomfortable that I shared that info with a practical stranger.

"No, he's not," I say but before I can explain, Quinn is reaching his hand out in front of him.

"Hi, weird bird-man. I'm Quinn. Nice to meet you."

Robert eyes Quinn and then slips his big paw in his, a chuckle escaping his mouth.

"I'm Robert. Grey and I go way back."

I mean, I wouldn't say *way back*. That infers some kind of long-lasting relationship. He bent me over a few times. Nothing more.

I watch their clasped hands pump up and down between them. I don't like it, them touching, and a breath I didn't realize I was holding leaves me as soon they release each other.

"Well, this is just a crazy coincidence, seeing you. What are you two doing up here? A little vacation?" Robert asks, turning his warm, hazel gaze back to mine. Tattletale's long talons grip his shoulder and I shudder. Robert tried to get me to hold Tattletale once and it creeped me out.

I'm not a fan of birds with their pointy beaks and their long claws. They're basically demons with wings and beady eyes.

"Yeah. Just a short trip," I say. "Quinn hasn't ever been to the UP."

"Oh yeah?" Robert asks. "Shame. It's gorgeous up here.

Like traveling back in time. How long are you two up here for?"

"Two weeks," Quinn says and then moves closer to me. "Grey and I have the whole trip planned out."

Well, that sounds like we planned this together, but I don't get a chance to clarify because Tattletale squawks loudly, causing Robert to prattle on once more.

But Robert is one of *those*. He liked the sound of his own voice too much. If I let him, he'd chatter on for hours. And I usually let him because how the fuck do you *nicely* tell someone to shut up?

You don't. You fucking don't.

And listen, when Robert stops talking, his bird starts up. It's like nonstop chatter. Just constant squawking.

"Where are you two headed today? I don't really have much planned..."

Oh shit. Oh, yes. I'd forgotten this about him too. He used to always hint at doing things, never outright saying what he wanted. Used to drive me crazy.

"We're actually going to the Soo today," Quinn replies, and my eyebrows shoot up. So he must have really looked at the itinerary. Memorized it, in fact, because even I didn't remember what we had planned for today.

"No shit, that sounds like fun. Mind if I tag along?" Robert asks. "I'd really like to catch up with you, Grey. It's been so long."

Quinn stiffens next to me, eyeing me, waiting for my answer. Both sets of eyes are on me now and I'm starting to sweat. Tattletales are on me too. He hasn't even moved his head, but his unblinking little eyes are carefully focused on me.

"Peekaboo," he squawks suddenly, and I jump a little.

Fucker. God, I hate that bird.

"Uh. Yeah. Sure," I reply, wanting him to just go away. But my response makes Quinn's eyebrows meet in frustration.

"For real?" he huffs so softly, only I catch it.

Robert smiles widely. "Awesome. Cool. I just need to get ready and then we can leave. How about in thirty minutes? Does that work?"

"You gonna bring the bird?" Quinn asks, and Robert startles a little, almost like he forgot Quinn was there.

"Yeah."

"Won't he fly off?"

"Nah, he can't fly anymore and he gets lonely when I leave him for too long. Parrots are really social, can't leave him alone for hours like that. Would be inhumane," Robert winks at me and then reaches out, touching my shoulder a little too intimately. It lingers, warm and hot against my shirt, and I start to squirm.

Don't know what I ever saw in this guy, other than his thick thighs and his broad shoulders. Looking back, the sex wasn't even that great.

"Gonna go get changed and then we can head out?" he asks me, squeezing me a little too roughly.

"Yeah. That works," I mutter, and then Robert is off, leaving me to watch him go, Quinn still at my side.

"God, he seems like a chatty asshole and he literally has

bird shit on his back," Quinn says, and a chuckle bubbles out of my throat.

"I forgot that about the bird."

"It's weird, Grey, that he totes it around on his shoulder. Like a fucking pirate."

"Yeah, well, we all have our quirks."

"He's also a Neanderthal," Quinn mutters, his brows still furrowed. "His muscles are too...big. He can barely walk. I mean, honestly..."

"Be nice," I chastise lightly, and Quinn's cheeks redden.

"Ugh, fine, I'll be nice for you. But why did you agree to let him tag along? Do you still have a thing for him?"

"Huh?" I ask, my eyebrows meeting my hairline because I haven't thought of Robert in ages. I'd forgotten he existed, to be honest.

"Grey, do you want to go to the Soo with Robert? Alone? That's what I'm asking."

"Hell no," I grumble. "Don't fucking leave me with him. He'll talk my ear off. My head can't handle it. And that bird is fucking eerie."

Quinn's lips twitch, his eyes twinkling. "Fine, I won't. I'll save you on *one* condition."

I meet his steely gaze.

"You don't treat me like a kid. I'm your equal. And..." He swallows, his cheeks flushing darker. "We're together."

My lips part and I just gape at him. Is he serious? Together?

"What does that mean?"

"It means I'm your boyfriend whenever Robert is

around," he says, and I nearly swallow my tongue. "It's the only way that dude will lay off," he adds.

"I don't know if that's needed..."

"I saw the way he looked at you. He was drooling. So yeah, it is. Unless you want him..."

I shake my head and blurt, "No." No, that ship sailed a long time ago.

"Fine, then those are my terms. Do we have a deal?"

He shifts on his feet, his hands clasping his coffee mug tightly, waiting for my answer.

I swallow, my lips meeting once more. Deep breath in and then out. This is a bad, bad thing to agree to, but I do it anyways. Bad decisions and all that...

"Fine."

Quinn grins at me. "I can't fucking wait."

Chapter Six

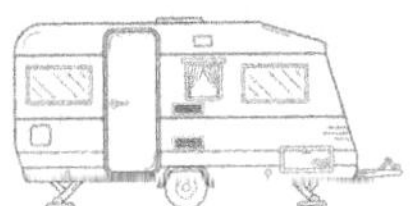

Quinn

I can't stop watching Robert watch Grey. After Robert lumbered back to his camper to get changed, he reappeared looking less shat on and pretty damn hot. It's making me start to feel unreasonably jealous. And I can't let it show. Not when Grey has promised to look at me like an adult.

And to make matters worse, Grey isn't keeping him at arm's length like he should, despite looking somewhat uncomfortable that Robert keeps putting his hands on him. Right now, Robert is leaning into him, that bird on his shoulder far too close for comfort. How does Robert not know that Grey hates birds? Not that I'm surprised. Robert seems like the kind of man who chats your ear off endlessly and never lets you get a word in edgewise. God, what was sex like with him?

He probably filibustered the entire time. He should work for Congress.

Robert reaches out and touches Grey's cheek, and the pencil in my hand is gripped so tightly, I think I may snap it in half.

I should go over there and insert myself, but I don't want to come across as too needy and jealous.

Even though that's exactly what I am. A jealous fucker. Jealous of Robert and those big thick arms and that parrot that is eyeballing Grey like he's a nut he wants to crack.

Suddenly the parrot speaks, something I can't make out, and Grey jumps a little.

Robert smiles widely and reaches out, steadying him with those big hands, his touch lingering a little too long if you ask me.

I've watched other men touch Grey far too often. I mean, not super often, but even once was enough. I've seen how Grey's cheeks flush crimson, how he pulls his lips between his teeth nervously, how he shifts closer, almost close enough that their cocks brushed.

I lurked like a creeper in the doorway of his house, watching him. I'm surprised Joshua never caught me loitering. I had no shame then, and I have no shame now. The only issue is now Grey doesn't seem to be enjoying these little touches Robert is bestowing on him.

Or maybe he is.

Fuck, I can't get a good read on him. When he finally detaches and makes his way back toward me, he is staring at me with a look I can't decipher. I scramble up from my chair, my sketchbook and pencil clutched in my hands as he ambles into the trailer.

The door closes behind him and he lets out a shaky breath.

"You okay?" I ask, setting my things down but keeping my distance. I wonder if my being close to him has made him uncomfortable, but then again, he's touched me just as much as I've touched him. So, I think we're okay, but still, I give him space.

"I'm fine. Just...just you know...."

I don't know, but I just stand there and watch him, wanting to pull him into my chest, wanting to run my hands down his back and grab on to his ass. Want to grind our cocks together.

Inappropriate, but there it is. There's no stopping it now.

"Robert was a little handsy," I say, and Grey's eyes slam into mine.

"He always was."

I stare at him, wanting him to tell me that he hated it, but he doesn't.

"I mean, it's really disrespectful since we're boyfriends and all..." I say, and Grey lets out a huff.

"He doesn't know that."

I pull my bottom lip between my teeth and shift on my feet. "Well, we'll just have to show him, won't we?"

Grey runs a hand over his head and stares at me carefully. "Yeah, suppose we should..."

"Unless you want him to touch you like that?" I have to ask, and Grey lets out a low grunt.

"Nah, I'm good."

And I motherfucking beam.

Yeah, that's what I thought. Grey's mine, Robert. Come and get him.

* * *

"So, to really sell this, we should definitely hold hands," I say as Grey drives us an hour north to the Soo. According to Google, Sault Ste. Marie is the oldest city in Michigan and it has these locks, or canals, that cargo freighters use to move through to their destinations. You can actually stand and watch the ships rise and lower as they move to the other side of the lake. And honestly, the thought of leaning against Grey, my hand in his while we do this is something I have dreamed about.

Listen, my dick will rise and lower the entire time we're out there, I'm sure of it.

If only Robert and his beady-eyed bird weren't tagging along, it would be perfect.

"Holding hands?" Grey asks, running a hand across the back of his neck. "I mean, we could just lie to him, like adults."

"Yeah, and where's the fun in that? Plus, I believe in showing, not telling. Makes it more convincing."

Grey lets out a chuckle and the sound lights me up.

I clench my hands tightly, resisting the urge to just crawl over to him. Ugh. If he let me, I'd so give him road head. I'd just lean over and suck him right on down.

Ngh. I want that so bad my mouth is watering.

"We should practice now," I say, setting my hand palm up

on the console because I'm an eager asshole, and I want it. Plus, the whole situation with Robert is making me insecure. Because as much as Grey says he doesn't want him, I know that he had at one point. And Robert and I couldn't be more different. So I'm feeling a little insecure and wary as fuck.

I just want him to hold my goddamn hand and make me feel better.

Make me feel better, Grey.

Grey eyes it and then swallows.

"Might be crossing a line if we do this," he murmurs, almost as if he's having an internal debate with himself.

Little does he know that I'd cross all the lines with him.

"It's not a big deal. And if we do this, it will subtly tell Robert to back off."

Grey seems to mull this over, for far too long, if you ask me. And then slowly, almost like he's moving through molasses, he slips his big hand into mine.

God, his fingers are rough, callused. I want to feel them dragging down my back as I push my way into him.

I let out a shaky exhale as my fingers curl around his, and I shift in my seat, my cock already hardening between my legs. See, up and down it goes. Although, right now it seems to just be in a permanent state of up. The only way this fucker is going down is if I'm inside of him. And even then, my dick would need to be maintained. I'd have to get off with him at least twice a day. Maybe more. That's how horny I am for him.

"You have really nice hands," I say, running my thumb across one of the veins near his knuckles.

"I didn't know hands could be nice," he says, glancing

down at where our bodies are connected. He is chewing on his bottom lip and I know he's questioning his decision to hold my hand, so I cling on tighter.

I'm not letting him go this easily.

"Oh yes, well, let me tell you a secret. They can be. And yours are…" I lean my head back and close my eyes, not sure if I should say it. But then I do. I just blurt it out. "I have a confession. I've drawn your hands, Grey."

His eyes widen slightly, obviously surprised. But really, Grey, you should know better with me by now. You should know how obsessed I am with you.

"When?"

"Remember that one day I came over and you showed me how to change a tire?"

"Oh. No shit."

I remember that day. In vivid detail. Two years ago, Grey's truck had a flat when I'd shown up with Joshua after school. I would always tag along just to ogle this man as he worked. Because Grey in a pair of jeans is…ngh. When we arrived, Joshua had trudged on inside to grab something to eat, but I lingered in the garage, letting Grey instruct me.

And let me tell you, I hung on every word he said, my eyes glued to him. The way his hands grasped the tire iron with a powerful grip, his long, thick fingers, nails cleanly trimmed. I imagined those hands grabbing on to me with the strength they exhibited. When I went home that night, I grabbed my sketch pad and drew them, not wanting to miss a detail.

I've drawn them several times since.

"Were you listening to me at all that day?" he asks.

I let out a small laugh. "Hell yeah, I was listening. I listen to every word you say, but I was also ogling your hands. Memorizing them. Those veins..." I trace one with my thumb, pressing against it. "Sexy as fuck."

He swallows loudly, his Adam's apple bobbing. I want to suck on it while he moans, want to feel the vibrations move from him into me as I come. My imagination is getting out of control, and pretty soon, if I don't get some relief, I'm going to combust.

We drive in silence for a few more minutes, my fingers tracing the back of his hand, my eyes on the scenery outside. Just shades of blues and greens.

Grey hasn't pulled away, and I'm not eager for him to. So I just hold on for a little while longer. There is so much I'd do to him, for him, if he'd only let me.

He has to let me. Eventually. I just need to tempt him into agreeing to it.

I glance in my rearview mirror and see Robert's jeep trailing behind us, and I let out a huff. Asshole, coming along and ruining my plans with his big muscles and sexy beard. His parrot should be a deterrent, but it's not. It makes him look even more rugged. Like some kind of ship's captain. How the fuck do you compete with a pirate?

I don't fucking know.

But I'm this close to gouging out an eyeball and wearing an eyepatch to win this one.

A sigh escapes me. I came on this trip to be alone with Grey, not to be hounded by an ex who looks like he could throw Grey around a room. Does he like that...being dominated in the bedroom? I'm not as big as Grey, but I could still make him come. I know I could make it good for him if he'd give me a fucking chance.

If he could just get over my age and the fact that I'm his son's friend.

"You know what would really sell this? If we kissed too," I blurt.

Grey jolts and the truck swerves a little as he lets out a nervous chuckle.

"Shit, Quinn. Warn a guy."

I squeeze his hand as my leg starts bouncing. "Okay, fine. We won't do that, but fuck, if Robert starts getting weird and gets all handsy, I'm going to. I'll take one for the team."

I can feel Grey eyeing me, probably not sure if I'm serious or not. But I am so serious. I'll even use tongue.

Hell yeah, I'd so tongue fuck him. My dick is already throbbing just thinking about it, and I shift to try and get comfortable.

Down boy, maybe later.

Yes, hopefully later.

"So, when did you and Robert meet?" I ask, knowing this will probably do the trick. Robert does nothing for me, even in those tiny shorts he was wearing. I have eyes for Grey and Grey only.

"Uh, a few years back," he says, his eyes still on the road. "Met at the grocery store."

"Huh," I say as I trace his forefinger with my thumb and resist the urge to pull it into my mouth. I'd suck on it.

Fuck, I want to suck on it.

"And why did you two break up?" I ask, pulling my thoughts away.

"Uh, yeah, we just didn't work."

"Sex wasn't good?" I ask, and he shrugs.

"It was fine."

Well, what the fuck does *that* mean?

"I shouldn't be discussing this with you," he says. "Should probably stop holding your hand too," he adds in as an afterthought.

I hold on tighter. I'm not ready for him to let go.

"Don't make it a big deal," I say. "It's not a big deal. And look, I'm not some virgin, okay? I've had sex. Loads of it."

Grey peeks over at me. "You're only nineteen."

"Yeah, so?"

He's working that one out. Look, yeah, maybe I am young, but when you have parents like mine, you're fucking by the time you're old enough to know how a dick works.

I mean, seriously, I had almost no supervision growing up. Their idea of a sex talk was handing me condoms and telling me to be careful.

So I was, I *am*.

I had to grow up faster than most kids. I always had to learn the hard way. They weren't bad parents, but there were times I wished I had someone who cared for me enough to give a shit about what I was doing and who I was with.

I wish I had a dad like Grey. Maybe that's why I'm so attracted to him.

His calm, steadfast demeanor just calls to me on a molecular level.

And he's fucking hot. The hottest man I've seen in real life.

I never stood a chance.

"Here we are," Grey says a moment later, his hand slipping from mine as he parks the truck. I feel his absence palpably. But I shake it off. He agreed to my asinine plan, so I'm going to try and be cool about it. I never thought Grey would even let me touch him like that, so I count it as a win.

I hop out of Grey's truck as Robert rounds the front of his Jeep, making his way straight toward us. The parrot is absent from his shoulder and my eyes narrow.

"Where's the bird?" I ask, and Robert thumbs over his shoulder

"In the Jeep. Don't worry, I got the windows rolled down."

"Aren't you worried he's going to shit all over your seats?" I ask and Robert chuckles, ignoring my question and moving toward Grey, who is looking far too vulnerable.

Oh, hell no. Robert is like some heat-dick-seeking missile. I need to take him out before he hits his target.

I step up to Grey, slipping my hand down his wrist and threading my fingers through his once more. The same shock of adrenaline hits me as soon as our skin touches and I bite down on my lips to keep the moan at bay.

I have to keep it together.

Fuck, it's so hard to keep it together. I'm falling to pieces just being near him.

Grey glances down at me, those brown eyes nearly glowing, and I squeeze his hand.

Robert's eyes snap down to where our hands meet, and he narrows them. Oh, challenge accepted, bird-man.

I am so going to win this.

Robert pulls his gaze away from our hands and looks at Grey, ignoring me completely. "So, what's the plan?"

Before I can answer in a snarky tone, Grey tilts his head to the left.

"Quinn really likes trying new coffee shops, so I thought we'd stop in here."

And there I go, a pile of goo on the floor. My eyeballs are emoting hearts, my skin flushed with adoration. Robert is completely forgotten. All I can see is Grey.

This man just knows things about people, always tucking information about those around him in these secret little compartments in his brain.

It's why he always knows what to get Joshua for his birthday and Christmas, despite his son never telling him a thing. Or why he knows these little facts about me, despite me never directly mentioning them.

Grey just listens and watches. He pays attention. He's thoughtful.

God, I am so into this man, he has no idea. It's ironic how my obsession with him is the one thing he's never noticed and the only thing I truly wish he would.

"I do," I say, my cheeks hot.

Robert clears his throat, and I wrench my gaze away from Grey. Enough staring. I get it, it is a little much.

Grey reaches out with his free hand and tucks a stray lock of hair behind my ear and there I go again. Just ded.

"You guys are very cute, in an odd way," Robert says, once more pulling my attention away.

Gah! Go away, Robert. I just want to stare longingly into Grey's hypnotic eyes. I want to will him to kiss me.

I would expire if he planted those lips on mine. My heart would stop beating and they'd declare me deceased.

"We aren't odd," I say, feeling suddenly defensive. And Robert with his stupid shit-shirt just smirks at me. Because I know Grey and I are different. I'm so much younger than him, and we don't look like we have anything in common. But who is Robert to judge? He wears a fucking parrot, for fuck's sake.

"Just meant you two seem like an odd pairing."

Unlike you and Grey, I think as my lips turn down in a frown. Well, Grey and I aren't together, but Robert doesn't know that. And yet here he is insulting us.

"We work just fine," I say and square my shoulders, Grey's hand in mine, giving me a much-needed confidence boost.

Robert raises his hands in mock surrender and then asks, "How long have you guys been together?"

"It's new," I say quickly.

Little does Grey know that it's not new for me. It's been years on my end. I don't even think he's looked twice at me, to be honest. He's not like that, not one of those older men who prey on younger boys.

And he probably would never have looked at me twice, except I kind of forced his hand by joining him on this trip. And by telling him I'm bi...and also by showing him my dick.

I have a fucking nice dick.

It probably doesn't help that I'm staring all gaga at him like he hung the moon. He can hang my moon anytime.

"New? Wow..." Robert chuckles, and I shrug.

"When you know, you know," I reply, and Grey huffs out a small laugh next to me.

"Enough of this," Grey adds and then nods to the door of the coffee shop. "Let's go in and order."

I lean into him as we enter, staking my claim silently as we move to the counter where two baristas stand taking orders and making coffees. I glance up at the chalkboards hanging on the wall and ask, "So what should I try, *boyfriend?*"

I say that word far too loudly, but I want Robert to hear it —to hear that this thing between us is serious, even if it's only pretend.

Grey curses under his breath, but still glances up at the boards. He runs his free hand over his jaw and I can hear the scratch of his stubble against his palm. I want that stubble to scratch along my thighs as he eats my dick.

"Well, uh, you like chocolate," he begins, and I feel my heart thunder in my chest. Here he goes. He's pulling up those little bits of information and using them to make me fall even more in love with him.

"And raspberry. So why not the raspberry white mocha?"

"With whipped cream?" I ask.

His eyes meet mine. "Yeah."

"Kind of juvenile...all that sugar..." Robert says lowly and I turn to glare at him.

"I'm young and not at risk for diabetes, old man," I hiss, and Robert narrows his eyes at me. If he keeps this up, his eyes will stick like that. God, I hope they stick.

Grey and I move up to the counter and I order my drink, noting how Robert has moved over to Grey while I do so, talking to him lowly. Honestly, he has no shame. No fucking shame at all.

Reluctantly, I let go of Grey's hand to grab my credit card, and Robert pulls him away from me, nearly dragging him to the other end of the store. He's pretending like he's showing him the mugs lining the shelf, but really all he's doing is trying to touch his dick.

I know it. The whole world knows it.

Dick touching Robert. He should be put away in jail with his bird. The creep.

God, is this how it's going to be? Am I going to be competing with this guy the entire time?

Fuck, it's on. I haven't waited four years for my chance with Grey, just to roll over and let someone snatch him out from under me.

I frown deeply, trying to strategize, when the barista hands me back my card.

"Good luck," she says, and I offer her a pained smile.

"Ugh. I need it. You see his shorts, right?" I glance over at Robert and roll my lips between my teeth. "His legs are amazing. Like those thighs. I can't compete."

Her eyes rake over me, and she shrugs. "Yeah, they're hot, but you have nice cheekbones."

Fuck. That's not much to work with. Who wants cheekbones when you could have tree-trunk thighs crushing you?

"And he's relentless," I say, and the girl bobs her head.

"Better be fierce then," she says and I nod in agreement. I can be fierce. I'm fucking Tiger King. I mean, sort of. You couldn't pay me to get in a cage with those big-ass cats. I like my limbs too much.

I stick a few dollar bills into the tip jar and then stride up to Grey, sliding my hands around his waist like I have every right to be there. Because I need to mark my territory. Like a dog.

The touch startles him a little.

Oh god, way to sell it, Grey. We really need to practice more so he can become desensitized to my touch.

Although, I don't really want him to be completely desensitized, just enough so he doesn't recoil when I touch him. I want him to want my hands on him. And eventually, my lips.

And then my dick. And my balls.

Robert lets out a huff of annoyance and I smirk at him. Game on.

I am so winning this.

"So, Grey was telling me you're nineteen," he says.

I nod my head. He wants me to feel ashamed, but I'm not. It's not my fault I'm young. Nothing I can do about it.

"Grey has no complaints. I have great stamina. I am *so young*, after all."

Grey's cheeks flush, and I pinch his side slightly, knowing that I'm probably embarrassing him, but not able to help myself. Not when Robert has thrown down a challenge like this.

I always was competitive.

I lean my head against Grey's shoulder, eyeing Robert as I do it, and let one of my hands slide into the back pocket of his shorts.

He jumps again, and I resist an eye roll.

"Grey, can I talk to you for just a minute?" I say, noting that my drink isn't ready yet. I have all the time in the world.

Robert opens his mouth to say something, but I don't have time for his blathering, so I just pull Grey toward the bathrooms on the other side of the shop. I open the free one and pull him inside, locking the door behind me.

"What—?" he asks, but his words are cut off when I press my hands against his chest, pushing him up against the wall. He lets out a surprised huff, his hands moving to grip my waist.

"We have a problem," I hiss.

"We do?" he asks.

"Yes. We do. You jump every time I touch you," I say, trying to focus on the point, but holy shit. I'm *touching* him and my dick is getting all sorts of ideas.

Like big-ass dreams. I could be President of the United States at this rate.

No one can stop me.

"Yeah, well, I wasn't expecting an ass grab."

"Expect it, your ass is fine. And Robert is trying to stake his claim and I refuse to let him win this."

"Jesus, I didn't know you were this competitive. I thought you just like winning at Monopoly," he mutters as his hands squeeze my hips, and I bite my bottom lip. Hard. His eyes shift down to my mouth, and his tongue darts out to wet those lips of his.

"I like fucking winning, Grey. A whole hell of a lot."

Suddenly the air shifts between us, those brown eyes of his darkening, and I swallow roughly.

"I'm sorry," he says softly, his voice rumbling between us. I feel it all the way to my balls.

"You should be. You're hurting my feelings, acting all afraid of me," I say with a crooked smile.

"I'm just not used to it."

That's right. Kevin. That coldhearted bastard he dated for years. I remember that night when Kevin told me intimate things about their relationship. About how incompatible they were. It took everything within me not to punch him in his stupid face, my anger rearing up within me. Because I could have been the one to satiate Grey's needs. Motherfucking me.

But I wasn't even on his radar. I had to bide my time.

And now is my time. Grey is *mine*. And like hell Robert is getting a piece of this.

"Do you want it? To be touched like that?" I ask. Because I could do that. I could touch him like this all day. Every day.

He swallows and his head nods almost imperceptibly. And that's it. I crack.

I move up to him, my hands pressed against his strong chest. God, I want to move my hands under his shirt, run my thumbs over his nipples, and slide my fingers through his chest hair. But that's for another time. Maybe tonight when no one is around, when we're cloaked in the shadows of night, he'll let me.

Instead, I let my hands wander across the fabric of his shirt, up his pecs, across his shoulders, and down his sides until Grey's head is tilted back against the wall, his lips open slightly.

"Like this?" I mutter, my lips impossibly close to his neck. "I could touch you like this all the time." I want to lean forward and bite down, suck his flesh until it bruises. But I just gently press my nose to the tendon that's bulging from his skin as my hands run down and then up his back, cupping his neck.

I shift my hips until I'm fully pressed against him, feeling his hard cock against mine, and a low, pained moan escapes me.

Fuck, if only we weren't in the bathroom of a coffee shop in the middle of nowhere. I would get on my knees and slide that big dick right to the back of my throat.

"This is wrong," Grey whispers, a plea in his voice.

"No."

It's a simple word, but he needs to hear it.

No, this isn't wrong. There is nothing wrong about it. If anything, this is too right.

I'm about to tell him as much when suddenly, a knock on the door startles us both.

"Shit," Grey mutters as I reluctantly pull away.

I glance down and see our hard cocks pressing out from the fabric of our pants, reaching toward each other. They know what's up.

"Grey. Quinn. Your drinks are ready," Robert's voice says from the other side of the door. And just like that, the thick tension surrounding us evaporates. He didn't need to interrupt us, but he did. He knows exactly what he's doing.

Grey moves to the sink, splashing cold water on his face, running some across the back of his neck.

I should probably do that too, to cool the fuck down, but there's no time. So instead, I tuck my dick under the waistband of my jeans and walk out of the bathroom.

Robert is waiting there in the hall, his thick arms folded over his chest.

"Got distracted," I say and then let myself smirk, allowing him to think more happened in there than actually did.

Let his imagination run wild.

It helps that Grey meanders out of the bathroom a moment later, looking flushed. Used. God, if he only knew what I'd do to him...the things my mind has already done. He'd be utterly wrecked if he let me have him.

I sip at my drink, feeling pleased as punch, and just like Grey predicted, it's exactly what I wanted. Of course it is. Nothing about him is wrong. Everything is exactly right.

Robert eyes the two of us and then squares his shoulders, not accepting defeat. He starts talking immediately again, filling the awkward space with more words, trying to pull Grey's attention back to him. But Grey's eyes are on mine. Electricity crackles between us and a small smirk pulls up the corner of my lips.

You can pretend that didn't happen, but I see you, Grey.

You were turned on by me.

And hell if I'll let that go.

Chapter Seven

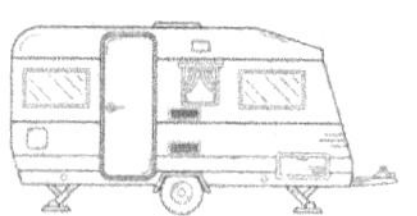

Grey

Well, fuck. Now I went and did it. I don't know what happened. Maybe it was his hand in mine for a good portion of the day, or the fact that he was pressed up against me in that tiny bathroom. Or, that I've been so fucking lonely for so long.

But my dick got hard when he laid his palms on my chest and moved them across my torso. My entire body was nearly trembling, my chest heaving with heavy breaths.

All from a simple, mostly innocent touch.

Bad. So very bad. And now Robert is watching me curiously. He's wondering why I'm with a nineteen-year-old guy who looks nothing like my usual type.

Well, fuck. I have no idea how it happened. It just did. And now we're together for the next thirteen days.

Am I even mad about it? Nope.

No, I'm actually looking forward to it. And I shouldn't. I *really* shouldn't.

This is so very, very bad. I am going straight to Hell. I've booked my fucking first-class ticket.

"So, the locks are really innovative," Robert is rambling again. "They're powered by gravity, and they use twenty-two million gallons of water to traverse a boat..."

Quinn leans into me, his fingers tracing a vein down my forearm before they link with mine once again. He hasn't let go of me once as we meandered through the downtown shops, and now we're standing on a small overlook, watching a freighter move through the locks. It really is fascinating, and I should be paying better attention, but my focus is solely on him.

I keep replaying what happened in the bathroom over and over in my head. How he felt, how he smelled.

"...and it takes about nine hours for a boat to pass through from the river system here..."

Quinn brings our hands up to his mouth and presses a kiss to my knuckles, and my entire body zings with pleasure. Robert's voice is just a hum in my ear as Quinn meets my stare.

He really is so fucking pretty. His hair has once again come loose from the confines of his ponytail, and a wisp curls around his cheek, blowing in the breeze. His dark eyelashes flutter whenever I move against him, and those pink lips that he keeps chewing on are puffy and just fucking...

They're just fucking perfect.

I could kiss those lips.

I've never wanted a guy like Quinn before, preferring to

have someone bigger than me, but suddenly, I can see the appeal. He's so different. Maybe that's what I was missing before. Maybe he can give me what those other men couldn't.

Maybe I just needed someone like him.

"He's not going to stop talking. He's trying to impress you," Quinn whispers and I roll my lips between my teeth because yeah, I noticed some animosity back there in the coffee shop, but I didn't know how to address it.

So I ignored it, like the cowardly man I am.

Robert isn't touching me, but he's standing really close and the bird is back on his shoulder, watching me intently.

"Goodbye," it says loudly, interrupting Robert's low drone, and I let out a small laugh.

If that isn't a sign, I don't know what is.

"You want to get out of here?" I ask Quinn softly, and his eyes widen.

"Where would we go?" he asks.

I swallow, not sure what the fuck I'm doing, but doing it anyways. "Anywhere."

He looks at me, something wild flashing in his eyes, and then nods. "Yeah, Grey, let's fucking go."

I turn my gaze to Robert who is, of course, talking again, not realizing that no one is listening, and I lay a hand on his arm. He startles a little and then smiles over at me.

Oops, probably shouldn't have touched him. Don't want to give him any ideas.

"Quinn and I are going to head back," I tell him, keeping my words short and to the point. Don't want him to convince me to stay when I don't wanna.

"Oh," Robert says and shifts on his feet. "You sure you want to leave? There is still so much we can do here...."

"We're good," Quinn interjects loudly and then pulls me to his side. "We're gonna go."

Well, that was a little rude, but I get why he did it. If you give Robert an inch, he takes a mile.

"We'll, uh, see you back at the campground?" I ask, and Robert narrows his eyes with a nod.

"Yep. I think I'll stay here for a bit and catch a tour."

"You do that," I say and then lie, "It was really good to see you again."

"Same here. You take care and call me...when you find yourself free again."

Quinn bristles at this, but I pull him away, not wanting to get into it with Robert, just wanting to escape it all.

I lead Quinn back to my truck and open his door for him. He flushes crimson as he pulls himself inside. I check out his ass for a second before wrenching my eyes away. But honestly, what's a little ogling when our hard dicks touched earlier?

I'm not sure it matters much anymore.

Not sure I can keep this train from chugging down its path.

Next stop is more bad decisions. Fucking choo-choo.

When I hop into the driver's seat, Quinn reaches over and pulls my hand back into his. There's no need to do this now that Robert isn't here, but I don't stop him.

"Want to find a place to eat?" I ask, turning my gaze to the road, and Quinn nods.

"Yeah, I'm starving."

We head back toward St. Ignace and find a small diner off the side of the road. After parking, we head inside and are led to a booth by the waitress. Instead of sitting across the table, Quinn slides in next to me, his leg bumping into mine.

Then suddenly, I feel his hand on my thigh, and I peek over at him. His gaze is on the menu in front of him, and I force myself to do the same, but I can feel his fingers tightening against me and my cock responding. It starts to lengthen down my thigh and my breaths come out in quick succession.

"You okay?" Quinn turns to look at me, and I manage to give him a small nod and a wobbly smile.

If Quinn placed his hand on my cock right now, who knows what I'd do.

No, I know exactly what I'd do. I'd behave *responsibly*. Like the adult in this relationship. Or, whatever the fuck this is.

"Yeah, just...you know...hungry."

He smiles softly at me. "Yeah, me too."

The way he says it makes me shift in my seat. It sounds like he wants to eat me for dinner, and to be honest, at this moment, I would probably let him. Which is why I need to put some space between us.

Things have gotten out of hand.

"I think you should sit on the other side of the booth," I tell him, and Quinn cocks his head at me.

"No thanks," he says, going back to the menu, and I huff. God, he doesn't even listen to me. I have no authority here.

Oh god. I am so screwed.

"*Quinn*," I say sternly, and he shudders.

"Say my name again, Grey. I love hearing it roll off your tongue."

I pull my lips between my teeth, and he watches them closely, almost like he wants to kiss me.

I must be going crazy to think that. But then again, his hand is on my thigh. And it hasn't left.

I gulp, feeling aroused and nervous and fucking confused.

The waitress brings water to the table and I grab my glass, the cold a shock to my system as I swallow it down.

Quinn removes his hand from my thigh, but his leg is still pressed up against mine and I scoot a little to the right. Needing space so I can think clearly.

I shouldn't have held his hand, or let him run his hands over my chest. Or press his cock against mine.

So fucking inappropriate.

"What are you going to order?" he asks me, his eyes on the menu, his fingers fiddling with the corners.

"Dunno," I say, clearing my throat.

"Want to share something? We could each pick some-thing weird and try it?"

I nod my head, twisting my glass, moving it around on the tabletop. Despite not wanting to, I should have stayed at the Soo with Robert and Tattletale. At least it would have been safer with him. But I'd been drawn away by Quinn, by my heart hammering in my chest. In that moment, I wanted nothing more than to escape with him.

But now that I'm here, I'm second-guessing myself, second-guessing my decisions.

"What's that look for?" he asks, having placed an order

with the waitress while I've been preoccupied with my thoughts.

I shrug.

"Do you really want me to move to the other side of the booth, Grey? Because I will. I don't want you to be uncomfortable."

I meet his stare, those dark emerald eyes, and feel myself melt.

"Probably for the best. Robert isn't here. So, no need to pretend anymore."

I don't mention how we held hands in the truck on the way here, but I digress.

He sighs, moving out from beside me and sitting on the other bench. Our knees knock but I don't shift to break contact. I kind of miss him next to me, to be honest. God, what is wrong with me?

What the fuck am I doing?

I am playing with fire. And let me tell you, I've been burned one too many times, and yet, here I am again. Doing stupid shit. I obviously haven't learned my lesson.

"Grey," Quinn says, and my eyes swivel to meet his. He pulls his upper lip between his teeth, and I am riveted.

"Yeah?" I breathe.

That lip pops out, wet and red. "It doesn't need to be weird."

I shift in my seat. "Nothing's weird."

He purses his lips and tucks a strand of hair behind his ear. "You're acting weird, so just stop it," he says lightly.

I toss some ice into my mouth and chew on it loudly. "Yeah. Okay."

"It was just holding hands, it's not like I bent you over."

The ice slides down my throat and lodges, burning, and I thump at my chest, trying not to die. Thank fuck it melts and slides down a moment later, and I inhale deeply.

"Jesus, Quinn."

He smirks, like it's fucking funny, and I reach into my glass, fishing out an ice cube, and chuck it at him. It hits his chest and falls to his lap.

His eyes positively twinkle. "Oh, Greyson," he says so softly that my cock perks up and takes notice. The way my name rumbles from his throat is sinful.

"Do it again and see what happens," he dares me. My fingers slip into the glass, closing around a freezing cube, and I hold it between my fingers.

"Do it," he whispers, and I flick it at him. It hits his chin and he grapples with it a moment, fisting it in his hand before the cube appears between his fingers.

And that little shit rolls it across his lips, a wet, reddened trail appearing on his skin before he slides it down his neck with a low moan emitting from his throat.

Is it just me, or has it gotten awfully humid in here all of a sudden? It's like a fucking sauna. I'm starting to sweat.

Before he can slide it down any farther, the waitress appears and sets two plates of food down.

"What is this?" I ask because I was too distracted earlier to hear what he ordered.

"Perch sandwich and Whitefish."

I stare down at it, my mouth watering. God, I love seafood. Joshua hates it, but apparently, Quinn doesn't because he's cutting into the fish and spearing some on his fork.

"God, I could live on the water," he says. "I could eat seafood every day. I was thinking about getting a houseboat and just chilling. Can you imagine that, Grey?"

I could. I so fucking could. "Good thing we live near the Great Lakes. You could make that a reality."

His eyes meet mine, his jaw working back and forth as he chews, almost as if he's considering it.

I could see him on a houseboat, just relaxing as the waves rock him back and forth. I could see myself there too, sitting next to him.

I shouldn't think those things, shouldn't imagine them. That's dangerous territory. It's too scary to dream.

Too heartbreaking when it doesn't pan out.

"It's weird that Josh doesn't like fish," he says. "Like, he has terrible taste."

I chuckle. "I know, who raised him?"

Quinn snorts softly. "The wrong fucking person, apparently."

My chest warms, and I pick up half of the sandwich, taking a large bite.

And that's how we spend the next twenty minutes, just slowly consuming the food on our plates until they're licked clean.

"Fuck, that's good," he says. "Should we get dessert?"

"You can," I say, and Quinn stares at me.

"I think I'll order some, Grey, and make you eat it."

I let out a stuttered breath. Probably a terrible idea, to be honest—for my cholesterol and my dick, but I still let him place an order for carrot cake and blueberry pie.

When it comes, Quinn spears a piece of the pie and leans forward, pressing the fork against my mouth.

"Open." And I do as he says, my tastebuds exploding. God, that's so damn good. I never let myself have shit like this, but here I am, eating it because Quinn is hand-feeding me.

A low moan escapes me, and Quinn's pupils dilate.

"Yes, so good, right?" he asks, his voice raspy.

I manage a small nod, and he sits back, feeding himself before moving forward and forcing me to consume the dessert I wouldn't normally eat in a million years.

When we finally make it out of the restaurant and we're back in my truck, Quinn folds his hands in his lap, almost as if trying not to reach out toward me.

Which is good. It's how it should be. No more holding hands, or whatever that was back there.

We're going back to appropriate now. Quinn is nineteen. He's my son's best friend.

I'm the adult.

I am the fucking adult.

I will behave like one.

Chapter Eight

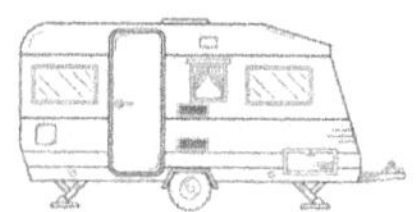

Quinn

I fed him that pie like I want to feed him my dick. I watched the way those lips engulfed my fork and my cock got all sorts of ideas. Not that Grey would ever let me. He put me on the other side of that booth like a kid in a time-out.

I'm not a fucking kid. But I can behave.

I got lucky holding his hand earlier, pressing my lips to his knuckles.

Feeding him.

I want to smear him in pie filling, stuff it into his hole, and lick it right out.

I bet he'd let me too.

Greyson Hart is into some stuff. I know it...heard all about it.

Fucking Kevin.

I hate that cunt, but honestly, the shit that spilled from his lips gave me all sorts of ideas. Things I've stayed awake at night and touched myself to.

"Gonna go sit outside for a bit," Grey says, and I grab my sketch pad and my pencil and follow him outside.

I don't want to crowd him, but I do anyways—can't help myself, it seems. Not when I've had a small taste.

I pull out a camping chair and unfold it, sitting down next to Grey as he sips his beer. He's leaned back, his thick thighs spread in front of him, and I force my gaze down to the paper in front of me. I'm going to draw those legs. I've drawn his hands, like I told him. But he doesn't know the other body parts of his I've sketched. If anyone were to find them, they'd think I'd gone insane.

I have. Partly. Grey makes me crazy.

I eye him, trying to be discreet, but it's hard to not put my pencil down and just gape. He is so damn gorgeous.

I wet my lips, thinking back to high school, to the casual hookups I've had throughout the years. Younger men, older men. I've fucked a lot of people for being only nineteen, but I swear to god, nothing would even come close to having Grey.

He would exceed all my expectations. There would be no other if I ever got to have him.

After drawing for a bit, I lay my sketchbook in my lap and lean my head back, soaking in the sun, feeling the humid air close in around me. Grey can look if he wants. And I know he wants. I can feel him watching me once my eyes slip shut.

It's like I'm incapable of not feeling him.

His eyes on me are like a brand, and he marks me with each lingering gaze.

I hear him stand up and his feet shuffle closer to me, so close I can smell him. I feel his finger brush against my lap, turning my sketchbook so he can see. So fucking nosy.

But I let him look. I want him to see what I see.

He lets out a huff but doesn't move, so I peek an eye open, catching him in the act.

"See something you like?" I ask, and draw my lips up in a smirk.

Grey falters behind me, his beer clutched in his hand.

"Just snooping, I guess."

"Snoop away, Grey. I'll let you snoop all day long."

He runs a hand across his head and then shakes it. "Gonna grab another beer."

"Want to go for a walk instead?" I ask. "There's a trail right up there. We can walk out to the lake."

Sounds all sorts of romantic to me. I want to romance him.

I've turned into some Victorian romance novel. But fuck, I'll keep doing it if it works. I'll shoot all my shots if it gets me a chance with him.

"Yeah, we can do that," he says. "Let me just lock up. Want a beer for the road?"

"Hell yeah," I say, surprised he's letting me drink when I'm underage, but then again, we're in the UP. Like, what else are we going to do?

I run inside, tossing my sketchbook on a chair and then meet Grey outside. He's holding two beers between his fingers and nods toward the trail that disappears between the trees.

"Ready?"

"Sure am," I say.

We walk in silence for the first bit, the sound of gravel beneath our feet. I can make out the waves hitting the beach in the distance. The Great Lakes are so enormous, they look like the ocean. It's my dream to one day travel to the coast and see what the real ocean looks like, feels like, tastes like. I want to skinny dip in it, feel that cold, salty water rush over me.

I want to do it with Grey.

"Ever been to the ocean?" I ask him.

Grey shrugs. "Nah, never made it out to the coast."

"You want to?" I ask, already planning trips with him in my mind, where we drive our trailer across entire states and set up camp and make love under the fucking moon.

"Never really thought about it, but yeah, I guess now that Joshua is gone...I guess I could."

"Yeah, we could plan it," I say, already inserting myself into his future. I want to plan all the trips with him. He could quit his shitty job, and we could just take odd ones as we move around, like nomads.

Grey peeks over at me. "We could."

I am already thrilled, so damn excited that he's even considering it that I nearly fall over, my feet catching on a groove in the pathway.

I stumble forward, but am saved from embarrassment by Grey's large hand steadying me and pulling me into him.

"Better watch where you step," he says softly, and I look up at him, my chest pressed into his. And there it goes. My dick is at full mast, just waving in the wind.

Hello, Grey, look over here! Down here!

But he pulls away, leaving me a little bereft and sad.

Wrap your arms around me again, Grey. Let me fuck you against a tree.

"You talk about traveling, but I thought you were going to college?"

I shrug. "Yeah, I got into a place, but I'm not sure I'm going to go, to be honest. Maybe I'll take a few years off. My passion is my art. I'd love to just do that for a living and it doesn't necessarily require college."

"I was always told art never makes much money," he says, eyeing me again. And I should be offended, but I'm not. Really, Grey would have to say something a lot worse to push me over the edge into anger. Like maybe, *your dick is small* or *I'd rather fuck Robert.*

"Yeah, well it might not, but at least I'd be happy. I'd wither being tied down to a nine-to-five job I didn't enjoy."

He runs his free hand across his head and nods. "Yeah, I can see that. It does take its toll on your mind and your spirit...and your body. My knees fucking hurt."

My eyes slide up and down his muscular torso, those legs I'm obsessed with. They look mighty fine to me.

"Why don't you quit?"

"Gotta pay for Joshua's college," he mutters, and the anger that refused to make an appearance earlier rears its ugly head. Because while he's my best friend, Josh is a spoiled asshole, a real entitled brat. Not that I can really blame him. He was raised by that wretched woman. How else was he supposed to turn out?

He has no idea what his dad is doing for him. I want to tell him, shout it in his face, but I'd never...not unless I was pushed to it.

Maybe when he grows up, he'll realize all the shit Grey's done for him, all the sacrifices he's made. But right now, for some mind-boggling reason, Grey refuses to tell him what's really going down.

But I know. I fucking know because I pay attention.

"Well, Josh could take out loans like every other person. Or Karen could help," I grind out.

Grey shakes his head. "Nah, it's my responsibility. I can do this for him."

Well, he doesn't need to do any more shit for Josh. He'll be eighteen soon. He can learn to take care of himself. Maybe if his dad didn't always step in and pay for shit when Karen drops the ball, Josh would realize how much his dad really does for him.

But I let it go, knowing I won't win this argument. If Grey is anything, he's stubborn. I can respect that. Maybe with these next couple weeks together I can convince him to stand up for himself a little.

I'd really fucking like that.

"Can I ask you a question?"

"Shoot," he says.

"What would you do if you didn't have to work that shitty job?"

He thinks about it a minute, his lips pulled between his teeth. I can almost see his brain working through the possibilities.

"Travel, I think. What you said...that sounds nice."

I peek over at him and just watch the way he moves as he walks. I can imagine him moving above me, underneath me, against me. I want to see his back arch off the bed, the tendons in his strong arms pop as he clutches the sheets.

I want to feel his ass strangle my cock.

I force my gaze forward. I need to keep my thoughts pure, which is impossible, but I can at least tell myself to behave.

It's getting harder and harder to remember how.

I don't know how I'll make it through this entire trip with this man. I am pretty sure that I'll end up inside of him at some point.

It would be careless of me not to at least try.

"There it is," he says, and my eyes are pulled forward to the blue expanse of Lake Huron. As we make our way down to the sand, Grey hands me a beer bottle, uncapping it for me before letting go.

I take a small sip, coming to a stop next to him, my arm brushing against his. He doesn't move away from me, which is progress in my opinion. I wonder what he'd do if I grabbed on to his head and pulled him in for a kiss. If I sucked on that bottom lip and slid my tongue against his.

I might scare him away, but then again, it's just us out here. Would it really matter? If I kiss Grey and no one is around to witness it, does it still count?

"Grey," I say, taking a sip of my beer and letting my fingers slide against his.

He doesn't move away.

"Why haven't you dated anyone seriously?"

He glances over at me and shrugs. "Never found someone I liked enough."

Me, he could like me enough.

"What are you looking for in a guy?" I ask as he takes a sip of his beer, looking out at the lake.

"Just want someone who will let me be me."

I curl my pinkie against his. "You don't want someone to push you, to try to help make you better?"

He thinks on that a minute. "I don't mind being pushed, but I don't want to be shoved."

"What's the difference?" I ask, my beer clutched tightly in my hand. This seems significant somehow, important. I'm listening so fucking earnestly.

"A push can be something gentle, a nudge in the right direction. A shove, it feels more aggressive. I'm too old to be shoved, Quinn. I just want someone to love me for who I am."

That's it, that's all I fucking need.

I reach up and grasp on to the back of his neck, pulling him down toward me. Giving him that push he needs.

His eyes widen a moment before our lips crash together. I keep my eyelids peeled open—I want to watch my first kiss with him. I want it seared into my brain.

He tastes even better than I imagined, a little like the beer he just drank, and I groan. I'm drunk off of him. So fucking wasted.

But it's over much too fast, Grey pulling his head away slowly, his breathing a little labored.

"Quinn," he grumbles, his voice rough.

I throw my head back and sigh. "I know. *I know.* I won't do it again. It was just a little push. I wanted to see what it would be like, kissing you."

Grey's eyes are focused on me, his beer dangling in his hand, and I fidget a little under his stare. God, did he hate it? I don't think he hated it. We barely brushed lips before he pulled away. I can do so much better than that. I could rock his world.

"And how was it?" he asks suddenly, and my hands start to shake.

"I think I'd need a larger sample size to make my determination," I reply, remembering that from my statistics class. It's the one thing I took away from that boring-ass course.

He mulls that over for a moment and then he reaches out, that big hand pulling me toward him, his lips lowering onto mine, and I nearly combust. My dick throbs between us, pushing against his abdomen.

He shifts impossibly closer, and I cling to his face, holding him still as I tilt my head and bite down on his bottom lip.

He grunts a little as I suck on it, nearly fainting from the sensation, but my eyes are open and locked with his. He hasn't closed his either. No, I can see the flecks of gold in his irises. They're so bright, he positively burns. He's so goddamn hot.

My tongue snakes out and presses between his lips, hoping he'll let me inside. His lips part like the fucking sea, and I plunge in, sliding my tongue along the length of his as he lets out a shaky exhale.

Oh god, yes. Oh fuck. He's enjoying this too, this electric current flowing from my body to his and back again. We're completing a circuit.

His tongue moves just slightly, flicking against mine, and I gasp, fucking into him slowly, taking my time. Savoring it.

But all too soon, he pulls away, and I'm left gasping, my hands still on his cheeks, my mouth feeling sensitive and under-used. I want it to be bruised from his. I want him to bite down on me until I taste blood. I want to walk away feeling him on me for hours.

"Better?" he asks, wetting his lips, and I just continue to hold him, his hand still clutching the back of my neck.

"God, Grey," I say softly, feeling my heartbeat in my ears. "Better? That was the best kiss of my life. I want to do it again."

His fingers flex against me, and he shakes his head. "Can't. And you know why."

"If Josh wasn't an issue, would you let me do whatever I want with you?" I ask, and his eyes meet mine, something unreadable in those depths.

"I don't know."

"No, you know. Tell me."

He lets out a deep breath and nods. "Probably...because that's just the kind of man I am."

"And what kind of man is that?" I ask, forcing him to continue looking at me. "A loyal one, a kind one, a hot one?"

"One who just kissed his son's best friend."

He lets those words sit between us, and I finally let him go. I know he needs to sit with that a minute, to think on it. I hope at the end he comes to the realization that we're both adults here, and we can do what we fucking like.

And there are things I want to do.

So many fucking things.

"We should head back," he says, his fingers touching his mouth. It's brief, but I catch it. He presses down on his bottom lip, the one I sucked on, and I swear to god, I see his hand tremble.

I want to watch him come undone.

I want to make him fucking cry for me.

Grey's hand drops and we turn back, chugging our beers and tossing them in a trashcan off the path. We make our way back to the trailer in silence, just the sound of the waves lapping at the shore in the distance.

That's okay, we don't need to talk. My mind is fucking chaos right now anyways. All I can think about is kissing him —rewinding and hitting play on each moment, pausing on the parts that made my skin burst aflame.

I am going to dream about him tonight.

I fucking know it.

Chapter Nine

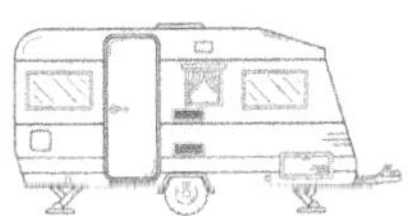

Grey

I have a lot of regrets in life, and I'm trying like hell to regret that kiss, but I can't quite make myself. He kisses like I'm his entire world, like the entirety of him begins and ends with me.

I stare at the small fan in the ceiling of the trailer. It's spinning noisily, and I run a hand down my face. I should be asleep. I should be fucking dreaming, but I've just been lying here thinking about his mouth on mine, trying to will my cock to soften. But it's relentlessly hard, aching and needy.

Quinn didn't bring the kiss up when we got back and made dinner. He didn't even say anything about it when we got ready for bed. But he didn't need to say anything. I could almost hear him thinking.

I turn onto my side and sigh loudly.

Go the fuck to sleep, Grey. Get your mind out of the gutter.

But it's there already, conjuring up filthy, dirty things—things I'd let him do to me with that tongue.

My hard cock throbs between my legs and I reach down to squeeze it, trying to keep it under control.

Jacking off to thoughts of Quinn as he sleeps just on the other side of the trailer is not something I'm going to do. And yet, still, my hand wraps around my dick and I stroke it, needing to take the edge off.

Fuck, that feels so damn good. It's been so long. So fucking long since I've gotten off.

My hand stills when I hear a thump, and I sit up straight, my head nearly knocking the lamp above me.

There's a slight whimper and then thrashing.

I don't even hesitate. I stand up, moving to where Quinn is sleeping. He's curled up, moving fretfully, his eyes closed, his brow furrowed. He's having a nightmare, something terrible lurking in his mind from the looks of it.

Fuck.

I lower myself next to him on the bed, my hands on his shoulders, and I shake him gently.

"Quinn," I say softly, not wanting to scare him. He shakes his head, a muffled sob escaping his mouth.

"Quinn," I say once more, a little louder, and his eyes shoot open. I can see it, the fear in his eyes.

He reaches out and clutches on to me, his fingers digging bruises into my skin.

"Grey," he croaks, and I pull him into me, his face buried in my chest.

My bare chest.

Oh fuck, I'm only wearing my boxers, the humidity nearly stifling.

And he's just as naked as I am.

His warm breath puffs against my skin as he trembles against me. I hold him tighter, needing to comfort him, knowing what it's like to wake up in a panic, your heart pounding, your mind reeling.

"You're okay," I whisper, my hand stroking up the bumps of his spine.

"Oh god," he murmurs, and I feel his nose coasting across my collarbone, his lips brushing against my chest. He seems so vulnerable, so needy in this moment that I just want to make it all better.

I want to take away whatever is haunting him.

His head tilts up and his lips part, just an inch, as he begs me with those sad eyes. I'm helpless to do anything but press my mouth to his.

Quinn groans, his hands pulling me to him, his heartbeat frantically pulsing through his veins. I can feel it in my fingertips, how much he needs this.

He pulls me harder and we fall onto our sides, my body pressed up against his, his tongue thrusting in and out of my mouth as his leg snakes around mine, pulling our groins together.

I can feel his hard cock against mine, both straining to touch.

Oh fuck, I need to stop. I need to end this, but I feel frantic, this burning need welling up inside of me. He teased me with a taste earlier and now I'm greedy and wanting.

"Grey," he moans as he bites down on my bottom lip hard, and I groan, growing louder and louder by the second. I can hear my rasping breaths bouncing off the walls of the trailer and the thunder of my heart in my ears.

My lip is pulled taut, still between his teeth, and my eyes meet his. He looks like he wants to eat me, consume me. He suddenly lets go, his hands on my face like he held me earlier, holding me in place. Almost as if to keep me grounded and present. With him.

"I need you," he says softly, arching his hips slightly, causing my eyes to roll back in my head. The friction of it, the heat. My god, I am on fire.

"Take my mind off it, Grey. Make me feel something other than that," he begs, and I groan, pressing into him, our dicks sliding against each other.

That movement is all the encouragement he needs. He slides a hand down my side, grabbing the waistband of my boxers and tugging them down over my thighs until my cock pops free. He reaches between us, his fingertips sliding against my thick length as he pulls my balls out, resting them on the fabric of my underwear.

The feel of him touching me. Oh my god. Those hands.

"So. Fucking. Hot," he whispers.

He rolls my balls in the palm of his hand and I grunt my need. I want him to stuff them into his mouth, I want him to tug on them gently, to make me see stars.

Quinn shifts, his hand suddenly gone from me, and I see him working his cock out from his boxers. It slaps against his abs as it pops free, big and uncut and so fucking perfect that I start to salivate. I want him in my mouth, want to taste him.

"Grey," he says as he leans over to kiss me again, our bare cocks now brushing, wetness spreading between us as we thrust against each other. We're humping frantically like a couple of horny teens.

He is a teen, my brain reminds me.

Oh fuck.

But those thoughts disappear as his hand squeezes between us and wraps around our lengths, pulling us together in his tight fist as his tongue and teeth assault my mouth. I whimper and moan and writhe against him.

The other campers here will be able to hear what he's doing to me, how he's taking me apart, piece by fucking piece. I cannot keep it in. I am nearly screaming.

"Grey," he moans as his hand strokes us, making me cry out, overly sensitive and needy.

"Listen to you," he gasps as his hand works faster. "Listen to how hot you are."

But I can't listen. I can't think. All I can do is feel as he expertly jerks us off, my body a live wire and ready to burst. My cum spills over his hand, endless streams of it until I am wrung dry. And then Quinn rolls and pushes me onto my back and jerks himself almost violently, using my cum as lube, shooting his release all over my chest.

Oh my god.

Oh my fucking god.

I cannot believe that happened. That was so fucking reckless, so fucking *good*.

Quinn whimpers, his chin against his chest, his body shaking from his release.

"Goddammit, Grey," he mutters, his hand still on his dick.

I can't move. I'm just lying beneath him, my cock and balls still out of my boxers, my chest heaving. I have his cum on my stomach, on my chest, on my dick.

There's no escaping it. I can smell it. He smells so fucking *good*.

"That, right there... You've wrecked me for other men," he says with a sigh, his eyes meeting mine, and I see the sincerity there.

It pinches my heart because I know he could find someone better. He's still young. He has his whole life ahead of him. Meanwhile, I'm pushing middle age, just tired and a fucking wreck.

"Do *not* fucking regret this," he mutters as he leans forward, his hand leaving his dick. He slides a cum-covered finger across my bottom lip, forcing me to taste him.

My tongue peeks out and I lick him up as he lets out a whimper.

"Oh, Jesus," he breathes, and then his fingers slide into my mouth. One. Two. Three. My tongue laps up the mess on his skin as he fucks his hand in and out of my mouth. It's filthy and degrading, but the way he's watching me makes me feel like a fucking king.

Like he's waited his whole damn life for this moment, right here.

"You are a dream," he murmurs when his fingers hit the back of my throat and he leaves them there, forcing me to swallow around him.

I shouldn't be doing this, and yet, here I am.

Like, I said, never a bad decision I didn't like.

He stares down at me and slowly retracts his hand until my mouth is empty. Our eyes lock and we just gaze at each other, awe and lust heavy between us.

His lips lower to mine for a soft, gentle kiss before he pulls away, standing up and moving to the bathroom.

"Don't move," he says, and then I hear the water running. He's back a moment later with a damp washrag, and he gently cleans me up until no trace of him is left.

Does it make me a bad man to wish he'd left a part of him on me, so I could feel him tomorrow? So I could remember this?

He tosses the used washrag into the kitchen sink and then lowers himself down next to me, our naked, spent bodies pressed up against each other once more.

"Don't run," he whispers, almost like he's reading my mind. I should run, I should run very far away, but I'm too tired to move. And honestly, what more could I really do? I already crossed all the lines. Lying here for a while longer won't change the fact that I fucked around with him.

Quinn turns his face and buries his nose in my armpit, inhaling me, his fingers running through the hair on my chest.

"What was your dream about?" I ask as my hand slides against his shoulder, pulling him a little closer.

"You really wanna know?"

"Yeah, I do."

He sighs, his fingers plucking at my nipple, causing my entire body to tremble with renewed lust. But I tamp it down. Now is not the time.

"Well, you've met my mom and dad, so you know how I

was raised. They aren't bad parents...but they kinda are, you know? They wanted me to be free-range or whatever, independent. So very early on, I was out doing shit that I shouldn't have...things that should have been supervised by an adult."

"Yeah, I noticed that about you."

His hand stills and he sighs. "Well, when you don't have much guidance or supervision like that, you don't come out unscathed. I've had some pretty close calls growing up. Got lost a lot."

My hand threads through his hair, and Quinn just snuggles further into me.

"That's what I was dreaming about. Getting lost on the walk home from school when I missed the bus. Not being able to find my parents when I needed them. Silly, I know, but as an eight-year-old who was a little too sensitive to be alone like that, it was fucking scary."

"I'm sorry, Quinn," I say. "I won't talk shit about your parents because that's not my place, but it does seem like they do things a little differently."

"Yeah, but different isn't always good. I like how independent I am now, but not how I got to this place. Did you know I was almost kidnapped once?"

My entire body freezes. "What? When?"

"When I was twelve. Got trailed by a creepy old dude on the way home from school. He grabbed on to me but I managed to kick him off. I always wonder what my life would have been like had my parents been around to protect me from stuff like that."

We're silent a moment and his hand slides through my chest hair again, his fingers curling against me.

"You're a good dad, Grey. A real fucking good one. I knew that the moment I met you. And you know how I know?" he asks.

I grunt, feeling my nose start to tingle and my eyes sting.

"Because you always made an effort to spend time with your kid. Even if his mom wouldn't let you. Even if Josh didn't appreciate it. You always tried to be there."

And then he buries his nose in my armpit again and holds on to me so damn tight. Well, fuck. My throat suddenly feels tight with emotion. I must be overtired.

Maybe I should get up and go to my own bed, put some distance between us, but my heart won't let me leave.

So I just stay, and we fall asleep in each other's arms.

Chapter Ten

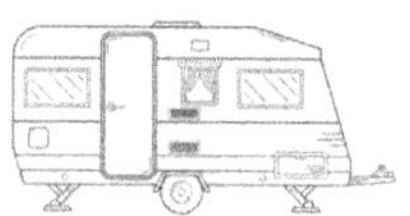

Quinn

I wake up pressed against Grey, and let me tell you, I am a horny fucker. He smells all musty and sweaty, and I want to bury my face in his balls and inhale. I want to do what we did last night all over again, and so much more. I don't care that we have morning breath.

My hips arch and my hard, naked cock drags against his hairy thigh. I fell asleep in his arms and didn't move. My body knows what's up. There was no way I was going to sleep apart from him. I'll be sleeping like this for the rest of this trip, that's for sure. I'll have nightmares every night if that's what it takes.

"Morning," Grey's deep, sexy voice rasps above me.

I thrust against him again, loving how he's built, how my cock drags along his thick thigh muscle. I could come just like this.

"Morning," I say and let my hand slide down to his dick, encircling it in my hand.

He lets out a low grunt, his length hot and heavy in my palm. I stroke it, loving how he fits so fucking perfectly against me. I know I'm being bold, but I'm taking what I want. Last night unlocked something between us and like hell I'm closing that door again.

It's gaping wide open and I'm walking through it.

"Shouldn't," he says lowly, but still thrusts his hips up, fucking into my fist.

Always so damn serious. He needs to let himself have something every once in a while.

Me, he could have me.

"Should," I counter and pump him faster, wanting to hear him grunt and pant for me again. What a fucking great way to wake up.

My stomach rumbles and I bite down on his pec.

Hmm, perhaps I should have a little snack.

I let go of him for just a moment before sitting up and scooting between his legs, and then before he can protest, I engulf his dick in my mouth, sliding my tongue along the underside of him.

Grey groans, his mouth open, his eyes screwed shut.

I could make him feel this good every day—every fucking morning, I'd do this.

My hands run up his thighs, and I spread him farther apart, needing access to the good bits. The hidden ones.

My mouth slides up and down his hard length, taking as much of him as I can, my eyes settled on his face, watching every single moment of this.

I pop off of him and Grey's eyes snap open, his cock wet and shiny. Our gazes lock as I pull his balls up and suck them into my mouth, rolling my tongue around as he groans deeply.

God, he's such a quiet man but when he's being fucked, he's so goddamn loud.

"Quinn," he grunts, and my name on his lips...oh my *god*.

I let his balls fall from my mouth and I'm back on his dick, sucking, letting my mouth glide up and down his cock. Our eyes meet and I memorize his sex face. I sear it into my brain, the way he's looking at me, how flushed his cheeks are, how utterly and completely fucked he looks.

His hand moves to my head, his fingers threading through my hair as he starts to move me, the rhythm just how he likes. God, yes. Take it from me. Take what you need.

I roll his balls in my hand, feeling how hard they are, like he's ready to come, and I can tell he's close. He's groaning and trembling, his cock hitting the back of my throat with each upward thrust.

Suddenly, his legs start to twitch and he's crying out, his cum sliding down my throat. I swallow, choking a bit, but drinking every last drop. Because it's him and I want to be full of him. I want to know that a part of him is inside me.

I keep him in my mouth, sucking gently, not ready for it to be over. I just need to cockwarm him for a minute. He lets me, too—his body limp beneath me, his muscles flexing ever so slightly as I mouth him.

His hand strokes my hair gently, and I nearly purr, my own dick straining between my thighs, needing release.

But right now isn't about me. This is about him, my man.

"You're spoiling me," he finally grunts, and I smile around him, letting him just sit heavily on my tongue.

My eyes meet his and his thumb brushes against my cheek.

"This is wrong," he whispers, and I suck on him roughly, causing him to wince.

This is so far from wrong, it's bordering on holy. I could go to fucking church right now and a priest would baptize me.

My mouth pops off of him and I crawl up his body, pressing my lips to his.

His big hands come up and pull me into him.

"Nothing about you and me is wrong, Grey," I say, and then roll off of him. "Come on, let's shower."

His eyes travel down my body to my hard dick, jutting out from between my legs.

I stand there, letting him look, letting him see what he can have.

Then those eyes snap up to mine, and I pull my bottom lip between my teeth.

"If you keep lying there like that I'm going to be tempted to do things to you," I say, letting my honesty pierce each word.

His body shivers, and he lets out a long exhale.

"Why do you assume I'm a bottom?" he asks as he sits up.

I want to straddle those thighs and hump myself up against him.

"Oh, Grey," I mutter, moving toward him and placing my hand under his chin, tilting his face up to meet mine. "You just beg to be fucked. It's in the way you talk, the way you respond to my touch, the way you look at me."

His eyelids flutter and he leans in, his forehead pressed to my stomach. I can feel the warm puff of his breath against my skin, and I trail my fingers across the back of his neck.

I feel his lips brush against me, and I dig my fingertips into him. I want him to drag his mouth down to my dick and suck on me. I want to fuck his face.

"We should shower," he mutters but doesn't move.

Neither do I. I want to see what he does. I don't want to shove, just want to gently push.

Push him onto my dick, but still. I'll be gentle about it.

But instead of doing what I've dreamed of, he stands up, his body brushing against my oversensitive cock, and he pulls me into a hug.

"You won't be fucking me, Quinn. That's...that's crossing a line we can't cross."

I grab on to his ass and squeeze, arching up into him.

"Oh, you keep telling yourself that," I murmur, and he lets out a huff, shaking his head.

"Let's grab our stuff and go."

He pulls away from me for real this time, and I feel slightly despondent, but I don't let myself dwell on my disappointment. He says these things, but he doesn't mean them. I'll get what I want.

Or I'll die trying.

We make our way to the campground showers in silence, but that's okay. I don't mind the quiet, as long as I'm with him.

We shower separately, but I let him hear me jack off. I even cry out his name while I do it. It helps curb this insatiable hunger I have for him. Until I look at him, that is, and then it's back.

God, when I finally get inside of him, he's going to be so sore trying to keep up with me. I am going to ride him into the mattress, going to rock that fucking trailer till the springs squeak.

"You ready for the next adventure?" I ask when we make it back to the trailer. The coffee is brewing on the stove and we're unhooking everything outside.

"Yeah," he says, meeting my stare and clearing his throat. Today we're headed up to Tahquamenon Falls State Park to see the waterfalls. God, what I'd do to get Grey under one of those. We'd probably both drown, but I'd still love to suck his dick while water washes over him.

Maybe we should stick to the shower for that instead. So damn tempting though. What a way to go out, with his dick in my mouth.

We shut all the external compartments, making sure everything is put away before we pour the coffee into to-go mugs and drive out of our camping spot.

On our way out, we see Robert lounging outside his motorhome, earphones in his ears, Tattletale on his shoulder. He looks...sexy, and I hate him a little for it, knowing that he was inside of Grey at one point. But whatever, I have him now.

He's mine for the next twelve days.

Grey slows down, the brakes of his truck squeaking slightly, and waves at him, letting him know where we're headed next. For fuck's sake, Grey, don't encourage him. It's better if he doesn't know where we're going so we can be alone. I want him all to myself.

But Robert just nods, not committing to anything, thank fuck. I don't want a third wheel on this trip. God, I hope Joshua doesn't end up out here with us. I mean, we messaged yesterday, but he didn't mention anything about reconsidering his decision to come on this trip. It would be so weird if he changed his mind though, because camping like this is so not his thing. But Hailey is a loose cannon. I wonder if she would convince him to change his plans. She seems adventurous and outdoorsy. So, who the fuck knows what will happen.

I glance over at Grey and feel a little guilty. I mean, I'd want Joshua here for his dad, to make Grey happy. I'm being a little selfish wanting the two of us to spend the rest of the trip alone, so I can explore him—his body, his mind, his fucking heart.

I want to know him so well that I practically become him.

Obsession doesn't even begin to describe what I feel for this man.

"How long till we get to the falls?" I ask, pulling up the itinerary. God, it's so detailed. I know how much work he put into this. I can't believe Joshua bailed on him.

Makes me mad just thinking about it.

"Probably an hour and a half. Maybe more if we stop."

"Oh, stop where?" I ask, imagining him naked under a waterfall once more.

"There's this little place called Paradise. If you want, we could stop there, grab some souvenirs."

I shift in my seat, taking a sip of my coffee. "Can we get matching shirts?"

He peeks over at me, his hands twisting slightly on the steering wheel.

"I mean, our dicks have touched, Grey. How much crazier can it get?"

His cheeks flush, and god, I'd lean over and bury my face in his crotch if he'd let me. Just let him drive me all the way to our destination with my head between his legs.

"I'm teasing you," I say softly, trying to rein in my crazy. Just a little. I mean, there's only so much I can do when it comes to him, but I also don't want to scare him away.

"Matching shirts should be fine," he says, and my lips turn up in a smile.

"Oh, I can't fucking wait. What size are you? 2X, right?"

God, he's big. He's like twice my size and the fact that he bottoms is so fucking hot. Like, you wouldn't expect it from a guy who looks like he does. He's the best kind of surprise.

"Yeah, 2X," he replies, and I watch as his biceps flex as he makes a lefthand turn.

"Maybe I should get you a size smaller, let it just stick to your skin," I say and he shakes his head, a chuckle escaping his lips.

"Jesus, Quinn. I didn't know you were like this."

"Oh, you have no idea. I am like..." I lean my head back against the headrest and stare at him. "I am like so fucking horny for you."

Grey's foot moves off the gas and the truck slows considerably. "That's...."

"Do not say inappropriate. Nothing about this is inappropriate. I'm nineteen, a consenting adult."

He tucks his lips between his teeth, rolling his neck slightly. "Yeah, I know."

"Ever been with anyone younger than you? Chatty Robert back there seemed at least a few years older," I ask, shifting my body so I can watch him more intently.

"Not as young as you."

"I've been with older guys," I say, and Grey glances over at me.

"That so?"

"It's so."

We're silent a minute and then I explain, "Now that was inappropriate. A sixteen-year-old with a thirty-year-old dude. So, yeah, Grey, I know what's wrong and what's not. And you and I...we're definitely not."

"Your parents know you were sleeping with an older man?"

I shrug. "Maybe. Not like they cared if I did. As long as I'm being safe and responsible, they're happy."

When Grey doesn't say anything, I nudge him. "Go on, spill. I know you have things you want to say."

"Not gonna trash-talk your parents, Quinn."

I lean over and bite at his ear. Fuck, he's adorable.

"You can trash talk them all you want. We both know what's up. Let me guess, you'd never let Josh date an older woman like that. And I totally agree. It's bad parenting."

He bobs his head a little and then takes a sip of his coffee.

"The only thing that's good about how much experience I have is that I know what I want."

"Yeah, and what's that?" he asks, his eyes on the road.

I don't even hesitate. "You."

He's silent, his body stilling for a moment, and then he clears his throat and takes another sip of his coffee. The road stretches out before us, just pavement and green trees. It seems almost endless.

"Listen, don't get your hopes up, Quinn. I don't...last night and this morning, it was a fluke."

I stare at him because that was no fluke. That was a goddamn miracle.

"I think we should have flukes more often then. I really enjoyed it."

"I'm just...you're young, you have an entire life to live."

"You make it sound like you're a hundred. You're thirty-three. You're fourteen years older than me. Big fucking deal."

Grey runs a hand down his face. "Fourteen years feels like an eternity sometimes."

"Well, it's not. It's just a fucking number." And like hell I'm letting him push me away over some math. I always hated the subject anyways.

But I'll let it go for now. Maybe tonight, when he's feeling lonely, he'll let me slide into bed with him and press my face into his chest.

If my dick presses into his hole while I'm at it, well, it can't be helped.

We wander into the roadside gift shop in the small town of Paradise in search of souvenirs. I find a keychain for Grey, one that will make him think of me when this trip is over. You know, just in case things don't go as planned. Maybe he'll look down at his keys every day and see it and think fondly of me.

Of the things we did together.

I clutch it in my palm as I move over to the t-shirts and peruse for far too long, searching for those matching shirts I promised him. It's a little hard since our sizes are so different. God, that chest. I want to see the fabric stretched across it. He's so damn big.

"What do you think about this one?" I ask, holding up a shirt with the state of Michigan across it. It's a little cheesy, but it works. I'm feeling a little desperate at this point. I want us matchy-matchy.

Grey eyes it and shrugs.

"It's the only one in both our sizes," I say, holding it up to him.

He stands completely still as I eye it and bob my head. "Yeah, we're so getting this one. We can grab another somewhere else, but you know, up here, things are few and far between."

Grey fiddles with the fabric. "I guess it works. I can get these."

"Nope," I say, pulling it away and striding to the counter. "I got it."

And before he can protest, I pull out my phone and pay.

I don't even have the cashier bag it. I just walk outside with it all in my arms. I plan on wearing this shit right the fuck now.

"Alright, give me your keys," I say, and Grey hands them over, not even questioning me.

I slip the keychain on, and he stares at the metal Q dangling there. Ridiculous, I know, but I never said I wasn't desperate.

"Don't want you to forget about me," I say with a wink, and Grey gingerly touches it.

"Don't think that's possible."

Oh. Oh fuck. Well, that just gives me hope. "And why is that?" I ask, taking a step closer, wanting to close the distance entirely. I want to plaster myself to him.

His eyes meet mine and I'm drawn in.

"You know why," he says, and I step in further, pushing myself against him.

"Tell me with words, Grey. I want to know what I've done so I can keep doing it."

He wets his lips, and I run my nose along the side of his cheek, feeling the stubble abrade my skin.

"You're relentless."

"Yes, when there's something I want, I go for it."

I brush my lips against his, soft and eager, and Grey melts into the kiss, letting himself *take* for just a minute.

When he finally pulls away a minute later, his cheeks are flushed and my heart is racing.

I'm going to end up in the hospital the first time I'm inside of him.

"Can we do that again?" I whisper, and his eyes sparkle.

"We have places to be."

I roll my eyes because we have all the time in the world, but he looks so damn hot right now, so I just smack another kiss to his lips, trying like hell not to tongue-fuck him.

"Fine, but when we arrive, no more excuses. You're mine."

He clears his throat and steps away. I follow him back to the trailer where I pull off my shirt and tug the cheesy Michigan one on. I hold out the other shirt to Grey and glare at him until he puts his on. It gives me a nice little peek at that chest again too. Maybe he should just drive us over to Tahquamenon Falls shirtless. In fact, he should just walk around nude all day long.

"You could just leave the shirt off," I say, and Grey chuckles, starting up his truck and putting it in gear.

"I'm not doing that," he says, and I shift in my seat.

"You could do it for me, so I can draw it. I've only seen it a few times and honestly, it's more impressive the longer I look."

"Didn't realize you were creepin' on me, Quinn."

I snort a laugh and then reach over and trace my finger across his arm.

"Oh, I creep like a pervert when it comes to you." I slink my finger up his shirt sleeve. "You have been my jack-off fodder for years."

He runs a hand down his face and peeks over at me. "Christ."

But I'm not deterred. "Remember that song about Stacy's mom? Well for me, it was Josh's dad. It's always been you, the hot-as-fuck dad."

My hand is fully up his sleeve now, groping his bicep. I've been let loose. Last night changed things for me. I feel freer about what I can do, what I can say.

I'm trying to put a leash on the horny, but I'm having a hard time.

"How much longer till we get to the campground?" I ask, my hand still up his shirt. My arm is kind of at a weird angle and it's starting to fall asleep, but Grey's not stopping me, so I refuse to retract it.

I'll need a cease-and-desist letter first.

And maybe some handcuffs.

"About fifteen more minutes. Can you hold it together?" he asks, and I smirk.

"I have been holding it together for four years, Grey. I can manage fifteen minutes."

He might not get that reference, but so fucking what? I'm all in now.

When we finally park the trailer, my hand has traveled down to his pec, my fingers playing with his nipple.

Grey hasn't said anything, but his breathing is a little more labored. As soon as he puts the truck in park, he turns to look at me. And I'm on him.

My legs carry me over the console, and I'm in his lap, my hands in his hair, my lips on his.

"Oh, fuck," I whine as I grind myself against him, my cock already so damn hard. It's been edged into oblivion.

"Fuck, I want you," I groan as I plunder his mouth with my tongue, and Grey meets me thrust for thrust, his dick hard against mine.

He wants me. He fucking *wants me*.

I gently bite my way down his face, licking my way across his neck. I'm feral, wild, unhinged. I want to rut up against him and spread my scent on him. I want to knot him and keep myself inside of him for hours.

"Quinn," he murmurs, his breath coming out in a raspy stutter. "*Quinn.*"

My entire body breaks out in goosebumps and I am so close to coming in my pants.

My lips latch on to the side of his neck and I suck and *suck* as those big hands of his cradle my ass. We are plastered to one another, rocking our bodies, almost like we're fucking.

I don't care who sees us like this. Let them look. Let them see how crazy I am for this guy.

"Let me fuck you, Grey," I whisper, my lips trailing up his skin. "Please."

He groans a low rumble, and I press my lips to his once more and lick my way inside his mouth.

But before my dream can come true, his body tenses, and I feel his orgasm as he falls over the edge. His body continues to rock against mine as he rides it out and then he collapses against the seat.

Fuck, that was hot. That was so damn hot.

I mean, my dick is still impossibly hard, but hell, I'd do that all over again, just to feel him break apart.

"Fuck, Quinn. What are you doing to me? I haven't...that hasn't happened to me in ages."

I reach between us and cup my aching dick. His eyes flicker open and our gazes meet.

"I'm just that good," I say with a smirk, and he shakes his head, his lips twitching.

"You are. *Jesus.*"

I perk up at the compliment as his gaze travels down to the bulge in my pants.

"You didn't come?"

He almost seems embarrassed by it, but he shouldn't be. It was too fucking hot. Nothing to be ashamed about.

"I didn't."

His head falls back and he closes his eyes. "Mortifying."

I reach out and grab on to his chin, forcing him to look at me, and his eyelids flutter open once more.

"The only thing *that* was, was epically hot. I want to do it again. And again. You can come in your pants for me anytime, Grey."

He swallows and then that big hand moves between us, cupping my dick and my eyes roll back in my head.

Here I am, surrounded by trees, with the big blue sky as my only witness that this is happening right now.

"This okay?" he asks, and I groan.

"You can do anything you want to me, Grey. Anything."

He squeezes me a little tighter, and I practically combust.

And when he unbuttons my jeans and pulls me out, I almost dic. My hypersensitive dick is happy to have Grey finally handling it with those thick fingers.

It takes him only a few strokes to push me over the edge, my cum spilling over his hand and onto his jeans.

"Fuck," I say, collapsing onto him, my breath unsteady.

"Feel better?" he asks, and I nod, gulping down air.

"I do. I mean, I'll be ready to go again in like two minutes if you want to fool around again."

He lets out a laugh. "I'm too old for that shit."

But I feel him hardening in his pants once more, and I glare at him, brow raised.

I know he'd be willing to give it another go. I think he's just as horny as me, but he's repressed it for ages because he's been so sexually unsatisfied. I get it, living with the disappointment. But I'm going to change things for him. I am going to show him what it feels like to ascend.

Just as I'm about to convince him to move into the trailer with me and give it another go, his phone buzzes, and I see Joshua's name pop across the screen. My heart drops.

Of course, *now* he decides to text his dad.

For fuck's sake.

Grey's face pales. For a minute, he forgot who I was to his son and now he's remembering.

I stuff myself back into my pants and move to the passenger side. My cum is still on him, but he's wiping his hand on his shirt before picking up his phone.

I don't want to see his disappointment, or shame, or whatever else he's got in that muddled head of his, so I just slide out of the truck and start hooking shit up. This campground doesn't have showers, so we will be using the small one inside the trailer. Probably means we won't be able to shower together, the thing is too damn small.

But it doesn't even matter because Joshua's text probably means that Grey is going to run scared in the opposite direction, leaving me to chase after him...again. I'm back at square one.

Fuck.

I'm in a mood when he finally appears. He looks a little

more put-together, not the sexy sloppy mess he was earlier, but he's quiet and won't look at me.

"You okay?" I ask, and he just grunts a response.

I bite back a snarky remark as we hook up the water and the sewer. When we're done, I don't bother waiting for him to grunt at me some more. I move inside the trailer and grab my sketchbook. I just need some space, and I think he needs some too.

"Going for a walk," I tell him, not even looking back at him.

I don't want to see it on his face.

The regret.

I'd rather remember how he came apart beneath me. I'll take that with me for now.

Chapter Eleven

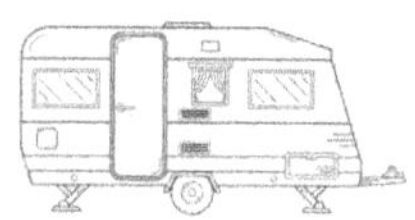

Grey

Guilt. I feel it most days. I never feel good enough. Never do enough. Never fucking *enough*. But for those few minutes with Quinn, I felt light, like I was his entire world.

But now the guilt is back.

Joshua.

I stare down at the picture my son sent me.

He doesn't usually send me shit, but he did for some reason, and my heart felt really fucking full. But then I remember what I've been doing with his best friend and cringe.

Goddammit, why does it have to be *him*?

I watch as Quinn walks away, his long legs carrying him down the dirt path, and I want to follow him. I need to explain that my mind is just a mess, but he doesn't look back. He seemed off after what happened in the truck.

He's mad, I can tell.

Fuck, I've ruined it. Not that I expected anything less from myself. I'm a champ at making things weird. I did it for years with Karen. I learned a lot during that time in my life. Apparently not enough though because I'm still fucking doing it.

I move into the trailer to change my underwear and grab a beer.

I should have shown more restraint when it came to him, but he's just so...alluring. I just can't keep my distance.

And the sex...best fucking sex.

The best. And we haven't even fucked.

I press my forehead against the wall of the trailer and take a deep breath. I can fix this, maybe. I can apologize and set some boundaries.

He'll respect those, I know he will.

Damn, but truthfully, I don't want boundaries. For once in my life, I want something for myself, something I shouldn't want, but do.

I want to be selfish. I want to take and take and *take*.

I move outside, the warm air hitting my skin and inhale deeply. It's all earth and wind out here. It's so damn beautiful, and I wish I could appreciate it more, but my mind's on other things.

I pull out the camping chair and plop onto it, facing the path that Quinn disappeared down. I'll just wait for him to come back and then we can talk.

Fuck, I hate talking. It makes me squirm and sweat. It's

why I've been alone for so many years. Because partnership requires communication and I'm shit at it.

I fucking suck at opening my mouth and talking about how I feel.

But I need to. We need to. We need to clear the air.

I glance down at my phone again, at my son beaming up at me from the picture he sent, and I feel my heart pinch.

Would he really care if I was with Quinn? Joshua hasn't ever really been interested in my life. I don't know if Quinn and I messing around would even bother him. Joshua is going to college out of state. But then again, am I willing to risk it—to risk this fragile relationship with my son?

It seems that I might.

It seems I'm willing to make all sorts of excuses to get what I want.

My legs are spread before me and I scoot lower in the chair, my eyes closing, my beer dangling from my fingers.

I'm just going to close my eyes for a minute and rest. When I open them again, Quinn better fucking be home.

When I wake a while later, I scan the area in front of me and don't see him. I don't know how much time has passed, but the sun is lower in the sky and he's still not back. God, I hope he didn't get lost. I think about how he told me how much he hated his parents letting him wander around by himself. I shouldn't have let him walk off alone. I should have gone with him, should have insisted.

I realize now that I messed up. He didn't need his space, he needed me to chase him.

Standing up, I run a hand over my face, my beer is on the ground, toppled over. I pick it up and toss it in the garbage can on the side of the path. And that's when I see him.

Quinn is chatting with someone else a few camping spots down.

A girl his age.

My heart flutters in my chest, an ugly feeling welling up within me. Something I can't quite define. Not so much jealousy, but more like rage, panic...desperation.

Because he's bisexual and she's young. Pretty. His age.

I stare down at my cum-stained jeans and frown. Oh fuck. I can't even compete, shouldn't even want to. I am not even comparable.

As if he can feel me staring, he turns to look at me and our eyes lock.

The girl turns her gaze too, and her brow creases in confusion. She probably thinks I'm his dad. Oh Jesus, if she only knew.

And yet still, I can't look away. To them, I probably look like a lost and pathetic old man. And to be fair, they're not wrong.

My hand clenches into a fist as I take in Quinn's neutral face. I can't tell what he's thinking. Usually he wears his expressions so damn loud, but right now they're muted and quiet, and I hate it.

His eye twitches and then he turns his gaze back to the girl, leaning in a little closer to her.

My breath stutters out of me, my chest impossibly tight.

It would be just about right for me to have a heart attack right now. I'd keel over dead and be eaten by bears.

Ridiculous. This whole thing is damn silly. I need to get a fucking life.

I need to change my clothes and maybe I'll take a look around the campground, get the fuck out of here. Let Quinn have his time with her. I'm not going to stand in the way of two teenagers who want to get it on.

I know when I'm not wanted.

I move inside the trailer and change into something clean, reminding myself that I need to go to the laundromat and wash my shit soon. If I keep coming in my pants like that then I'm going to need to buy some new stuff. This is getting ridiculous.

I brush my teeth and run a hand over my head, staring at myself in the mirror. I have lines near my eyes and mouth, and in this moment, I feel a hundred years old.

I can't look any longer or else I'll get down about things I can't change, so I move outside instead, striding down the path that Quinn escaped to earlier. I don't look over my shoulder at him. I tell myself I don't want to disrupt them.

But in reality, I just don't want to glance over and see him not looking back at me.

So I just push forward, losing myself in my thoughts. I know that I'm quiet, uttering very few words, but my mind is the complete opposite. It's a cacophony of noise and chatter that I can't escape. Sometimes I wish my mind would shut the hell up and leave me in peace and quiet.

I can't wish for things that won't ever happen.

My legs carry me toward a small wooden bridge and I

stride across it, my eyes on the scenery in front of me, but not really seeing it. It's getting a little late and I know that I should head back, but I'm not ready.

I just need to walk a little farther to clear my head.

My mind flashes to Quinn, to the taste of him, the feel of him. The way the loneliness that's infiltrated my very being for so many years seems to lessen when he's around. But I can't ever have what I want, right?

And do I even want him?

I think back to him in high school—showing up at my place, sitting with me, chatting with me, just genuinely enjoying my company—and I feel my chest constrict.

Not many people can handle me. But Quinn doesn't seem to mind how I am. He seems to like it.

Or he did.

I may have ruined that by being weird.

My feet carry me to a river and I clutch the back of my neck as I stand there, listening to the water rush over the rocks in the creek bed.

My anxious thoughts are so loud and consuming that I stand there for far too long, just ruminating. Turning things over and over again in my mind and getting nowhere.

By the time I start my hike back to the campground, the sun is setting and the katydids are chirping loudly. When I finally arrive back at the trailer and pull the door open, Quinn is standing there, his hair half out of its ponytail, his eyes a little wild. He looks utterly and completely undone.

"Where the fuck were you?" he asks lowly, his hands in fists at his sides as I step past him. "You left hours ago."

I meet his stare, and his eyes flash.

"Went for a walk."

"That was a motherfucking journey, Grey."

I shrug and move toward the fridge, feeling overly warm. He was worried about me. He was fucking *worried*.

"Didn't figure you'd miss me."

Quinn's breathing picks up and he growls, sounding almost feral.

"Why would you think that?" he asks, his voice danger- ously low.

"Figured you made a new friend."

He stops breathing, and then I hear him say, "Maybe I did."

I peek over at him and see his cheeks flushed. My mouth goes dry. He's so goddamn pretty.

"Gonna make something to eat," I manage to say and try to move around Quinn, but he blocks me. I could easily move him, just lift him and set him aside, but I don't. I just press up against him, and those cheeks of his darken.

Oh, he's angry. He looks so hot when he's mad. God, I want him to pound into me, to teach me a lesson, to use that anger and spank my ass red.

"Don't feel like you need to stay here and keep me company," I say softly, and Quinn snaps. His hand reaches out and wraps gently but firmly around the front of my neck, pushing me back against the fridge, holding me in place.

"Shut the fuck up," he mutters as his hand flexes against my throat and my dick instantly perks up. Oh god, yes. This. *This.* "You want me to go fuck her? Is that what you fucking want, Grey?"

I gasp as those fingers of his move up and he tilts my face so my eyes are forced to meet his.

"You think I want that pussy?" he mutters, and I wet my lips, my cock leaking.

"Dunno."

He steps into me, his body nearly shaking.

"You don't know?" he hisses, and I groan when he moves his hips against my cock.

"You fucking know, Grey. You're fucking blind if you don't."

And then he's right there, his lips against mine, not kissing, just lingering.

"Do I even stand a chance with you, or is this all for nothing?" he asks, arching up against me once more, and I let out a huff. "Tell me," he says, his lips brushing mine, and I cling to him, holding him against me.

And when I don't answer, he bites down on my bottom lip causing me to groan.

"She thought you were my dad. What would she think if she knew I was fucking you?"

He licks his way up my cheek and my eyelids flutter closed.

"We're not fucking," I manage to say, trying to think clearly, but it's so damn hard when he's so close. He's crowding me, forcing me to face this. I don't want to. I want to fucking hide.

But he's holding me in place and making me *see*.

"Oh, I know. I fucking know."

Our breathing is heavy between us as his hand squeezes my neck and I let out a shudder.

"Get on your knees," he says softly, and I blink at him. "On your fucking knees."

I don't even hesitate. I just fall to them, my face now level with his crotch. Quinn runs a hand over the top of my head and pulls me forward so my face is smashed into his groin.

I inhale deeply, my hands landing on his ass, holding him to me. God, he smells good.

"This is what you fucking need."

His hand runs across the back of my neck and then he bows his hips away from me, pulling his dick out.

He's hard and angry, and I should think about this, should have some fucking commonsense, but I can't stop. I just pull him into my mouth and take his dick all the way into the back of my throat.

Nothing has ever felt this right.

Quinn groans lowly, both of his hands cupping my face as he fucks into me—gently, slowly, killing me with each thrust.

"I don't want anyone but you," he says as drool pools from the sides of my mouth and drips down my chin.

I look up at him, our eyes locking, and I feel my dick jerk between my legs. He's so gorgeous, his hair falling across his cheekbones, that septum piercing through his nose, those freckles.

Those eyes.

They lock with mine as he picks up his pace. I gag and gurgle around him, choking on his dick.

"Oh fuck, I'm not going to last. You're too fucking good," he groans and I take him further into me. His hands clutch me tightly, his fingernails digging into my cheeks, but I relish the sting of it. I hold him against me as I lick and slurp and bob my head.

Suddenly, he explodes in my mouth without warning. I choke on it, his mess sliding down my chin and neck, but I manage to swallow some before he pulls out of me.

Then he's crouching down, pushing me back, so I'm sprawled out on the kitchen floor. Those lithe fingers hook into the waistband of my pants and he yanks them down until I'm only wearing my shirt. His hands are all over me, his mouth is licking and sucking at my balls, and I arch up, crying out.

"Yes, louder. Let her hear who owns me," he says as he engulfs my dick.

I lose my fucking mind, nearly screaming as he takes me over and over. Abruptly, my legs are being pressed up to my chest and his tongue slides down my taint and twists around my hole.

I nearly black out as he rims my spasming hole.

Oh fuck.

He's moaning against me, his tongue pushing into me over and over, and I'm sliding up the linoleum until my head hits the wall. I reach up and hold on, pushing my ass back against his face, needing him further inside of me.

"Fuck. Fuck!" I cry out as two fingers press inside of me and his tongue swipes around them. My dick leaks profusely as he presses inside and hits my prostate, like he knows exactly where it is. God, why am I even surprised? He's memorized me.

"*Quinn,*" I shout, and he does it again and again until I'm sobbing, my entire body on fire. My cock aching.

When he stuffs his third and fourth fingers inside of me, nearly fisting me, I break apart, my untouched dick bursting across my shirt.

My entire body falls limp, my ass still full of his fingers, my cock twitching between my legs. Oh my god.

Oh my fucking god.

Quinn lays his cheek on my hip, his breathing labored.

"Goddamn," he whispers, and I swallow roughly, unable to speak.

That was like a sexual awakening. And I've been gay a long-ass time.

"You're so fucking loud," he laughs, wiping at his damp face with his free hand.

I try to lean up to see him, but I can't fucking move. I just lie there, letting myself feel stuffed so impossibly full.

When he finally pulls his fingers free, my hole is loose and empty.

His face appears before me, and I blink up at him, still in a daze.

"Did I break you?" he asks, his lips puffy and red.

"Mhmm," I say, and he grins.

"Good. Fucking *know this*, Greyson. You're mine. And I'm yours. I don't want anyone else."

He leans down and runs his cheek along the wetness of my own, and I reach up and hold him to me. God, if anyone could see us like this. Messy and wrecked on the floor of my trailer.

I've come completely undone.

I've completely lost my motherfucking mind.

And it feels so fucking good.

Chapter Twelve

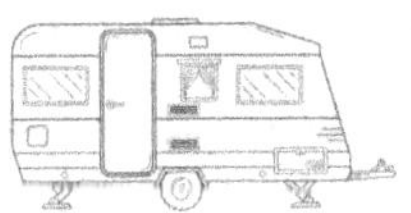

Quinn

We make a simple late dinner in companionable silence, my eyes drinking him in. I'd eat his ass for dinner if he'd let me because, let me tell you, that was a highlight of the last nineteen years.

We finish eating and then clean up before sitting outside, our camping chairs pushed together, my ankle hooked around his. We just sit, listening to the wind rustling through the trees and the insects chirping.

"You know," I say softly, reaching out and running a finger down his arm. "If you keep screaming like you do during sex, the forest rangers are going to come investigate. They'll think there's been a bear attack."

"I am a bear," he says, and I crack a wide smile at that.

"Kind of are," I say. "So fucking big and hairy."

I feel my dick chub up just remembering how he looked

sprawled out on the floor. Oh hell. I want to do that again. I want to fuck him through a wall.

Grey runs a hand along his chest and eyes me. "I'll try and keep it down next time."

"Like hell you will," I say and then grab on to his arm, squeezing it. "I like you loud."

He stares at me for a moment and then turns his face back to the darkness in front of us. The only lights are those of the stars above us, the moon, and a few trailers in the distance.

"Should we head in, go to bed? We can get an early start in the morning, see the falls," he says, and I shrug. I could go either way as long as I'm with him.

"Sounds good," I say and then we stand up, moving inside. We brush our teeth and use the restroom, and when it's time to finally tuck ourselves into bed, I move to where he's sprawled out on top of his sleeping bag.

I don't even bother asking and just take what I want. My hands pull his boxers off, needing him naked, needing to feel nothing between us, and then I lose my own clothes, crawling in beside him.

"What are you doing?" he asks, not really all that confused, but pretending like he is.

"Sleeping with you," I say, refusing to let him push me away. "Would it help if I said I was sleepwalking?"

He chuckles and scoots over, making room for me.

"You usually chat while you sleepwalk?" he asks.

"Dunno, maybe," I murmur, trying to get comfortable.

"You're too big for me to move," I add, my hands running up his side. "Turn over."

He does as I say, turning onto his side, facing away, and I scoot over so my cock is nestled right between his ass cheeks. Like a hot dog in a bun. Fucking cozy is what this is. Like a campout.

"Not gonna fuck you," I tell him, pressing my nose into the back of his neck. "Just gonna hold you."

He grunts, and I let my hand fall to his hard abdomen and then down to his cock. It's semi-hard against my palm, and I sigh.

I'll get up close and personal with it in the morning, but right now, I just want to hold him, to fall asleep with him in my arms.

Tomorrow, we have tomorrow.

* * *

Blinking my eyes open, I realize that Grey is draped over me —his head tucked into my side, his thigh over mine, his arm stretched across my stomach.

Good fucking morning to me.

I shift onto my side so I'm facing him and let my hand slide up his hip, watching as his skin breaks out in goosebumps.

My dick perks up and stretches out toward his, wanting to touch, wanting to play.

"Morning, Grey," I say softly, pressing a kiss to his forehead.

It wrinkles and those eyes I'm obsessed with blink open.

"Mmm," he growls, stretching out lazily, his dick sliding against mine and forcing a moan out of me.

"Want me to eat your ass for breakfast?" I say, and he freezes, his gaze snapping to mine.

"You just like to see me get all flustered," he mutters, his cheeks turning a delicious shade of red. Like candy. I want to gobble him up.

"I just like telling you your options," I say as I reach down and clutch our dicks together.

He stares at me as I stroke us lazily, the morning fog in my brain slowly dissipating with each flick of my wrist. Fuck, this feels good, the two of us pressed together like this. One day, I'm going to slide my foreskin over his cock and dock him.

I'm going to love watching that, watching him pant and whine while I release all over him.

Right now, his eyes are watching me closely, his mind moving much too fast for this early in the morning. He's thinking too fucking hard. He pulls his lip between his teeth, worrying it a moment, and I wonder what the fuck is going on in that brain of his when he suddenly twists out of my grasp. For a moment, my heart sinks because he's pulling away, putting an end to our lazy frot session. But then he turns onto his stomach and shifts his ass up into the air, and I almost *pass the fuck out.*

Oh my god, he's offering it up to me on a proverbial platter. He wants this, he's begging for it without words.

I scramble behind him, wasting no time. I don't want him to change his mind or think I'm not into this. I am *so* into this.

Quickly, I palm his cheeks and spread him open, stuffing my face into his crack and inhaling. He groans lowly as I stick out my tongue and lick across his hole. I do it again, loving the taste of him.

I want inside so fucking bad. I ache from needing it.

My tongue slides around the rim of him, teasing him for only a moment. And because I lack any and all patience when it comes to him, I spear him on it, making his hips jerk forward violently.

Oh hell. Nothing about him is wrong. It's all so perfectly right.

He's perfection.

I press my tongue in and out of him again and again, making him writhe beneath me until he's a sweaty, sloppy mess. He's groaning and grunting and coming completely undone.

"Need more," he gasps as I slot my tongue inside of him and wiggle it around. He cries out, desperate for something only I can give him.

"You want my fingers?" I ask, pressing the tips of two against his loose, wet hole.

He grunts his affirmation and I fuck into him slowly, all while sucking a hickey on his ass cheek, marking him.

Mine. All fucking mine.

"Quinn," he groans as I twist my wrist and peg his prostate. He likes that. He so fucking does because he cries out, his hands fisting the sheets, pushing back at me each time I rub against it.

And the sight, the feel, the taste of him...it makes my dick leak like a drippy faucet. Honestly, this man. This fucking man is so damn hot. I want my dick to be inside of him; I want to slide inside his wet hole and lose myself in it.

"More," he mutters and I add another finger. Three. Four.

Practically sticking my damn fist up in him, and he just takes it like a champ.

"You want my whole fucking hand?" I ask, and Grey whimpers, his entire body trembling as I fuck into him again and again.

I reach down and take my cock, stroking myself furiously as I press my face into his crack once more, licking him, stuffing him full of my saliva. God, he's wet. He's so fucking wet from me. I can hear the way my fingers move in and out of him, the filthy, degrading squelch of it.

"Want me to fuck you, Grey?" I ask, slipping my fingers out of him and getting up on my knees behind him. I slot my eager cock right at his hole, and I swear to god, it wants in. Knock, knock, Grey. Here I come. I pause and wait for his slight nod, his face buried in the pillow.

Okay, good enough for me. I shift my hips forward and Grey cries out as I press just the tip inside. I don't want to hurt him, but fuck, I'm desperate. And he's so eager, so wet.

I know he can take me.

I grab on to his hips to steady him, to keep him still, but he thrusts back, his hole swallowing every inch of me.

My soul leaves my body.

Oh, fuck.

I need lube. I'm not sure my saliva is enough, but Grey keeps pushing back further, his slutty hole so damn needy for my dick.

"Grey," I gasp as I finally bottom out, my eyes glued to where my dick disappears into his body.

I am fully inside of him. He's so tight and so warm, and I never want to leave.

Grey shifts and moans, breathing raggedly like he's just run a mile. I can't believe he did that—that he just stuffed himself full of me like that.

Jesus, can this man get any hotter?

No, no he cannot.

"Oh fuck," he grunts into the sheets. And for a second, I wonder if he hurt himself, if he took it too fast, too hard. His breathing is ragged, and I swear he's shaking.

But before I can ask if he's okay, he pushes forward and slams back on me.

I black the fuck out as he fucks back against me. Because it's Grey, his ass. There has never been another that compares. I've never done this raw before.

I feel *everything*.

The drag of his insides against my cock feels so damn good.

Our skin slaps together as we fuck, my balls hitting his and I don't last, I can't last.

A wheeze escapes me, wanting to prolong it, but not being able to. I come so hard my heart skips a beat and then I'm falling onto his sweaty back, reaching around our bodies and jacking him off.

He comes on a scream, long and pained and feral. And then it's quiet, just the sound of our ragged breaths filling the trailer.

"Oh fuck," I say, still inside of him, refusing to leave. "Grey, what the fuck was that? Are you okay?"

He swallows, his throat clicking.

"Mmm, fine," he says, his entire body trembling.

But I just did him raw with no lube. I mean, there was a

lot of spit, but Jesus. I knew Kevin spewed all sorts of confidential shit to me that day, telling me the things Grey liked, but I didn't really believe most of it. I thought he was just shit-talking after a nasty breakup. Apparently, he wasn't exaggerating. Grey is a power bottom in more ways than one.

I run my hand up his chest and cup his neck, feeling his thundering pulse beneath my fingertips and then slowly, pull my hips back, slipping out of him.

He hisses as I make my exit, and I can't help but look down at his swollen, pink hole and the cum that lingers around the rim.

My cum.

"I need a picture of this," I say as Grey flops onto his stomach and buries his face into the pillow.

"Go ahead," he murmurs and sighs. "I'll be here a while."

I spread his cheeks and press my finger against it and it puckers under my touch. Oh, hell. I want to fuck him again already.

In all the positions.

But not now. Later. With lube.

I remove my hand from his sore ass and move off the bed, grabbing my sketchbook and then a washrag. I clean us both up before sitting cross-legged next to him and sketching his ass—the one with my hickey right on the cheek. It's purple and blue, and I reach out to touch it.

I marked him, like a beast.

I felt like one in that moment. I lost control of everything as we fucked each other like animals.

Grey doesn't seem to notice. He doesn't even move, his

body just draped across the mattress. Hell, I fucked him into a coma and I'm not even mad about it.

I shut my sketchbook and move toward him, pressing a kiss to the base of his spine.

"I'm gonna make you breakfast. Is that ass too sore to hike today?"

He shakes his head, sighing. "I'll be fine."

I reach out and squeeze his butt before pulling on the boxers I discarded on the floor last night.

"Alright, babe, you rest while I make you something to eat and then we'll go."

He grunts and must immediately fall asleep because when I come back in a little while later, I have to jostle him awake.

"Goddamn, Quinn," he groans as he sits down at the small kitchen table and starts to dig into his eggs and toast.

"Ass sore?" I ask, feeling a little proud.

Grey's eyes meet mine, and he smiles softly at me.

"In the best way," he replies and then shifts his focus to his food. I just watch him dreamily for a few minutes, conjuring up things—like our wedding day—before I finish off my breakfast. I wonder for a moment how this will change things between us. Because fucking Grey like that, having him so raw and unfiltered changed so many things for me.

I was one hundred percent obsessed with him for years, but now I am fully committed to making my dreams come true. And my dream is him.

Him and me.

After breakfast we shower and take off on our hike, our

hands brushing against each other as we make our way down a trail that will eventually lead us to the lower waterfalls.

As we walk, my phone buzzes in my pocket and I pull it out, seeing my best friend's name on the screen. I know it makes me a bad person, but I want to pretend like he doesn't exist, just for a moment. I don't want him piercing this bubble I'm in with his dad. I just don't fucking want him to ruin it.

JOSHUA:

Having fun in the UP with my dad?

I stare down at his words, pulling my lip between my teeth. Because fuck yeah, I am. I am so damn glad he bailed on his dad because now I get this time with him.

ME:

Yup.

I'm leaving it simple. I don't want to give anything away. Josh has no idea how I feel about Grey. I've kept that so close to my chest, no one knows. Just me.

"You okay?" Grey asks as I shove my phone back in my pocket.

"Yeah, just a friend checking in," I say, not wanting to tell him it's his son. I don't want him to pull away like he did the other day.

He shifts his small backpack on his back and eyes me another moment, probably wondering if he should push, but he doesn't. I'm glad he lets it go. I mean the make-up sex was fabulous, but I'd rather not feel any kind of animosity between us. I hated those few hours. They caused my entire body to lock up with anxiety.

"Hey! Quinn!" a female voice suddenly says behind me. My footsteps falter, and I turn to see Becca jog up behind us. Becca is the girl Grey saw me with before he disappeared for hours.

I met her yesterday when I was walking back from my hike and ended up chatting with her for a while. She's a freshman at the University of Michigan and an avid photographer. We're both artists and we bonded over things like color and lighting and our manic minds.

My lips turn up in a smile as I wave to her. I can see Grey's footsteps slow as he finally comes to a stop.

He turns to glance at her and then me.

Yes, well, don't you worry, boo. I have no interest in Becca. I only have eyes for you.

"Hey," I say as she comes to a stop next to me, the camera around her neck swinging side to side. She really is gorgeous with that dark hair and dark eyes, and if I was anyone else, I'd be all over that. But I can't see past Grey. I never have and never will.

If he discards me when this trip is done, I will pine after this man for all eternity.

"Hi! God, sorry, I was trying to catch up but you two walk super-fast, and I am obviously out of shape," she says on a wheeze.

She gestures to her body which doesn't look out of shape to me, but I don't say anything. I'm not sure if she's fishing for a compliment or if she's just trying to be funny. I sure as fuck won't be giving out any compliments when Grey is around— don't want him getting any mixed signals.

"No worries," I tell her and then gesture to Grey who is

standing a little too far away from me at the moment. "This is Grey. Grey this is Becca. We met yesterday. She's making her way across the UP with her family, just like we are."

Grey gives her a small wave and then thumbs over his shoulder.

"Cool. Well, uh, I can head out. Give you two some space," he says, and I roll my eyes.

"Babe," I tell him and his cheeks darken at the term of endearment. "We are going to the falls *together*. Like we planned."

Becca watches all of this, her eyes moving back and forth between us. I didn't tell her what Grey and I were because I don't really know myself. But she can make assumptions about us with the information at hand. I don't mind.

Presume away.

I walk up and link my hand with his, and he just stares down at it, his breath coming out a little heavier. Well, hell, that's making me think about fucking him, and my dick is perking up.

I clench his hand and peer up at him. He wets his lips, and I want so desperately to lean into him and press my mouth to his. I want to eat him.

Click.

My eyelids flutter, and I turn my gaze to Becca who is standing there, the camera pressed against her eye.

"Ugh, I know. So rude, and I can delete it if you want. It's just...the way you two look at each other. I just had to capture it. Look."

She sighs dreamily and then moves toward us, angling the screen of her camera so we can see. We both glance down and

I feel my heart thunder in my chest. Fuck, she's right. The way we are looking at each other...there are no lies here, just the absolute truth. Passion. Adoration.

"Can you email this to me?" I ask her, and she nods.

"Do I have your permission to snap more pics of you two along the way?"

Grey shrugs, running a hand over his head and I nod enthusiastically.

"As long as I get to keep them, go ahead."

She beams and then we begin our walk up the trail, my hand still in Grey's.

Yeah, this is a pretty good start to the day.

Chapter Thirteen

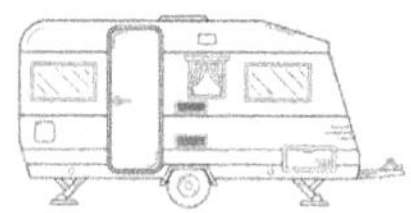

Grey

I can't pretend like I didn't like him fucking me. I can't even pretend like I don't want him to do it again.

I have never had sex like that before in my life.

And I've been a bottom a long-ass time.

"She sent me the pictures. Wanna see?" Quinn asks as he crawls into bed next to me. He doesn't even bother lowering the kitchen table to give the illusion that he's going to sleep on it. No, he just stripped us both down and moved right in with me. And I can't even complain.

I want him here.

"Sure," I say, shifting so our heads are touching, our naked bodies impossibly close.

Quinn runs a hand down my chest, holding the phone up with his other, and slowly swipes through the pictures Becca sent us.

One of us looking longingly at each other.

One of us from behind, holding hands.

One of us kissing at the waterfall, Quinn's hands cupping my cheeks.

I can see his need in those pictures, but what's worse, I can see mine too. It's so transparent, it's scary.

Can he tell what he's doing to me? Can he see how desperate I am for him, despite how inappropriate this is?

"Look at us," he says with a smile, turning his head and pressing his lips to mine. "We're hot together, right? I mean, look at you, Grey. You're a total babe."

I huff in disbelief, but he just keeps going.

"You're like every queer boy's wet dream. The things I have imagined doing to you. Do you know how impossible it was to wait for you all these years?"

My eyebrows rise at that.

Quinn leans up on an elbow and glances down at me.

"I wanted to make my move when I finally turned eighteen, but I thought you'd never give me a chance if I was still in high school, so I waited. A whole other year, Grey. I waited."

"Were you the oldest in your class?" I ask as he presses his hand to my neck and visions of him squeezing it the other day cause my dick to plump up.

Fuck, I want him to do things to me, like this morning—just take control and wreck me all in a matter of minutes.

I can't ask him for that though. I already feel desperate enough.

"Yeah, my mom tried to unschool me for a few years. Didn't work out and really set me back," Quinn says. "So that's why I'm nineteen. I was held back a year."

"Shit, sorry," I say, not sure what else to say. I mean, I have no fucking clue what unschooling entails, but his parents are quite odd.

"Doesn't matter. All that matters is that I'm here now. And it was torture waiting for you, but I am so fucking glad I did." He rolls his lips between his teeth and then mutters, "You'd never have gone for me if I was still in high school, right?"

I shake my head. "Nah."

I mean, I'm barely going for him now. Oh, who the hell am I kidding? I so fucking am.

"Want me to send these pics to you?" he asks.

I stare into his jade-colored eyes and let out a shaky exhale.

"Yeah," I say because I want them. I want to remember this. There is no way I can let this continue once we get back. But up here in the UP, so far removed from everything, I feel like I can let go. Let myself have something I want.

Fuck, this is going to end disastrously.

He fiddles with his phone and I see my screen light up, knowing those pictures will be sitting there, waiting for me to look at later.

"Grey," Quinn says, his teeth gnawing on his bottom lip. Some of his hair has fallen out of his ponytail and slides against his cheek. I reach up and tuck it behind his ear and those eyelids of his flutter. "There are so many things I want to do to you. Things I've imagined. Will you let me? I have been so damn patient...."

I swallow as I put my hand on his lower back, pressing my palm against him. His skin jumps beneath me and I pull him closer, needing him near.

"Is that a yes?" he gasps as his thick cock drags against my thigh.

"Yeah," I mutter.

His head drops forward, his lips lowering to mine.

"I'm going to fuck you with lube this time. I'm going to make it so good for you."

He slants his head and licks into my mouth, long and slow and torturous. One of his hands is on my cheek, keeping me in place. Not that I'd run. I'm not moving. Not today.

"I want you to ride me," he says, grinding his cock against my thigh. "I want to see you over me, feel your weight on me."

I can imagine it, straddling him, sitting on his dick, taking him inside me over and over.

"Yeah," I whisper, and he kisses me almost frantically like just the thought of it is driving him wild. And it affects me—I grow a little savage thinking about it.

Suddenly, Quinn rips his lips from mine and he moves into the other room, knocking into the wall on the way.

"Getting lube," he tells me before reappearing almost instantaneously.

I glance down at the bottle in his hand and then meet his gaze.

"I have condoms too, if you want to use them..." he adds.

I glance down at my straining dick and then back at him. "We didn't the other day."

"I know. That was on me. But I'm negative. My panel is clear."

I wet my lips, feeling my heart rate increase. "Same."

Quinn groans loudly and then uncaps the lube. "So that's a yes then, right? Because I'm good either way, Grey. I just want in you."

I shouldn't. This is so irresponsible, but I nod anyway, giving him my consent. I want him in me raw, want to feel his cum dripping out of me when he's done using me. That was so hot last time. I've never let someone have me like that.

Quinn groans again and says, "Wanna watch you work yourself open for me. Show me how you fuck yourself."

My skin flames at the thought of him watching me do this, but it's not enough to deter me. I hold out two fingers to him, letting him squirt some gel onto them. He's gazing at me intensely, those pretty eyes never leaving me as I press a knee against my chest. I reach my hand down, dragging it along my balls, and then spear myself with my fingers.

His hand grips on to his dick and he starts to pump it rapidly.

He likes this, watching me, and I like showing him what I can do, what I'm capable of.

I slide my two fingers in and out of my hole before adding a third.

"Fuck, look at you, Grey. *Look at you*," he gasps, leaning down and sucking my dick into his mouth, like he's so eager he can't wait to have me.

I groan, fucking myself harder, needing him inside of me.

He grabs on to the hand that's thrusting into my hole and he takes over, twisting it and pounding it into my ass, and the entire time, his mouth never leaves my dick. He's sucking my brains right out of me. My free hand shoots up and clutches on to the wall behind me, using it to ground me.

But it's not enough. I need his dick.

I pull my fingers out and push Quinn off of me. His mouth slides off my dick with an audible pop and then I'm pressing on his shoulders, forcing him onto his back.

He falls back without complaint and I crawl on top of him, grabbing the lube and smearing it across his uncut cock.

"Oh, fuck yes," he murmurs as I place his straining dick right at my hole and sink down onto it.

I take it all in one long-drawn-out slide and Quinn's entire body bows up off the mattress.

"Jesus, Greyson," he groans as I lift up and slam down onto him again.

Oh fuck. Oh fuck, this is even better with lube. He's so big, so fucking long. I can feel him hitting my prostate each time.

His fingers curl into my thighs and my hands press against his chest, riding him slowly with a frantic kind of need that only comes from being celibate for far too long. I need this like I need air.

"You are such a cockslut," he says as he bends his knees and fucks into me.

My head falls back and I just let him impale me. Yes, a cockslut. *His* cockslut.

"Yours," I say loudly as our skin slaps together. "*Yours.*"

I am so lost, so fucking gone that I don't even know what I'm saying. But I can see that Quinn sees it. His eyes widen with each of my downward thrusts, and his hands move to my hips as he guides me, forcing me to ride him like he wants.

My thighs burn and my balls are drawn up against me, but I don't stop. No, I just keep going until I feel my release welling up within me.

When Quinn reaches down and starts to pump my cock, I explode, my hole clenching around him repeatedly. Quinn lets out a low growl and releases inside of me, and I swear I can feel it, his cum marking my insides.

I want to remember this...want to remember the best sex of my life.

My shoulders slump forward and I fall onto him, pressing kisses to his lips. We kiss lazily, slowly, not a worry in the world. He's still inside of me, plugging me, and I like it. I want to keep him inside of me for as long as I can.

"God, you are exquisite," he says. "I want to sculpt you riding me."

I press my nose to his cheek and inhale and exhale shakily. I'm not sure what to say because he'd sculpt me when we return home, and I don't know if I can promise him that.

Can I?

His hands rub up my back, soothing me. I should answer him, tell him that yes, he can sculpt me, but I don't. I can't form the words.

"It's okay," he says softly, soothing me. "You don't have to make any promises."

God.

I press my face into his neck, loving the connection to him. We lay like that for a long-ass time, just being together, until I finally shift up and off of him.

"Let me clean you," he says, moving toward the bathroom. He's always so good about aftercare, unlike so many of the men I've been with.

After we've cleaned up, Quinn tucks me into him, using me as the little spoon, and it should be weird because I'm so much bigger, but it's not. I fucking love it.

I love that my size does nothing to deter him from taking what he wants.

I feel the puff of his breath against my neck and the warmth of him surrounding me lulls me to sleep.

We spend the next day hiking and driving up to Whitefish Point to see the lighthouse. We hoofed it up to the highest point of that damn thing and looked over Lake Superior, Quinn's arms wrapped around me from behind, holding me against him. I didn't want to leave.

"There are so many shipwrecks submerged in this lake," Quinn said.

"Three hundred and fifty," I'd replied, as his lips brushed against the skin of my neck. His hands had snuck up my shirt, brushing across my stomach and causing butterflies to erupt within me. I love his hands on me.

When we were done, we wandered around a shipwreck museum and ate lunch in a small diner outside of town. That night we crawled into bed and spent hours fucking, his hands on me earlier the perfect kind of edging. I was ready for him, eager, tearing off my clothes and arching my ass up, begging for him. He took me hard over and over, the trailer squeaking and rocking as he slammed into me. It was punishing and rough and perfect.

My ass is sore the next morning, throbbing as I drive us to the campground in Grand Marais, one of the friendliest towns in Michigan. It's artsy and quirky, and I think that Quinn will love just poking around.

"So are we really going to kayak out to Pictured Rocks?" he asks, talking about a scenic shoreline on Lake Superior that features cliffs streaked with colors, making it seem almost as if they've been painted on. You can kayak up to them, reach out, and press your hand against the stone.

"Yeah, I booked a tour for two o'clock."

"I can't wait," Quinn says, shifting in his seat and glancing out the window. "Fuck, it's going to be hard to go back home after this."

He reaches over and links his hand with mine and I stare down at them, the way his fingers fit so perfectly in mine. Those magical fucking fingers that bring me over the edge like nothing else can.

"Yeah," I say, not telling him that going home means so many different things that I can't really think about right now.

He brings our entwined hands up to his lips and presses his mouth to them.

"How about," Quinn says softly, mischief in his eyes. "If you're not too sore, we get set up and fuck."

The blunt way he goes about it makes a laugh burble out of me. God, this guy.

"We could break in the campsite. Christen it."

I peek over at him, my hole already clenching around nothing, ready for it.

"What do you think?" he asks, squeezing my hand. I can see his pants tenting, and I snort softly.

"You think you can manage to hook up the trailer with a hard dick?"

"Gives me an incentive," he replies quickly. "I can work really fast under pressure."

I smile at him and he smirks back.

"And then when you're nice and sore, we can go explore. From what I read online this town is amazing. Have you ever been?"

I shake my head. "This will be my first time."

Quinn quirks an eyebrow at me and then slides one of my fingers into his mouth. I don't know how I manage to drive us safely to the campsite, but I do. It's hard as fuck with him sucking on my fingers like he's going down on me.

By the time the camper is hooked up and we're back inside, we're on each other, ripping our clothes off, our hands greedy, our tongues tangled.

"Fuck," I groan as he pushes me up against the wall and grinds against me.

I never in a million years thought that I'd be fucking my way across the UP, but I am. Quinn grabs my face, holding me in place as he bites down on my bottom lip, sucking on it with that lush mouth of his.

I just stand there and let him do what he wants. I've always been submissive in the bedroom, which has been an issue more often than not because most people look at me and expect something different. They expect me to take control, when I want nothing more than for my partner to make the decisions for me.

I'm so fucking tired of being in control. I just want someone to take the reins every once in a while.

And Quinn seems to like doing that.

Fuck, I like it too. He's smaller than me, but he can still manipulate me around the bedroom, taking exactly what he wants each and every time. He takes what he wants so well.

He knows how to turn me into putty.

"Turn around," he says, his hands on my hips, spinning me to face the wall.

My breath comes out as pants, and I splay my hands out in front of me.

"Ass out," he says as he roughly tugs my pants down.

I arch back, needing him. Now.

But he doesn't give me what I want, instead, he makes me wait. His hands grab my ass cheeks, kneading them, pulling them apart slowly, working me into a frantic mess.

"Please, Quinn," I moan, my forehead rolling on the wall in front of me. I am so goddamn empty and I just want to be stuffed full, impaled on him. I want to feel him press inside of me and stay there.

"Please what, Grey?" he asks, his finger sliding up my crack and teasing my hole.

My mouth falls open in a gasp and I rock back against him.

"Please fuck me."

He leans up against me, one hand cupping my cock, the other pressing against my ass cheek.

"God, to hear those words come out of your mouth. The things I have let myself dream about. Well," he begins as he pumps me faster, "they're my reality now."

He pulls away quickly and I hear the lube uncap. Then a second later, I feel the press of his fingers entering me. Yes. *Yes.* More of this.

"God, you're so tight," he mutters as he pushes in knuckle deep. "You're a fucking work of art. I'm going to draw this. My hand up your ass."

I groan as he continues to work me open, stuffing me full until I'm slippery and wet. And then I hear the snap of his jeans, the sound of his zipper lowering, and then his cock is pushing its way inside.

I love that he never waits too long, that he doesn't treat me with kid gloves. I can take it. I can so fucking take it.

"More," I grunt, his knees hitting the back of my legs as he thrusts up into me.

I feel my voice crack as I groan loudly, taking his punishing pace over and over. I should keep it down, try to muffle these moans, but the way he arches into me, the feel of his cock dragging over my prostate has me seeing stars.

"You. Fucking. Come," he grunts as he slams up into me. I just lower my chin to my chest, trying to hold out, to calm this orgasm building within me, because this feels too good. I'm not ready to finish. I want more time. I need more time.

But he doesn't give it to me. No, he can't wait, always so damn eager. He reaches around me, pumping my dick, and I can't do anything but watch his hand on me.

Oh fuck, that's too good. Too fucking good.

My balls tighten, and I feel the tingling in the base of my spine.

My mouth falls open and I cry out, a loud, wild shout that reverberates around us. My cock jerks and spurts its release, my hole clenching around Quinn's cock, milking him. His body tenses against mine, his hand tightening around my dick as he empties inside of me.

We're left standing, still connected, our breathing shaky and uneven.

"It never gets old," he whispers, his lips on my shoulder. "It fucking never gets old."

I agree. I can't imagine sex with Quinn ever becoming a chore. He's always so into it, like I'm everything to him. I've never had it like this before. Never.

"I don't want to leave you," he says softly, his cheek resting against my back, his hand still clutching my cock.

"I know," I say with a weak nod. I don't want him to leave me either, but fuck, we have to get cleaned up. He can't stay inside me forever.

"Okay, fine," he murmurs and then slips out of me. I press my forehead against the wall and inhale deeply through my nose, trying to get my bearings.

Quinn moves to my side and reaches out, turning my face so I meet his gaze.

"You, Greyson Hart, are perfection," he says, leaning in and pressing a kiss to my mouth.

I blink at him, not sure how to respond because I don't feel perfect. I'm sure—almost positive—that this is just a teenage obsession. As soon as this trip is over and we've parted ways, he will forget about his crush. About me.

My ribs ache at the thought...of becoming nothing more than a distant memory to him.

But I have lived a life full of disappointment.

What's one more? I've come to expect it.

"Come on," he says, tugging me into him. I sag against him, my entire body aching as he leads me into the small bathroom. We barely fit inside, and when I look at myself in the small mirror, I see how wrecked I look. Red cheeks, wild eyes.

"Look how hot you are," he says, reaching over and wetting a washcloth. He gently wipes at my ass, cleaning up the cum that is leaking out of me. I just let him do it, my hands curled against the countertop, as his green eyes watch me.

He leans into me, pressing his lips to my shoulder and his gaze meets mine in the mirror.

"Look at us."

I do, I fucking *look*. And what a pair we make. I have never been with someone so different, someone so much smaller than me...younger than me. But we look good together. We just...fit, somehow.

"I'm so fucking ready to go explore," he says, excitement lining his voice as we pull on our clothes and get ready to escape this trailer and walk around the small town.

I love his voraciousness for life, how he just meets things head-on, always ready to try new things, his eyes always wide with excitement. I wish I was like that, I wish I could experience the world like he does, but years of disappointment have eroded it—years of being told I wasn't good enough, that I needed to do better. Those criticisms take a toll on a person, they slowly crush a spirit. I am half the man I could be, I know it. I know I could be something else entirely if I had never married Karen, if I had come out sooner, if I had made different choices.

Yet, a part of me feels a little more alive when I'm around Quinn, like I can experience the excitement of life through him. He's breathing new life into me, my spirit that was once withered is starting to bloom. I'm starting to feel like maybe, just maybe there is hope.

Maybe things could end up differently for me. Maybe with Quinn things could be different.

"I wanna see everything," he says, as we step out of the trailer, his hand in mine. I glance around and see a few people milling about the campsite and blush. Because I'm pretty sure that they heard me getting my ass fucked.

"Don't worry about them," Quinn says, reading the blush on my face like a book as we walk to my truck. "They're just jealous that their love lives are boring as fuck."

Love.

I rub at my chest as I climb in and start the engine.

This isn't love.

No, this is just...lust. Lust and bad decisions.

Chapter Fourteen

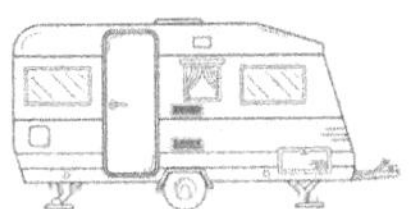

Grey

Thunder rumbles in the distance signaling a summer storm as we make our way through Grand Marais. Quinn is in his element here, his eyes alight with anticipation.

"I want to learn to sail," he says, our hands intertwined as we walk down the wooden boardwalk which overlooks Lake Superior. "You know how?"

"Nope," I say and then shrug. "Never got a chance to learn."

"We could take lessons next summer," he tells me, pulling his lips between his teeth, the wind moving across the lake, whipping his hair across his cheeks. God, he's fucking beautiful. I don't dare tell him that there will be no sailing lessons with me. I don't dare crush his dreams.

He's young and happy. Let him have this.

In the distance, I can see the sailboats he's talking about bobbing in the lake, and for a moment, I let myself wonder what it would be like, letting myself do *this* with *him*. And I can feel it, the sensation of being alive coursing through me—before I crush it.

It's better to always set your expectations low so when the disappointment comes, it's not so debilitating.

"Don't do that," Quinn says softly, moving up against me and wrapping an arm around my waist. "Don't think those things."

I eye him, wondering if reading my mind is a superpower of his. Or maybe I make it too easy for him, being so vulnerable and open.

"Let's go walk the shore and then we can go look in the shops when it starts to rain...if it rains."

I glance up and see the darkening sky. Those sailboats better get out of the water before the lightning strikes. But my thoughts are derailed as Quinn tugs me down to the sand, his smile wide, his eyes wild.

He'd fuck me right here for all to see if he could. If I'd let him.

God, I'd probably let him.

He picks up his pace, forcing me to move faster, and pretty soon we're nearly running down the span of the shore, sand kicking up into our shoes, his laugh floating through the wind as we race. When we finally stop, our chests are heaving, our skin flushed and damp.

It's humid and the wetness in the air sticks to our skin. He's shining, practically glowing.

"God, that felt good," he says, tilting his head back and breathing deeply.

I can't help it—the pull toward him is so damn overwhelming—I lean over and lick a stripe right up his cheek, tasting the salt on his skin.

Quinn's eyes snap open and he stares at me, his lips open in surprise.

"You motherfucker," he says with a smile. "Why'd you do that?"

I shift on my feet and then reach out and pull him into me, slanting my mouth across his and pushing my tongue into his mouth.

He melts into me, his hands clasping my arms as we kiss and kiss and *kiss*. We only pull away when a crack of lightning lights up the sky.

He gasps, his fingers linking with mine once more, and then we're running back the way we came, seeking shelter from the impending storm. My legs and lungs burn as we run down the pier, back to town.

"Wait," I say, gasping as he pulls me under a storefront eave. Quinn pushes me back against the brick wall and presses his lips to mine as we pant into each other's mouths. I'm exhausted, wrung out, but so fucking *alive*. I can feel it coursing through my veins, it's like a drug being here with him.

"Come on, in here," he says, pulling away and leading me into the small gift shop just as rain starts to fall from the sky, leaving Quinn with raindrops smattered across his face.

I reach up and brush one away, watching his eyelids flutter at the contact.

"You keep touching me and I'll keep getting distracted," he says, pressing a kiss to the pad of my thumb.

I feel the press of his lips all the way to my heart.

Will feel it for days to come. Years, even.

We pull away, just now noticing the older man behind the counter, his glasses perched on his nose, his eyebrows raised.

"Can I help you?" he asks, and Quinn smiles widely.

"Looking at the artwork," he says, gesturing to a wall full of paintings. I hadn't even noticed them when we stepped through, my eyes solely on Quinn.

"Local?" he asks, and the man nods.

"Yep, made by people born and raised here."

Quinn moves toward the wall, pulling me with him and then we just stand and stare at it, splashes of color across canvas. I don't know what I'm looking at, but Quinn certainly does, his eyes alight with something beautiful.

I want to see him, one day, in a gallery of his own, surrounded by his art.

Maybe, in a different life, we could move here and he could run this place. Turn it into something of his own.

In another life...

"Isn't this fucking wonderful?" he asks me, his voice full of awe.

I take him in, absorbing everything that is Quinn.

"Yeah. It fucking is."

Chapter Fifteen

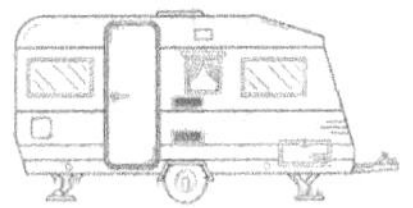

Quinn

Grey seems lighter here, as if the farther away from home we get, the freer and younger he feels. I'd bring him all the way to California if he'd let me. I want to watch him be twenty-one again.

I don't think he was ever carefree though. Having a kid at fifteen changes a person. But maybe I can give him that back, in my own way...

"You didn't need to buy me this," I say, glancing down at the bag hanging off my wrist. A miniature painting of Lake Superior sits inside. It was expensive, and I'd thrown a minor fit over it, but Grey had insisted. So I let him.

I'm going to hang it on my wall and stare at it, remembering this time with him.

Or maybe I can look at it while he's wrapped around me.

I can hope. I can fucking *hope.*

"Wanted to," he says simply. I glance up at him and lean over, pressing my lips to his cheek.

I'd kiss his mouth, but people are watching, and I know that once I start, I won't be able to stop.

I am insatiable.

"Well, I love it," I say.

"I know."

The humid air clings to us as we make our way back to his truck, and I just hold on to him, needing to touch him at all times. We spent the afternoon kayaking to Pictured Rocks, staring up at the red, yellow, and blue sandstone cliffs. Well, I took a peek for a few minutes and then spent my time staring at Grey because honestly, what is more beautiful than him?

Nothing. That's what. Fucking *nothing*.

He's like one of the Seven Wonders of the World.

"Want to go grab food from the store and we can head back and cook? Or do you want to eat here?" I ask.

Grey eyes me. "Could do either."

I roll my lips between my teeth because I want to be alone with him and I'm trying to figure out the best course of action to get what I want as soon as possible.

"How about we grab something to eat real quick and then we can head back," I say, already growing excited. My favorite pastime is spending time alone with Grey.

I don't know how much longer he'll let me have him, so I have to absorb it. I need to tuck it inside of me so far that no one can reach inside and pull it out. I need it safe and guarded, so I can peer within myself and *remember*.

There aren't a lot of places to sit down and eat in this small town, but there is a saloon that I think Grey would like.

I know after a long day of work he likes to crack open a cold one and their website says they have a good selection on tap.

"Forget you're not twenty-one sometimes," Grey says as we walk toward the restaurant. "Hopefully they'll let you in."

I shove at his shoulder. "Oh, you fucking joke now? Funny. Ha. Ha. But listen, I grew up real fucking fast. I've had my share of drinks and drugs, Grey. I'm basically forty years old."

He squeezes my hand and glances over at me.

"I know that. But you deserve to be cared for," he tells me. "To have someone you can rely on."

"You offering?" I ask with a smirk, and his cheeks flush. *Ngh*, he's so fucking hot. I'd have parents like mine all day long if that meant that Grey would offer to be the man I can come home to every day.

I open my mouth to tell him this when a high-pitched whine distracts us.

Our gazes are pulled to the right, and lingering in some bushes is a ragged-looking golden retriever. I mean, he's mostly a retriever—something else is mixed in there, as well.

"God, look at him," Grey says, and I turn to eye him.

"Be nice," I say with a small smile. "Not everyone can be super sexy and handsome."

Grey rolls his lips between his teeth and rocks on his feet. "He has one eyeball."

"Yes, well not everyone is born with two eyeballs."

Grey smiles widely at me, and I lean up and kiss the corner of his lips.

"I'll be nice."

"You better be, or I'll have to dole out a punishment," I

say, and Grey's cheeks flush. Now I'm imagining him bent over, his pants pulled down his thighs, his ass jiggling with each swat of my hand.

The dog whines again, and I force my gaze to it, meeting its one-eyed stare. The doggo is a little worse for wear. I mean the one-eyed thing is unfortunate, but it also has this rogue tooth sticking out of its mouth. It makes him look a little derpy.

"Hey," I say, leaning down a bit and speaking softly. "Hey, you."

The dog wags its tail, doing small tippy-taps, seemingly happy to see us. But then again, most dogs do this, right? They really are the best of friends. I had one growing up, but she got out one night and never returned.

I always wondered what happened to her. I'd like to think happy thoughts, like maybe she went into the woods and met some friends.

I don't like to think of the alternative.

"Does it have an owner?" Grey asks, sounding a little doubtful, as we move closer. The dog woofs happily and pants, its tongue lolling out of the side of its mouth as we approach.

"It's pretty scraggly-looking. I think it must be a stray," I say, leaning down and scratching at its ears. It doesn't have a collar or any identification. As I pet it, the dog whines happily as it peers up at me with twinkling eyes, and I melt. Derpy and all, everyone needs love, and I am a total sap when it comes to this shit.

"We need to see if anyone knows anything or something…" I begin, already plotting a course of action. I've basically adopted this mutt. It's mine now.

"I mean, look at it. It's a pretty distinct dog. You'd think someone would notice if it was missing," Grey says, tucking his hands into his pockets, almost like he's reluctant to get attached.

"Should we ask someone?" When he doesn't respond, I nod. "Yeah, let's ask. Someone should know something. There's like a couple hundred people in this town. I'm sure they all know each other's middle names…"

I move inside the restaurant, leaving Grey outside, and speak with a waitress, confirming what I already thought. No one's lost a dog with one eyeball and a snaggletooth. The dog outside is probably a stray. Then she gives me the address of the local vet in the area, which I punch into my phone.

When I make my way back outside, I expect to find Grey standing at a distance, but instead, he's on the ground, his legs stretched out in front of him, the dog sniffing at his face. A smile curves his lips up and I die a little at the sight. I want to sketch it.

I'll fucking sketch it.

"No one seems to know anything about a stray or a missing dog and you'd think in such a small town, they'd know. Especially one that looks like him. The server suggested we bring it to the vet to get checked out," I say, and Grey's gaze turns up to me.

"Sounds good," he says, and the dog nuzzles up to him.

"I see the one eyeball didn't deter you for long," I say, trying to bite back a smile, but failing.

"He was lonely, so I figured I'd sit down here with him and hang out for a bit."

Like he needs to explain it to me. I think it's fucking amazing. I want to marry this guy for being such a damn marshmallow. I'll be his graham cracker, his s'more. Just as long as he's mine.

"Mhmm. So it's a boy?" I ask, keeping those crazy thoughts inside. No need to scare him off prematurely. I've already nearly blurted that shit out multiple times...usually when I'm stuffed inside of him, but still.

I need to play it cool.

"Think so. Vet can confirm it," he says as he pushes himself up and brushes off his pants. "They say where the vet is?"

"Yep, gave me an address and general directions."

We head the way I think we should go on foot, the dog trotting happily beside us, panting loudly. It's almost like it knows we're its new family.

This is our dog.

I believe in signs, and this is a good fucking sign for me. Dogs mean permanency and commitment. Everyone I know that has settled down or gotten married, has gotten a damn dog.

So I know this means maybe we stand a chance. Maybe there is a future for us.

After a few missed turns, we find the vet. It's a bright blue house on the corner of the street with a wooden sign outside. Not like we could miss it. This house is a beacon. We approach the bright yellow door and push inside, the bell chiming above our heads as we cross the threshold.

There is no one at the front desk, not that I expected anyone to be here. This isn't a bustling town. I'm surprised there's even a vet in the first place.

"Hey, there," a deep voice says and my eyes swivel to the small hallway as a man emerges. And let me tell you, I expected someone old with wispy gray hair and glasses. I did not expect a hottie in a lab coat with big muscles.

A guy who is currently eyeing Grey like his next meal, like he already wants seconds. Well, listen up, hot man. This is not the Shire. We don't do that here. And we definitely do not do that with Grey.

Honestly, this is just my fucking luck. First Robert and now this dude.

His thighs are enormous too—they could crush a head, easily. He looks like he hikes through the Serengeti and works with the hippos.

At least he's not wearing short shorts. I can't compete with that. My legs are not that impressive.

"Hi," Grey says, and looks far too hot just opening his mouth. I mean, honestly, could he just be a little less impressive? But his build, coupled with his voice makes the vet's cheeks flush in attraction. Bet he doesn't get men like Grey up here every day.

He's probably going to try and shoot his shot.

Not that I'd let him. I'll block that shit. I'll take a bullet for Grey.

"Oh, what do we have here?" the vet says, bending down and petting the dog's head. "Look at this handsome fella."

Well, now he's just sucking up because this doggo is not handsome.

"Found him outside the restaurant," Grey says.

"Ah, well, you did good bringing him here."

Grey perks up a bit at the vet's praise, and I purse my lips. I'm feeling ridiculously jealous right now and I know it's absurd, but whatever. I just got him. No way do I want competition right now, and like hell I'm going to share.

"Want me to see if there's a microchip? Maybe someone's missing him..."

"That'd be great," Grey says, and the vet holds out his hand to Grey.

"I'm Michael, by the way."

Fucking Michael. Couldn't have a weird name or something, could you?

"Greyson," Grey says and my eyes narrow at that. Oh, he's pulling out the formal name? Sly, Mr. Hart. Sly.

"Nice to meet you, Greyson. You passing through?" Michael asks.

"Yup," Grey says and shifts on his feet. I fold my arms across my chest, watching this exchange. I notice that Michael hasn't asked me my name. It's almost like I'm invisible.

As long as Grey still sees me, then we'll be fine. I won't have to rage.

"Alright then, let me take this guy to the back. You wanna come? It should just take me a minute," he says.

Probably wants to get him alone. Like hell I'm letting him.

"We're fine here," I say and Michael startles a little as if he forgot I was even here.

"Oh, hi," he says, and I narrow my eyes at him. I could be

polite, but I'd rather not. I think I'll just be a surly teen right now. At least I have an excuse.

"This is Quinn," Grey says, and Michael nods.

"Nice to meet you both. Well, okay, just wait here..." he says and bends down, patting his leg. "Right, okay, come here, boy." The dog woofs once and trots along after him. Well, the dog has some shifty loyalty, but I know I'll win him over eventually.

When Michael's out of hearing range, I lean into Grey, inhaling him. God, he smells good. I can't even be that mad at him. He's like excreting some kind of pheromone or something. All the single gay dudes flock when he's around. They can't help it.

"*Greyson*," I say dryly, and Grey's cheeks flush.

"Don't know why I said that," he mutters.

"Hmm, you don't? Well, it seems to me like you were flirting with sexy vet man. Do you mind not doing that while I'm around?" I ask softly, trailing my hand up his back.

Grey peeks over at me and cocks his head. "I wasn't flirting. I was just talking."

I shift even closer, running my nose along his jaw as I cup the back of his neck.

"Fine, talk away, but you're mine, Greyson Hart. Fucking mine. I don't share."

His breath comes out a little shorter and his pupils dilate. Good. He likes it, me being possessive.

I can do this all day long. It comes naturally, especially when it comes to him. I am jealous to a fault. I don't know how I managed to keep it together all those years of watching him with other men. Men who weren't me. But I was biding my time back then. No more, though. No, I have what I want. I'm not giving it up easily.

"Nope! No chip here. Seems like a stray to me," Michael says, moving back out to the lobby, the dog once more happily trotting along next to him. Doggo seems to be smiling a bit too. He probably liked all the vet's attention.

Well, he'll like me just fine once we get him home. I'll pet the shit out of him.

"Seems like we're gonna take him then. We can't just leave him outside," Grey says, and Michael nods.

"Want me to make sure he's up to date on vaccines before you go?"

Grey looks at me, a question in his eyes and then nods. "Sure, yeah, that sounds good and then maybe you can tell us where we can get some food and whatever else we'll need..."

"The local store will have some things. I can give you a leash and a collar," the vet offers helpfully. Far too helpful if you ask me—probably trying to win Grey over, trying to lure him into his bed.

"That would be really helpful," Grey says, and I sigh, trying to get a grip.

Beggars can't be choosers. It's not like there's a Walmart around here that we can just pop into and grab what we need. We gotta take what this man is offering.

Alright, sexy vet man, you can give us some handouts, but I will not be thanking you.

"Come on, boy," Michael says, and the dog follows the vet into the back, not realizing that he'll be getting shots in just a few minutes. Maybe after that, doggo won't like him much anymore.

One can only hope.

"We should probably name him," Grey says as he watches them go.

"Yeah. What are you thinking?" I ask, my eyes sliding back to Grey.

He shrugs, pulling his bottom lip between his teeth. "Never was good with names."

"You named your son. And I think Joshua is a pretty damn good name."

"That was Karen. I wanted to go with Bernie."

A snort escapes me. "No, you fucking did not."

Grey smirks at me and I pull him in for a long-drawn-out kiss. Ridiculous man. Grey's hands move to my hips and he pulls me against his chest and I cling to him, loving the taste of him, the feel of him against me.

"How about you give me some ideas," Grey says, his hand in my hair, making some of the strands slip from my ponytail.

"We could go traditional. Max, Milo, Koda...or we could come up with something once we learn more about him."

Grey's eyes meet mine and I lean up and press my lips to his once more, needing more of him already. I cannot wait until tonight when I can crawl in next to him and feel him scoot against me, resting his head against my chest, my fingers sliding up his neck.

I am obsessed with sleeping next to him. I want to wake up every morning with him against me.

"All done," Michael says, forcing our lips apart. Michael's cheeks are flushed and he's looking intensely at us, probably sad that his dreams of wrangling Grey to his bed are dissipating before his very eyes. "Gave this guy a brief check-up.

Looks healthy. Maybe a little malnourished and dehydrated, but with proper food and water, he should be good to go."

"We know how old he is?" Grey asks.

"Yeah, looking at his teeth, I'm thinking he's probably five or so."

"Ah, so an oldie," Grey says.

"Midlife. Still got some good years left in him," Michael replies, and Grey smiles.

Okay, enough bonding over being old. I can't relate. It's not my fault I'm young.

"Sounds good, thanks," I say, taking the leash that doggo is now attached to. He trots next to me and sniffs at my pants, his tail wagging behind him.

"How much do we owe you?" Grey asks, pulling out his wallet, but the vet shakes his head.

"No, I've got this. It was my pleasure."

I'm sure it was, I think, as we make our way out onto the sidewalk and move toward the small local store, in search of some stuff to get the three of us through the next few days.

"Can't believe we have a dog now," Grey says, reaching down and threading his fingers through mine.

"Believe it," I say. "This is a motherfucking sign, Grey."

"A sign of what?" he asks, his brows furrowed.

"Dunno, but we'll find out, won't we?"

Grey looks down at the dopey dog beside us and nods. "Yeah. Guess we will."

* * *

"Think I came up with a name for him," Grey says. His head is on my chest as we lay in bed, his big hand splayed across my shoulder, massaging it lightly.

"Yeah, and what's that?"

I've been watching him mull this over all day and damn, if it wasn't cute as hell. He even ran a few choices by me, but I want the name to be his. I want him to choose.

I think Grey has lived a life where he's done everything for everyone else and never took a thing for himself. All he wants to do is to make everyone around him happy, but for once in his goddamn life, I want him to pick something that makes *him* happy. I want this name to be his. His choice.

I'll love whatever he comes up with.

He pauses a moment, almost as if he's unsure, and then softly says, "Winter."

"Winter," I say, letting the name roll off my tongue. "I love it."

"Yeah?" he asks, leaning up and looking down at me. My hand moves up to cup his cheek, feeling the stubble lightly abrade my skin. "Thought because he's a little older that it fits."

"It fucking fits, Grey," I tell him softly.

His hand travels up my neck and weaves through the hair at my temple. My entire body breaks out in goosebumps. I haven't had him in hours and I am dying for it.

We spent the afternoon buying what we needed for Winter and then came back to the trailer and gave him a shower. Winter just sat there calmly, letting the water wash over him, his tail thumping against the floor, his tongue lolling out of his mouth. Now he's sleeping on a makeshift doggie bed on the floor in the other room, snoring loudly.

For being a stray, he's ridiculously well-behaved.

"Think we can fuck without waking Winter up?" I ask softly, leaning up and pressing my lips to his.

Grey's entire body trembles, just as eager for it as me.

"Can you be quiet?" I ask, my hand sliding to his mouth and pushing two fingers inside. I feel his warm, wet heat surround me and my cock aches thinking of those lips around it—how he looks on his knees.

Ngh. I need him like that all the time. It's the thing fantasies are made from.

Grey's eyes flutter shut as he sucks on my fingers, his hips starting to arch up against my thigh. I can feel his hard cock pressing against me and I'm ready for it—ready to feel him come apart.

"I'm going to fuck you nice and slow," I whisper, my free hand moving down to his ass. "I'm going to take my time with you."

He whimpers, and I pull my fingers out and press my lips to his, licking into his mouth and sucking on his tongue. He lets out a gasp as I tug on it, reaching between us and stroking his hard length. God, he's desperate for it. He just craves it.

I pull away after nearly bringing him to the edge and then just stare at him, his swollen lips, his flushed cheeks.

He has utterly wrecked me for other men.

"Can I tell you a secret?" I say, my hand still gently squeezing his dick.

He nods, his breath coming out stunted.

"Kevin told me how you liked being fucked," I admit,

sliding my hand down his boxers and stroking his bare cock. "He got drunk one night and told me everything…"

"God, he's such an asshole," he mutters, but still pushes his hips up.

"Yes, but shit, Grey…the things I imagined doing to you after that conversation. I'd jack off almost nightly envisioning it."

Grey's eyes are hooded, his entire body trembling.

"I hate that cunt, but I am so fucking glad he told me. Because now I know exactly what you want. You are a wet dream. My wet dream."

Grey groans lowly, and I lean down to kiss him, fucking wildly into his mouth before ripping away from him.

"Strip. Then on your side," I tell him, reaching for the lube as I wrench my boxers off. We're trying to be as quiet as possible because the last thing I want is for Winter to trot in and watch. God, imagine? His one eye glaring at us in disapproval. Please stay asleep, Winter. Do not cockblock me.

I move behind Grey, my front to his back, my fingers already slick with lube, and I watch as Grey reaches down and exposes his hole to me. I slip my fingers inside of him so easily and hell, he's just a dream come true.

His hands clench the pillow he's resting his head on, and I see his bottom lip pulled between his teeth. He's trying to keep it down, to muffle those whimpers, but he's so fucking loud. He can't help it, and I love how he falls apart when he's getting fucked, every single time. I wonder if the sex he had with other men, like Robert, was just as good. Is being with me special somehow? Fuck, I hope I'm special. I want it to be only me who makes him this crazy.

I twist my wrist and press my fingers against his prostate, causing his hips to jerk frantically, fucking himself back against me.

Damn, I could watch this all day. I just love how desperate he is for it.

"Oh god," he grunts as I pull out my fingers and grab my cock, putting it at his hole, and sliding inside. He doesn't even resist the stretch, just sucks me inside. And when I'm balls deep, Grey turns so he's partially on his back, his leg thrown over mine as he pulls me in for a bruising kiss.

"Tell me what you're thinking?" I whisper when our lips finally part. I'm rocking into him slowly and he grunts with each thrust. I can see his cock bobbing against his abs, see the precum beading at the tip.

"You feel so good inside of me," he admits, his hand threading through my hair as he breathes into my mouth. "You feel so fucking good."

"Tell me I'm the best you've had," I say, licking my way across his mouth.

"The best. The fucking best," he groans as he starts to fuck his cock with his fist, his grunts turning into moans.

His admission makes my entire body light up. He just gave me something...he just gave me hope that maybe this thing between us is different.

I start to rock my hips faster, slamming into him, and Grey lets out a loud cry, assuredly waking everyone nearby.

I shove two fingers back into his mouth to keep him quiet, but the damage has already been done. I can hear the clink of Winter's collar as he gets up from his bed in the other room and then I see his head peer over the top of the mattress. His one eye blinks at us, and I groan.

"For fuck's sake, Grey," I say with a laugh. "You woke him up. He's watching us now."

Grey sucks on my fingers harder, his fist working his cock frantically. He seems unbothered by the fact that we have an animal watching. Jesus, of course. He's too far gone.

I have never met another man who gets so lost in sex.

"Shit," I mutter as I shove another finger into his mouth and arch up into him roughly. "Go away, Winter. Give us some fucking privacy."

Winter only huffs loudly, probably thinking we're wrestling. Or maybe he's a perv. Maybe he likes watching.

"I swear to god, Grey. If he comes up here, I won't be able to finish. This is weird enough."

But Grey isn't listening. He's groaning around my fingers while Winter pants at the end of the bed. And goddammit, I'm getting nervous. I can't perform with an audience.

I pull my focus back to Grey and immediately know he's close. A tear slips out of his eye, and I slide my tongue across his skin, licking it up as I fuck into him harder. He sucks on my fingers roughly, his teeth biting into my skin, and then I feel it, his entire body tensing as he comes. I feel his hole clench around my cock and it pushes me over the edge, my orgasm ripped out of me.

I slam my hips into him, riding on the tail end of my release, and then collapse, my fingers still shoved in his mouth, my cock still inside of him.

Winter is whining, his tail thumping against the wall.

"Jesus," I say, pulling my fingers from him and resting my

forehead on his. "I didn't realize getting a dog would be a cockblock."

Grey lets out a small laugh and then sighs, his eyelids drooping.

"Let's get cleaned up," I say, pulling out of him, and Grey groans.

"Wish you could stay inside of me," he says softly, and I freeze.

I lean over him and he peeks an eye open, looking completely relaxed.

"Next time, I'll fall asleep inside of you."

His lips twitch, and he throws an arm over his eyes.

"Yeah, Quinn. I'd like that."

God, can this man get any better? I don't fucking know, but I want to stick around to find out.

I manage to scoot past Winter without him smelling my junk and move into the bathroom, grabbing a washrag and bringing it back to clean us up. I love this part—taking care of him. I'd do it forever if he'd let me.

"Can't believe Kevin told you all my shit," Grey grumbles as I slide the washrag against his skin.

"Yeah, well, he did. And now I know."

He sighs, his limp dick settled right against that hairy thigh.

"So glad we broke up. He was toxic. I never did anything good enough for him."

"He's an idiot, couldn't appreciate a good thing."

Grey huffs, and I know he's worn out. I mean, his ass took a beating, I know he's ready to pass out.

I tug on his boxers and then pull on mine, lowering

myself next to him once more. Grey hesitates a moment before he lowers his head to my shoulder and throws an arm across my abdomen. This. This right here is exactly how it should be.

"Should let him up here. He's probably lonely," Grey says after a moment of silence.

I lean up and glance down at Winter who is resting his head on the mattress, his eye on me. I can't even be mad at him. He's so damn ridiculous. And he's ours.

"Alright," I say and pat the space next to me. "Come on, boy." Winter hops up, the mattress dipping beneath his weight, and lies down next to me, nuzzling his wet nose against my arm. Grey reaches over and pats Winter's head before he throws a leg over mine and presses a kiss to my neck.

"Get some sleep, Quinn," he mutters, and for a moment, I internally protest because I don't want to fall asleep just yet. I want to memorialize this. But my eyes eventually close and I drift off.

Dreaming of him.

Of us.

* * *

Things are fucking perfect the following day. We spend the day walking along Lake Superior with Winter and then head into town, perusing the few shops once more. I mean, we've seen it all already, but we do it again anyways. Then we head to the grocery store where we have to tie Winter up outside. He whines and looks so damn sad that Grey ends up staying outside with him while I head in to grab the items we need to make dinner.

I love him even more for doing that, for never wanting to cause harm, even to an animal.

Tomorrow we will pack up and head out to Marquette, an hour's drive across the UP with some stops in between. I can't fucking wait to pull over and see the falls and the dunes, and to just be with Grey.

And Winter. He's fast becoming a favorite of mine. I cannot wait to see what he thinks about Grey's home when we finally get back. I wonder if Grey will make him sleep on the floor or will invite him into bed every night.

There might be a discussion to be had over this. I want to be able to access Grey all the time, without interruptions.

Hmm, I may need to do some convincing.

"We have a feast here," Grey says as he pulls things out of grocery bags and sets them on the counter. I'm making us steak and mashed potatoes. I was going to get green beans and then decided against it.

Who needs green things? Not me, that's who.

I got ice cream instead.

"Only the best for my boo," I say, already imagining what I'm going to do with that ice cream later.

Suddenly, Grey's phone rings.

He glances down at it and smiles softly, tapping on the screen and placing it to his ear.

"Hey, Josh," he says cheerfully, his entire face breaking out in a grin.

Oh, my heart. My fucking heart. Josh has no idea how much his dad loves him. I don't know how he doesn't see it, that longing in his eyes. I've never much liked his mom, but I never knew if that was because I was so fiercely into Grey that anyone who hurt him immediately became an enemy.

But the more I get to know him, the more I realize that Karen did a lot of things to Grey with the sole purpose of hurting him. She kept Joshua away from his dad, not because it was what was best for her son, but because she knew how desperate Grey was for that relationship.

"Of course. Yeah. Of course. We'd love that," Grey says, his cheeks flushed.

My brows meet at his expression and the way his voice has changed. What's Grey agreeing to? I pull my phone out immediately, having set it on silent while we were out, and see that I missed some texts from my best friend.

Fuck. This is so my luck.

"See you soon," Grey says and then hangs up, his eyes meeting mine, and my heart sinks.

"Goddammit, Grey," I mutter, and he runs a hand over his head, huffing.

"Yeah, I know."

I know he's split between being excited his son is coming on this trip and knowing that it will put a damper on the two of us. There is no way we can behave like we have been when Joshua is here. We will have to go back to how it was before.

I don't know if I can handle it. I don't know if I can survive it—not when I've had him, when I've had a taste.

"I'm assuming we aren't telling him about us," I say, and Grey runs a hand down his face, his lips turned into a frown. He doesn't know what to say. I don't blame him. I don't know what to say either.

I get why he would want to keep it a secret.

"It's gonna be damn hard for me, Greyson," I tell him, being completely honest.

"I just..." he resumes pulling stuff out of the grocery bags, his voice trailing off. "I just don't know how I'd even approach that with him, Quinn. You're his best friend. I'm his dad."

"And we're both adults."

He peeks over at me and nods.

"Yeah, but he might not see it that way, and fuck, I don't want to ruin anything between us before he goes off to college. Then he won't ever want to visit."

Part of me wants to say, *what about me? What about us? Aren't you worried about ruining things between us?*

But I don't. I bite it back because I get it. Joshua is his son. He will always come first. He should always be a priority. But shit, I want to come first every once in a while. I want to be someone's first choice.

"When will they be here?" I ask.

"Tomorrow, around noon. They want to travel to Marquette with us. You okay with staying an extra day here and then we can head out?"

I shrug, trying like hell to keep my disappointment at bay. "Of course."

Grey sighs, reaching out and pulling me into him. His lips are in my hair, his hands clutching me to him.

"I'm sorry about this. I don't want to hurt you."

"I'll be fine," I say, lying through my teeth. I'm not sure I will be fine, but there's no reason to say anything now. Joshua is coming and that means this happy little bubble that we've been existing in is about to burst.

I just hope that when his son shows up, Grey remembers what we were like, how good it was between us.

"You look worried," Grey says, reading me so easily.

I shrug, placing a mask over my face, burying those feelings so damn far inside of me, even I can't feel them anymore. I don't want to stress him out. I just want us to enjoy our last free evening together.

"I'm not worried about a thing," I say, forcing a smile on my face.

And then I make myself believe it.

Everything will be fine. Just fucking fine. I'll will it into existence.

Chapter Sixteen

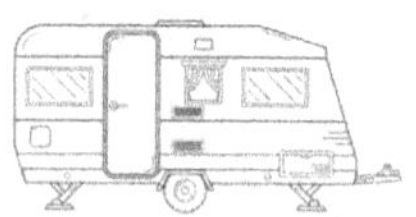

Grey

"Goddamn. How do you put up a tent?" Joshua asks, eyeing the heap of canvas on the ground. He has his hands on his hips, his eyebrows meeting in confusion. "Looks complicated."

I stare at my son, happy and content that he's here. But also, I'm trying like hell to ignore how sore my ass is. Quinn railed into me last night, and then again this morning. I feel like he wanted me to be sore so I wouldn't forget about him. I know he's nervous and trying to hide it. But I could never forget him, and it will be damn near impossible to let him go. I can already feel his absence and it's only been thirty minutes since Hailey and Joshua rolled into camp.

Damn, I'm excited to have them here. But I am going to miss Quinn's hands on me.

There is no way in hell I'm going to risk doing something

that would jeopardize any of us. It's not worth it. I can be mature about this. I can be the adult.

I glance over at Quinn who is chatting with Hailey, helping her pull the tent rods out and piece them together.

"Maybe you could learn a thing or two from Quinn. Seems he knows what he's doing," I say, and Joshua rolls his eyes at me.

"Yeah, well, maybe I'll just let them get it set up. They seem like they have it handled. I think I'd just mess them up."

I throw my arm around him and he lets me give him an awkward side hug.

"Glad you're here," I say. "We both are."

He glances up at me as my arm falls to my side. He looks a little like me, but more like Karen. He's thinner than I was at his age, with a runner's build and a tangle of black curls on top of his head. Joshua also has Karen's disposition too. He's full of passionate emotion and attitude, whereas I'm just...not. It's what drew me to Karen in the first place. She was just so full of fire and life, and she was my best friend in middle school. I, of course, was too young to know how people could change and how things could end so badly.

"I'm sorry I bailed last minute. Hailey made me realize it was a shit thing to do," he says, worrying his lip between his teeth. "But I'm glad Quinn could tag along. He's always down for an adventure."

I look over at Quinn and he must feel my eyes on him because he turns and our gazes lock.

"Yeah, I've learned that about him."

Quinn's eyes shutter and he turns back to Hailey. I met Joshua's girlfriend once before and liked her almost immediately. She seems different than the girls Joshua usually brings around, and from what I know of her, I think she's good for him.

Finding out that she's the reason they're here now makes me like her even more.

"Oh god, and that dog, Dad," Joshua says with a laugh. "I can't believe you adopted him."

I see Winter raise his head from where he's lying on the ground. It's almost as if he knows he's being talked about, and I can't help but bend down and pat his wiry head.

"Yeah, me too."

"Thought you didn't like dogs," Joshua says.

"Nah, I just knew I'd never be home enough to have one. Wouldn't have been fair to the dog."

Joshua eyes me. "And you will be now?"

I shrug, not really sure what the fuck I'm gonna do. I don't know if I can go back to the way things were before all of this happened. "Well, Quinn and I found him, so I figured we'd split custody."

Joshua snorts, his lips turned up in a smile. "Yeah, I'm sure Quinn will be thrilled about that."

"Thrilled about what?" Quinn asks, walking up and nudging Joshua with his elbow.

I glance over his shoulder and see that the tent has been assembled and Hailey is crawling inside, her dark-blonde hair braided down her back.

"Thrilled that you share custody of this dog."

Quinn's eyes meet mine and he smiles softly, a shared secret moving between us.

"I don't mind. Winter is cool," Quinn says, moving up next to me, his arm brushing against mine.

Just that small amount of contact has tingles shooting through me, and I feel my heart burst alive. Fuck, the next few days are going to be torture.

I'm not going to survive it.

Winter hears his name and wags his tail harder, his one eye blinking up at us.

"Yeah, well, I'm sure he'll grow on me," Joshua says, reaching out and patting Winter on the head just as Hailey calls out, asking Joshua to bring her something from his car.

We watch him walk off and Quinn's smile drops.

"Was he insulting Winter?"

"Don't take it personally," I say. "Shouldn't you know by now? You are his best friend, after all."

Quinn looks at me, those dark green eyes so fucking expressive. I want to reach out and bury my face in his neck, but instead, I just shove my hands into my pockets and stare intently at the trees in the distance. I wonder what kind they are—probably birch, maybe maple. Should go over and have a real long look.

"Yeah, well, I do. Just...I'm just tired already, Grey, and it's only been an hour."

"Been more like thirty minutes."

Quinn rolls his neck and I hear a pop.

"Fuck this, let's just leave while they're sleeping," he says, his voice low. "Let's just go and never come back."

I start to chuckle and then realize he's deadly serious. Oh shit. He'd so run away with me. He's not even joking.

He watches me as I shift on my feet because fuck, I do

want to leave. It was so nice living in our own little world and now that it's been invaded, it feels like a special kind of carnage.

"We can't do that," I say solemnly. "We can't just leave when he just got here."

"Yeah, we fucking can."

I roll my lips between my teeth and shake my head. "We'll manage. We can be adults about this."

Quinn doesn't look so sure, but he lets it go. And thank fuck for that. I don't want him to be mad at me, but I can't just come out and tell Joshua. Not yet. Probably not ever.

But the thought of keeping us a secret puts me in a bit of a mood as we finish helping them get settled and wander around town once more. We hike along Lake Superior with Winter, listening to Joshua and Hailey fill us in on the last of their summer plans.

They're heading to Mackinac Island after this for a few days and then over to Traverse City to spend time with some friends. After that, they're off to college.

"You gonna come see me off, Dad?" Joshua asks me, and I about wilt from the question. Because I hadn't planned on it. Karen hadn't invited me and neither had Joshua, so I expected to just say my farewells privately.

He never seems to want me around for the big moments. Never. I was lucky to sit across the street during prom and snap some photos of them before they left in their limo, not wanting to ruin their moment by showing up uninvited. And his high school graduation, I sat in the very back because Karen didn't save me a seat.

"Yeah, I could do that. Could drive down with you to the dorms."

Joshua smiles and nods his head. "Yeah, that would be cool. As long as you and Mom don't fight the entire time."

Quinn pipes up then. "It's never Grey who starts those fights, you know that."

Joshua's eyes swing to his best friend and he bobs his head. "Yeah, Mom gets a little...weird about stuff. I get it. I'll make sure that we're cool. I'll tell her you're coming."

My heart pitter-patters in my chest as we continue walking, and fuck, I want to reach over and thread my fingers with Quinn's, to pull him into my side and share this moment with him. But I can't. Because if I did, it would ruin whatever Joshua is finally trying to build between us, something I've worked so hard to accomplish in the past. I don't want to tear it down. I don't want to destroy this.

But I also don't want to destroy Quinn either.

I may have already begun unknowingly. But I don't know how to fix it.

He glances at me, and I feel my chest constrict. Those eyes. Those fucking eyes looking at me like I'm his everything.

How did I never notice it before? How did I not see?

I'm an idiot, it seems. Not seeing what was right under my nose all those years. Not that I would have acted on it, but still.

He looks at me like I've hung the moon, like I can do no wrong. But I can. I have. I will probably continue to fuck up without meaning to. I could hurt him and not mean it. I'd never mean it.

Oh, Jesus.

After meandering through town and eating dinner, we head back to the trailer and sit outside to chat, watching the sun slowly set below the horizon. It's almost eleven o'clock when we finally part ways, Joshua and Hailey crawling into their tent, while Quinn and I move into the trailer.

As soon as the door snaps shut, leaving us alone, Quinn lets out a shuddering breath.

"Fuck," he murmurs, his hands carding through his hair. His shirt rides up his waist, showing me the skin of his abdomen and the hint of his tattoos, and I feel my mouth water.

He's so damn perfect.

"Don't tell me to sleep over here," he whispers, glancing at the kitchen table. "I can't bear it."

I bite down on the inside of my cheek and don't say a word. I can't. I can't turn him away, but doesn't he see how risky this is? What if Joshua finds out? What if he sees?

"I won't fuck you. I just want to hold you," he says softly, his voice laced with desperation.

A low hum of panic starts to spread through me because I don't know what to do. I don't know what decision is right.

"I'll lock the door. He'll never know."

Winter whines between us, almost as if sensing something is off, and I pat his head, offering him some comfort where I can offer Quinn none.

Or maybe I can.

"Please, Grey. Don't make me start this all over. I won't survive it."

I feel my chest constrict, feel my skin start to sweat, and I know that if he sleeps separately that I too won't be able to bear it. I'll be a miserable mess until morning. I've grown used to being next to him, falling asleep in his arms.

"Lock the door," I finally say, and Quinn's shoulders sag in relief.

The lock clicks and he moves toward me, his hands on my face, his lips on mine. We are back in our little cocoon, sheltered from the outside world, and oh, to be in his arms again. It's fucking heaven and feels so absolutely right.

"I'll make up this bed out here, so he'll never know."

"It's so deceptive," I murmur against his lips. "He'll be so angry if he finds out."

"Don't care. Don't fucking care, Grey."

"But I do. He's my son."

"Then stop me," he tells me, pulling away, his hands still on my face. "Tell me to back off and I will."

But I can't. I can't utter the words because I don't want him to stop. I want Joshua in my life and Quinn by my side. That's what I want.

"I'll help you set it up," I say instead.

Quinn lets out a long sigh and then we work on moving the table into a bed, rolling out his sleeping bag and placing his pillow at one end. We stare at it for a beat and he rumples it a bit. Then Quinn links his hand with mine and leads me to the bedroom. He shuts the windows and pulls down the blinds as I undress and then we're crawling onto the bed together, our bodies pressed up against each other.

"Can I kiss you, just for a bit?" he asks, his nose nuzzling against my neck.

"Okay. Yeah," I say, and he lowers his mouth to mine.

We kiss for long moments with the background noise of Winter's snores.

When Quinn finally pulls away, I ache, desperation rampant within me. I want him inside of me again, but I can't ask him to do that. I can't risk it. When he fucks me, he owns me, and I can't keep quiet. I know for a fact that even with the windows closed, Joshua and Hailey would hear what he was doing to me.

There would be no hiding from the truth then. And Joshua only just got here. I don't want him storming off angrily in the middle of the night because I couldn't keep a dick out of my hole.

Quinn shifts onto his back and tugs me up against him.

"No more thinking about it," Quinn says softly, his hand massaging the back of my neck lightly. His touch relaxes me instantly, and I melt into him.

"You're a good dad," he says after a moment of silence, almost as if he can read my muddled thoughts.

"Not really," I murmur, my hand curling against his stomach, because if I was a good dad, I would have resisted temptation. I wouldn't have fucked Quinn, wouldn't have been so selfish as to jeopardize their friendship and my relationship with my son.

"No, Grey. I know all the ways you showed up for Josh, despite being kept away. I know that you deserve recognition for a whole hell of a lot. I *see* you."

My throat closes up, and I feel my eyes begin to sting. No one has ever called me a good dad. No one has ever said those words to me. Except for Quinn.

"I haven't done anything remarkable."

"Says you. I know you picked up an extra night job so you could buy Josh his car. I know that Karen calls you every time Josh has something planned, like a school trip, and asks you to pay for it. I know that she never told him that it was you who funded his way to Mexico last year or to D.C. the year before that. And I know you're paying for his college..."

My nose burns and I blink rapidly, feeling my heart thunder beneath my ribs.

"How do you know all that?"

"Because I pay attention. Because I spend all my time at Josh's mom's house or at yours and I hear things, notice things. I notice everything about you, Grey. I know that you work your ass off each and every day for your son, and he will never know it because you never tell him."

"He can't ever know," I whisper.

"And why not? Why can't he?"

I am silent a moment, letting my thoughts settle, and I let out a shaky breath, holding Quinn to me. "Because...because for years I pretended I was someone I wasn't and everything that's happened to Joshua and Karen since then feels like my fault. This seems like my penance."

Quinn stiffens beneath me. "Horseshit, Grey. Everyone comes out in their own time. You were young and Karen is just a spiteful bitch."

A small snort escapes me and I sniffle loudly. "You don't mince words, do you?"

"Yeah, well no. Not when it comes to her. I've seen her in action and have heard enough of her lies. You've done nothing wrong. You have spent your entire life making sure Joshua has a good life, even making sure Karen has one.

You've more than made up for any hurt you caused. Enough is enough. No more, Grey. You need to start standing up for yourself."

I sit with that, my thoughts a jumble of emotions. I scoot closer to him, letting my ear rest over his thrumming heart. It's strong and steady, and it reminds me so much of Quinn. And while part of me believes him, another, much larger part, still thinks that he can't possibly be right. I could never tell Joshua the truth. It could possibly destroy his relationship with his mother and I'd never want to do that.

So, as much as Quinn wants me to start standing up for myself, I just can't. I'm going to keep all those secrets stuffed away inside of me. Maybe one day Joshua will figure it all out for himself. But I'm not going to be the one to tell him.

Hopefully Joshua can come to want a relationship with me without knowing all of the things I've done for him. Maybe he can love me for who I am.

I breathe in the scent of Quinn and let my eyes close.

I am just going to file this all away for later. Right now I am just going to relish in my time with Quinn because tomorrow we have to pretend like we don't know each other in this way.

We have to go back to keeping our hands to ourselves.

I hold him tighter.

We still have tonight.

* * *

We pack up camp in the morning and drive over to the Grand Sable Dunes before we head to Marquette. We park on the side of the road and trek up the slope, and when we get to the top of the mountainous sandy dunes, we pull our shoes off, holding them in our hands as the four of us look *down.*

"Should we race to the bottom?" Joshua asks, and I glance over at him.

"If we run down there, we have to come back up."

"Too old, Dad?" Joshua jokes, and I crack a smile at him. I feel old at the moment, but before I can open my mouth to say that, Joshua is running downhill, sand kicking up as he moves down the dune at breakneck speeds. Hailey glances over at me and smiles, following him down, her braid swinging back and forth as she runs. Quinn nods toward them.

"Race you?" he asks, and I bite my bottom lip, contemplating it before I jerk forward, nearly toppling over as I follow my son and his girlfriend down the steep incline. Winter trots along beside me like this is no big deal, his woofs and pants piercing the air.

As I descend, my heart is thundering in my chest, Quinn's laugh filtering through the wind behind me. And minutes later, we finally stumble to a stop at the lake shore.

All of our chests are heaving, our bodies covered in a thin layer of sand, our hair mussed and our eyes wild.

"Fuck, that was steep," Joshua says and swipes a hand over his head.

I glance behind me and look up, up, *up* and groan because we have a long hike back to our vehicles after this.

"Come on. Let's not think about that. Let's walk for a bit," Quinn says, thumbing over his shoulder. Winter laps at the waves, his paws getting wet as we move down the shoreline.

Joshua grabs a stick and throws it for him and he happily chases it down, bringing it back to us, his eye twinkling in delight.

"So, Joshua tells me you two are going to the same college," I tell Hailey as Joshua throws the stick once more.

She bobs her head. "Yep! We are. Indiana University has a great ESL program there. I know Joshua is still undecided, but I think they have some majors that he seems interested in."

I glance over at my son and he nods. "I have time to figure it out. Two years right?" When I just bob my head, Joshua asks, "Quinn, you ever reconsider going to that art school in New York? I know you were debating it."

My heart drops in my chest because this is the first I'm hearing of it. I thought Quinn would be attending a school nearby, if he was attending at all. That was the impression he gave me, at least.

Quinn's cheeks flush and he shrugs. "I turned them down. I want to stay close to home."

I eye him warily when Joshua reaches out and shoves at his shoulder. "But that was your dream school."

"Not really," he mutters and peeks over at me. I try like hell to school my face, but damn, it's hard. When Hailey and Joshua take Winter's leash and jog down the beach a ways, I slow my steps next to Quinn.

"Didn't know you were considering a school out of state."

"Yeah, well, I applied on a whim and then turned them down."

I swallow roughly. "And why's that?"

He glances at me and sighs. "You have to know, Grey."

My heart flip-flops in my chest.

"But you must have made the decision to stay months ago. We weren't...." I let my words fade away into the sound of the crashing waves on the shore.

"Yeah, well I was holding out hope. I knew you'd come around. I knew I had a shot once Kevin was out of the picture."

I run a hand over my head and glance up, seeing Joshua and Hailey talking animatedly in the distance.

Shit, I'm fucking up more than one life by getting involved with Quinn, but I don't know how to give him up now.

"Please don't overthink it," he says, his voice almost desperate. "It wasn't my dream school. I don't even want to go to college. I'd be happy in a studio apartment with you and making art. As long as I had you."

I swallow roughly, keeping my feet moving forward, keeping my eyes ahead of me. Because if I look at him, I am going to crumble.

"We can talk about it later tonight," I say and see him shuffle a little closer to me. His hand brushes mine and I resist the urge to twine my pinkie with his.

"Yeah, we can talk more if you want, but there's really nothing to discuss. I made my decision and I have zero regrets. New York can go fuck itself."

I hold those words in my head and repeat them to myself as the day moves on, trying to remember that he's an adult, that he can do as he likes. But I can't help but wonder if he's made the right decision.

Chapter Seventeen

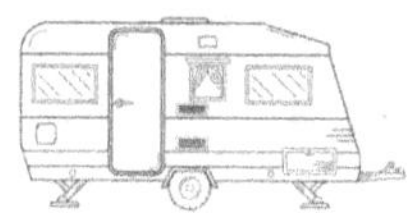

Quinn

Goddamn, Grey is being weird. And I'm not much better, honestly. I am antsy as fuck because I can't touch him. It is a special kind of torture because, after unlimited access to him, I now have to wait until we are locked inside the trailer to touch, to kiss. And we can't even fuck because he's so damn loud.

It's been two days since Joshua and Hailey arrived, and I've behaved. I have been the best boy. I haven't so much as looked at him weird, but it's getting harder and harder to do. I am teetering on the edge.

Two nights ago, after trailing across the dunes near Lake Superior, Grey had seemed upset to find out that I had chosen him over an out-of-state art program. It took a lot of words to get him to understand that he was what I wanted, that I didn't care about some prestigious college or a stupid degree that comes with a load of debt. None of that would help me much anyways. I would be just fine either way, mostly resigned to living simply and making art as I traveled.

I don't need much in life. But I do need him.

Yesterday, we walked through Marquette, eating lunch downtown and then spending some time touring the museums. I saw how happy Joshua and Hailey are, always touching and kissing, and it took everything within me not to push Grey into a darkened corner and press my mouth to his, to just swipe my tongue into his mouth and taste him. Just once.

"Thank fuck they're leaving tomorrow," I tell Grey as we work on getting dinner ready. We spent the day walking around Houghton and debated going on a six-hour ferry ride across Lake Superior but decided against it. Joshua would puke and I'm pretty sure I would too. Those waves on the lake aren't anything to sneeze at, and I don't want Grey to see me barf. I'd rather save that for another time, like maybe after he's heard me fart. Then maybe a little puke would be okay.

So instead, we just wandered through the town, enjoying our last day together before Grey and I head off to Copper Harbor.

Grey chuckles a little, peeking over at me.

"Tell me how you really feel," he says softly, and I lean toward him, wanting to just fucking kiss him.

"I can't wait to be inside of you tomorrow. As soon as they leave, I'm fucking you."

He lets out a stuttered breath, and I beam. His cheeks are flushed and I can see that vein in his neck pumping blood furiously. Oh yes, he's ready too. I wake up next to him each morning, feeling his cock pressed up against my body. It's just as eager as he is.

It's been two days of edging ourselves, just bringing ourselves to the point of no return over and over.

I haven't even jacked off, just waiting until I can explode into his ass.

I am going to fill him up so much. He's going to leak for hours afterward.

"Hey, guys?" Joshua calls as he and Hailey barrel inside.

Grey quickly steps far away from me, and I sigh unhappily. I mean, honestly could he just maybe stand a little bit closer? It's not like I'm going to latch on to his neck and suck. I mean, I am resisting the urge to slide to my knees and suck his dick, but I would never. I would never do that in front of someone else...unless he asked me to.

I'd so be down for that if he was into it. I'm into anything he is.

"We were just talking about where we are headed after you guys take off tomorrow," I say.

Joshua sits down at the small kitchen table and Hailey scoots in next to him.

"So, where you headed next?"

"Copper Harbor. And then up to the Porcupine Mountains," Grey says.

"Damn," Joshua says and runs a hand over his head, so much like Grey, it's funny. Even though he wasn't raised by his dad, he still has some of the same mannerisms.

But he's very much like Karen in how he blows things out of proportion. I get why Grey doesn't want to say anything about us. I can see Joshua flipping his lid over this. It's best we discuss how to break the news to him after they're gone. Then we can handle this like adults.

I think once Joshua is away at school things will be easier to handle since he won't be as close. Maybe he won't even give a fuck. I just don't know. At times, he can be such a wild card. And I get that this is a little unconventional, but Joshua doesn't understand my feelings for Grey. He has no idea how many years I've pined for this man.

"Wish we could tag along," Hailey says, the bun on the top of her head bouncing slightly. She has her chin on her clasped hands, her eyes watching Grey and me curiously.

A little too curiously for me. I shift on my feet, feeling suddenly a little nervous. We've been so careful. There is no way she could know something.

"But I'm sure you guys will have fun without us."

The twinkle in her eye and slight smirk is telling. My cheeks flush and I feel a flutter in my chest. Dammit. She so knows.

"We will," Grey says, reaching around me, his arm brushing against mine, and my eyelids flutter closed.

I snap them open immediately and see Hailey's head cocked.

So maybe I haven't been as careful as I should have been, or maybe these feelings I have for Grey just can't be contained. Either way, she knows. I wonder if she will tell Joshua or if she will let it go.

I hope like fuck she lets it go. There is nothing wrong with what we're doing, and I want to be the one to tell Joshua. Grey and I should tell him together.

She smiles softly at me and I feel a sense of relief because that's not conspiratorial at all. That's just someone who sees and understands.

Her eyes shift away, and I let out a breath I didn't realize I was holding.

Thank fuck for Hailey being reasonable and mature.

"You guys wanna play another game after dinner?" Hailey asks, linking her hand with Joshua's.

Grey bobs his head, reaching into the oven, and my eyes can't help but swivel down to his ass. God, soon. Tomorrow I can be inside of it.

I can't fucking wait.

* * *

I should tell Grey about Hailey, that I think she knows, but I keep it to myself. Joshua hasn't come storming into the trailer, demanding answers, so I tell myself to let it go. Plus, Joshua and Hailey are leaving soon, which means I get Grey all to myself in just a few short minutes. And that's all I can think about at the moment.

I finally get Grey alone again.

Right now, he's hugging Joshua, saying something to him that I can't make out, and I'm squirming. God, I love my best friend, but just go the fuck away now, please. I cannot keep my hands to myself a moment longer. They're starting to grow a mind of their own. They reach out for Grey unbeknownst to me. It's only a matter of time before I run them up his chest, down his thighs, around his dick.

I can't stand not touching him.

Finally Grey and Joshua step away from each other, and I

move over and slap Joshua on the back, pulling him into a quick hug.

"You and Hailey have fun," I tell him. "Don't go all crazy without me."

Joshua snorts a laugh and then rolls his eyes. "Yeah, like you're ever crazy."

It's true. Being with Grey is the most reckless thing I've ever done. Usually, I'm the one holding Joshua back from doing something stupid. Although, Hailey seems reasonable and able to keep him in line, so maybe Joshua doesn't need me around anymore.

I meet her eyes and she smiles at me, so I pull her into a brief side hug.

"Thanks," I say softly, and she meets my stare.

"Of course. That's your business," she replies, and I feel myself blush at how kind she is. I really hope that things between them continue. Joshua needs someone stable in his life, someone level-headed.

Moments later, they're climbing into their car and Grey is waving as their car fades from view.

And I can't wait another moment more.

I tie up Winter, patting him on the head and murmuring a quick apology, and then grab on to Grey. I eagerly pull him into the trailer, the two of us nearly stumbling up the steps. And as soon as the door slams shut, I'm on him. My mouth smashes into his and my hands travel down his chest, lifting and wrenching his shirt up over his head.

My fingers travel through his chest hair as I lick my way into his mouth.

"God, you feel so good," I say as I rut up against him,

feeling the strain of the past few days melt away. Finally. *Finally*, I get to have him again.

Grey seems to feel the same because his moans are growing louder and louder, not at all muffled by my mouth on his.

I yank his pants open, reaching behind him and palming his ass. God, that ass. The one I'm going to be inside of soon. My finger swirls around his hole and he cries out, his body trembling against mine.

Fuck. Yes. Soon.

I'm shaking as I fall to my knees, pulling his pants down as I go, and when his cock bobs free, I just consume it. My lips stretch around the thick length, and I take him all the way to the back of my throat, swallowing around him.

Grey is wild above me, his hands fisting my hair, his head thrown back as he fucks into my mouth.

Oh yes. Fuck yes.

Louder. *Louder*.

Suddenly, a loud crash has me pulling back, and I see Joshua standing in the doorway, his eyes wide, his mouth agape. Grey shoves me away, nearly tumbling over trying to right himself.

Oh god. Why the hell is he here? And why didn't I lock the door?

"What the fuck!" Joshua yells, his eyes wide, his cheeks flushed. He slaps a hand over his eyes and gags.

"What the fuck was that!?" he adds, his entire body shaking.

I don't know what to say, so I swallow it down and steady my breathing.

"You can look now," I say, trying to remain calm when I feel like throwing up. Oh god, what he just walked into. It would have been better had we just told him when they first arrived, not given him the shock of his life like this.

Joshua's hand falls to his side and he stares at us. He looks so damn confused and embarrassed and...there it is...*angry*.

"Dad?" he asks and then shifts his eyes to me. "Quinn, what the fuck are you doing to my dad?"

I shift on my feet, meeting my best friend's stare.

"You know what you saw."

"I thought he was being murdered," Joshua says and then covers his ears, almost like he's trying to erase the sounds from his mind. "Oh my god, are you guys...fucking?"

His voice is a screech, and I wince at the sound. Grey looks like he's going to pass out, his face devoid of all color.

"We are," I say softly, hoping it lessens the blow.

It doesn't. It only makes him angrier.

"Oh my god. How long has this been going on?"

The way he says it, so accusatory, has me standing up taller.

"Just since this trip. There was never anything going on before that..."

He doesn't seem to believe me, his eyes wild, his throat working overtime.

"How do I know you're telling the truth? My dad could be some kind of pervert!"

That makes something ugly rise up inside of me, and I take a step toward my best friend, my hands slowly curling into fists.

"He's not. Shut your damn mouth."

I've never spoken to Joshua like this before. Never. And the shock of it has him stumbling back a little, his body slumped over the chair behind him.

"You're fucking *my dad.*"

I give him a clipped nod.

"It's wrong," he whispers.

"And why the fuck is it wrong? I'm nineteen. An adult..."

"He's my dad!"

His voice is raised once more, his hands fluttering around him. He's having a hard time processing this, so I take a step back, giving him some space. Grey hasn't moved from where I left him, his body in shock.

Oh fuck. I should have just waited to get my hands on him until later tonight. If I hadn't been so desperate, all of this could have been avoided. But no. I was greedy and now I've ruined things for all of us.

I don't think my friendship with Joshua will ever be the same after this, and I'm not sure Grey is going to let me touch him again.

But maybe it will all be okay. Maybe, by some miracle, it will all work out.

God, it needs to work out.

"I can't believe you'd do this, Dad," Joshua says, his eyes searing into Grey's pale face.

Grey winces, looking like someone's slapped him.

"I'm sorry."

Those words hang between us, and Joshua swallows once. Twice. Before he utters, "You're so damn selfish."

And I see red, my entire body boiling with anger. I step forward, my body crowding his.

"Take it back," I hiss, and Joshua's eyes narrow as he shakes his head.

"I won't because it's fucking *true*. I came on this trip because I wanted to give him a chance and look what he did behind my back. He's a fucking selfish asshole—fucking my best friend."

"Shut your mouth!"

"Quinn," Grey croaks, but I can barely hear it over the roar in my ears. God, Joshua is such a prick, throwing hurtful words around like that, knowing what they'll do to his dad. They're cutting him wide open, I know it.

"He knew what this would do to me and he did it anyways..."

"Stop it," I say between clenched teeth. "You don't know what you're saying."

"You are both perfect for each other. Selfish dicks who only think of yourselves..."

"Enough!" I roar, and Joshua's eyes widen at my outburst. "Shut the fuck up, Josh! God, you are such a prick. Do you know half the things your dad has done for you?" I let loose, my words tumbling out of me. "You don't fucking know because your bitch of a mom has lied to you all these years. Lied about it all, taken credit for all that Grey's done. So fuck you. Fuck you for making him feel bad for taking something for himself, for once in his goddamn life. And if you must know, it was *me* who pursued this, who pushed it. Grey was too concerned about his dick of a son to make any moves."

My chest is heaving when my words finally trail off and silence hangs heavily in the trailer.

"It still doesn't make it right," Joshua says, and I shove at him, hating him so fiercely in this moment. Because he didn't hear a word I said. He's too focused on the fact that Grey betrayed him. That I did too.

"I'm not giving him up for you," I say, and Grey moves up next to me. And for a moment I think he'll stand by my side, that he'll emphatically say that he won't give me up either, but instead, he just runs a hand across his head and looks utterly broken.

"It shouldn't have happened," Grey says, and I let out a shaky exhale, feeling my entire world knocked sideways.

"No, it fucking shouldn't have, Dad. God, you disgust me."

And without thinking, my fist pulls back and plows into Joshua's cheek with a *crack*. His head jerks back, his hand flying to his cheek, and I just let my own arm fall to my side, my fist opening and closing, an ache spreading across my chest.

"What the hell?" Grey says, moving toward his son who is just looking at me with confusion. Hurt laces his eyes, but doesn't he see? He's cut us both so much deeper by being so uptight about all of this. The entire world doesn't revolve around him for once and he can't fucking stand it.

"He deserved it," I say, my voice cracking because Grey is trying to comfort his son, his focus not on me. Not at all.

"Quinn," Grey says softly, his voice hurt and strained. "You should go."

My entire body locks up, and he sighs, his eyes darting between Joshua and me, running a nervous hand across the top of his head again.

"Just outside, for a minute. Let you both cool off."

But before I can protest, Joshua jerks away, moving toward the door.

"Don't bother. I'm fucking going. You two have a nice trip. Don't bother coming to see me off for school. I don't want you there. Either of you."

And then Joshua is stumbling out the door, a broken sob leaving his mouth as he rushes toward Hailey waiting in the car. Whatever he'd come back for is forgotten and then it's just Grey and me standing in the trailer, the air heavy with regret.

I turn to look at him and he sags against the wall.

"We'll get through this. He'll forgive us," I lie, and Grey glances away, not even able to look at me. But I'm not letting him just fucking run from this. I can't.

"Please don't shut me out," I say softly, and Grey swallows, stepping away from me. I can hear Winter whining outside; he knows something is wrong.

Because it is. It's so fucking wrong.

"I'm gonna go for a walk," he says, and I feel my soul slowly wither from what this could mean. "I'll be back later...I just need some space to think."

And then he's gone.

Leaving me alone. Leaving me to wait for him to come back to me.

Chapter Eighteen

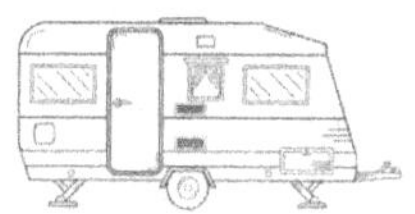

Quinn

I sit outside on the steps, waiting for Grey to return to me, barely moving, my eyes glued to the tree line. Winter is by my side, his chin on my lap. He wonders where Grey went too. He can feel this as palpably as I can, this utter and complete ruination of me.

Grey can't be gone for long. He can't just leave me here like this, in this state of misery.

My phone beeps and I fumble with it, reading the message across the screen.

JOSHUA:

Fuck you. I cannot believe you would do this.

Just to be clear, we aren't friends. Not anymore.

I sigh, feeling my stomach clench and my heart drop. He's my best friend and I punched him, knocked him right in the face. But he had deserved it, spewing all that hateful shit. I couldn't let it go, although I could have handled it better. I should have. Perhaps if I had behaved more maturely, Grey wouldn't be running away right now.

No, he'd run anyways. He's broken over this. I could tell. He was so happy those few days, his relationship with his son on the mend. And I went and ruined it.

Fuck, I ruined everything.

I run a hand through my hair, the strands tangling in my fingers and I sigh. The elastic band is long gone, having fallen somewhere since Grey left and I lack the motivation to find it. I look unhinged, I'm sure. Wild. Like some kind of crazed teen in love.

I am a crazed teen in love.

I should leave.

The sudden thought is so jarring, I stuff it down, far down, trying to hide it. But it keeps popping back up the longer he's gone.

I don't want to leave.

I chant that to myself, pacing in front of the trailer, gnawing at my sore lips.

I want to stay.

Still, what if he wants me to go? Fuck, he might want me to. I roll that idea around in my head until I'm nearly hyperventilating. But I move into the trailer anyways and pack my shit. Just in case. Just in case he kicks me out.

Not sure where I'd go, to be honest. It's not like I can get an Uber home, we're so far out here, in the middle of nowhere. I should probably call Becca and see if she can come and get me. She and her family shouldn't be far behind us, and I know she has her own car for the trip.

God, he can't just throw me out. Right?

Motherfucking right?

I'm tossing the last of my things in my duffel bag when Grey returns. It's been hours, and he looks wrecked in the worst possible way. He looks older and worn down, and my heart skips a beat in trepidation.

I stand by the kitchen table, tense and wary, as we just stare at each other.

"Grey," I manage to say, my voice cracking, and he winces, looking pained. Like it physically hurts him to hear me speak.

"Sorry I was gone for so long," he says, glancing away and running a hand over his head. His eyes fall on the duffle bag and he sighs.

"Are you leaving?" he asks lowly, and I swallow the lump in my throat.

"If you want me to," I whisper.

Those words hang in the air between us and Grey glances away from me.

"I don't want you to..."

I let out a breath I didn't know I was holding.

Thank fuck. *Thank fuck.*

"But maybe you should."

It's just a whisper of words, but it's powerful. My whole world caves in and I feel my head start to spin. Because he's not choosing me. I'm not enough. I don't matter enough to fight for this.

"Maybe I should?" I ask in utter disbelief and he nods, not meeting my eyes.

"Maybe it's for the best. We've...we've ruined enough."

"Ruined what?" I ask, even though I know the answer. We've ruined what he was building with Joshua and my relationship with my best friend. And we ruined what we had between us.

Before it even had a chance to fully develop, we ruined it.

"You know," he says and then those sad brown eyes meet mine, and I collapse into the chair. Winter whines, coming up to console me and then looking back at Grey, unsure where he should go.

To be fair, I think I need Winter more. I've loved Grey far longer than he ever loved me.

He doesn't love me. No, if he did, he'd fight for this. He'd fight for me.

But I'm disposable.

The thought almost makes me sick. My stomach churns and rolls.

"There's no arguing with you is there?" I ask, scraping my fingers through my hair and breathing deeply through my nose.

"No. We both knew it couldn't last..."

"*You* knew that, but I sure as fuck didn't," I hiss, and Grey winces.

I stand up, jerking my duffle bag over my shoulder.

"Fine. You want me to go, I'll go."

Grey jolts upright and his eyes widen. "I didn't mean right this second. It's late."

"I'll be fine," I murmur, my eyes filling with tears. I turn away, not wanting him to see me cry. No, this is all humiliating enough.

I bend down and hug Winter before pushing my way out of the trailer and begin walking toward the entrance to the campground. The soles of my shoes hit the gravel and I hear the crunch of it. I focus on the sound, trying to swallow down the sting in my throat.

Do not cry. Not yet.

Not yet.

I'll cry when Becca gets here. Whenever that is.

"Quinn, wait," I hear Grey call out, and I stumble to a stop. My heart is racing as Grey approaches, his cheeks red, his eyes a little wild.

"Please let me drive you. I can take you home."

Oh god, he didn't come back to ask me to stay. He came to ask me to leave again. That's even worse.

"No," I say and then continue walking.

Grey moves up to my side and continues following me, and with each foot forward, I feel like my heart is cracking more and more. I wish he'd just go away.

I wish he'd stay.

Stay with me, Grey.

Don't make me leave.

"I'll wait with you until your ride gets here," he says softly, and I press a clenched fist to my mouth and bite back a sob. I can't respond, so I just keep walking.

When I get to the main road, I find a bench just near the campground sign. I hear it creaking on its hinges as I sink down, pulling out my phone and finding Becca's number.

I had texted her earlier, vaguely letting her know my situation and asking her to keep her phone on, just in case.

Well, it's time to call in a favor. She responds immediately, saying she can be here in a couple hours.

A couple hours of hell, sitting next to Grey and waiting for him to change his mind. Or not. He probably won't.

But he's here, steadfast and quiet, his body far too close. I can smell him, can almost taste him. I want to lean over and let him gather me in his strong arms and hold me. I want to lean up and kiss him one last time, to have him just for one more moment.

But I don't. I can't. He doesn't want me.

Instead, I just face forward and wait and fucking *wait*, feeling my heart shrivel inside of me with each passing minute. This is a special kind of hell. This longing and utter need for another person who is right there, right next to you, but you still can't have them.

I will never be enough for him.

Finally, Becca appears in her run-down car and Grey stiffens next to me. He knows what this means, that this is over. I stand up on shaky legs and move toward the passenger-side door. Grey follows silently.

He reaches down, brushing past my side, opening the door for me.

That's when I let the first tear fall. Meeting his stare, I pull my bottom lip between my teeth.

"When you're ready to make this work, find me," I tell him, and Grey's nostrils flare.

This means that I love him and that I'll wait for him to come around.

I'll fucking wait.

Before he can respond, I slip inside the car and the hinges creak as Grey closes the door behind me. He stands there, his hands in his pockets, his lips in a pained frown as we drive off. I can't look.

I can't stop looking.

"You gonna be okay?" Becca asks, her dark eyes flicking over to me.

I pull my knees up into my chest and shake my head.

"No. Nothing is okay."

Chapter Nineteen

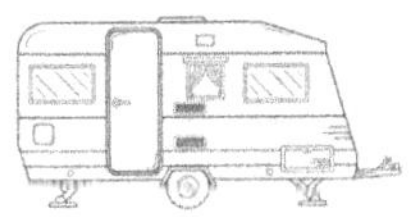

Grey

I spend the next two days in my camper, face down on the bed, Quinn's pillow tucked against my face, Winter whining next to my still form.

I'm in a bad way, a bad place.

Depressed is one word for it. Utter ruin might be a better term.

I did a bad thing and wrecked it all. And what hurts the most is not the angry texts from my ex-wife or the radio silence from my son, but the absence of Quinn.

I shouldn't have told him to go. I should have made him stay.

I should have kept one thing for myself, one goddamn thing, instead of pushing him away. But I didn't. I was too afraid of what it could mean, losing Joshua forever. But it didn't matter because I still lost Joshua. And now I've lost Quinn too.

"I made a mistake, Winter," I murmur, his one eye blinking sadly at me. I swipe at my cheeks which are damp from the tears. It's all I do now—just cry into his pillow like a sad sack.

"Shouldn't have let him go," I whisper, and Winter whines in agreement. He knows what's up. He's been silently judging me this entire time.

I don't blame him. At least he's stuck around. God, imagine if Quinn had insisted on taking him? I'd be all alone out here to wither and rot.

It says a lot about him that he didn't do that—that he didn't intentionally try to hurt me back, when it's obvious I hurt him. He had my back even when I didn't have his.

"You miss him, huh?" I ask, and Winter's tongue darts out and licks a stripe up my cheek.

I huff and turn my face into Quinn's pillow and inhale. The scent of him is disappearing and I am distraught over it.

"I do too," I say and then turn over and stare at the ceiling. Winter scoots over to me, placing his head on my shoulder, as if he's giving me a hug, and I wrap my arm around him, breathing in his doggy scent.

Fuck, I need to get up and shower...and move. I cannot just lie here forever.

I mean, I could. But poor Winter doesn't deserve that.

I let out a long exhale before I roll over and stand up. My body shakes from not eating enough the past two days, and I feel lightheaded. Stumbling into the kitchen, I pull out a box of crackers, stuffing a bunch into my mouth, swallowing as best I can. Crumbs litter my chest and fall to the floor, but I ignore them and move to the bathroom where I peel my clothes off and turn on the shower.

The water is scalding hot, but I suffer through it, washing myself quickly before brushing my teeth.

And when I feel somewhat more human, I make myself some coffee and sit down at the kitchen table to try and collect my thoughts.

I need to head home; I need to face this. I'm sure Karen will have something to say about it. I know she will. She's already blown up my phone the past few days, but I've ignored her calls and her texts. I can't deal with her right now.

When I get home, she can stop by and we can talk like adults.

And then I can figure out what I want to do about Quinn.

What the fuck do I want to do about Quinn?

I don't know. All I know is I miss him. And I worry that he's going to get tired of waiting and decide that I'm not worth it.

I may not be worth it.

I never have been.

I don't go home immediately, putting off the inevitable. Instead, I cart Winter up to Copper Harbor, where I'd planned to do things like kayaking and hiking with Quinn, but I end up just sitting outside the camper drinking, feeling worse with each passing hour. I should keep going, just finish off my trip, but I can't. I don't want to finish this journey without *him*.

I pack up the following day and head home, that Q dangling from my keychain winking at me each time I turn a corner. The pictures on my phone that Becca took while we hiked that day are seared into the front of my mind.

This was his intent, to force me to remember. And I do. I fucking remember it all.

This trip had started out as a way for Joshua and me to reconnect, but ended up with me discovering Quinn. And now it just feels empty without anyone to share the journey with. I'm so damn tired of being alone.

After the long drive home, I tell myself I should unpack the camper, but end up leaving most of it for later. I'm unmotivated, and honestly, it can wait. I have better things to do, like sulk. I flop down on my bed and try to sleep, only to wake up early the next morning, my mind full of the things I can't put off any longer.

I send out texts as I'm making coffee, and now that they've gone out, there's nothing to do but wait. I sit and wait for the responses that may never come, at least not from the people I want to hear from the most.

My phone finally buzzes midafternoon, and I glance down, my heart thumping frantically in my chest. I wanted it to be my son or Quinn, but it's Karen, demanding that when she stops by later, that I answer the door. As if I've ever ignored her in her entire life. If anyone had been cast aside in all of this, it's been me.

But I digress.

The fact is, I'm dreading this, dreading the confrontation.

But I know I can't hide away from her forever. I know that ignoring her the past few days did more damage than good, but I just needed time to process without her voice in the back of my head.

Walking out onto the front porch, I lower myself into a chair that overlooks the street, and memories of Quinn sitting next to me on my birthday all those years ago come flooding back.

He was just a kid and yet, even then he seemed to get me like no one else ever could. Not Kevin, not Karen, not bird-man Robert.

I lean my head back and breathe deeply, Winter lying down next to me.

And that's when I hear it, the slam of a car door, the familiar *click-clack* of high heels moving toward me. I peek over at Karen, seeing her curly brown hair perfectly situated over one shoulder, her lipstick red and neatly applied.

She's just as beautiful as she's always been, full of fire and energy...and anger.

I wince internally, knowing what's to come.

I stand up and shove my hands in my pockets, bracing myself.

"Grey," she says, her lips turned down in a frown, her arms folded across her chest. Oh, she's gonna blow.

"Karen," I say and let out a long breath.

"Josh called me and told me what happened," she begins, and I run a hand over my head, feeling ridiculously nervous.

"Yeah."

Her hands fly out in front of her, not trying to strike me,

but fluttering like angry wasps. "How could you! Seriously, Greyson. Quinn? He's only nineteen!"

"You and I were fifteen when we messed around," I say and then groan because that was the wrong thing to say.

"Are you saying you and Quinn have been going at it since he was *fifteen*?"

"Of course not!" I nearly shout. "I never looked at him like that."

"But you did on this trip," she hisses, and I sigh.

"Yeah. I did." I looked real hard too. Fuck.

So glad those words didn't seep from my mouth because now she's seething, her cheeks red, her eyes glinting with fury.

"Joshua is never going to forgive you for this."

"I already know that. If that's why you came over, you didn't need to bother."

But my words are lost on her. She's powering ahead, full fucking speed. "He was broken up about it. Quinn *punched* him," she says, her eyes wide, and I nod, swallowing roughly. Because I remember that moment distinctly, the sound of it, the way my son's eyes widened with shock, the dismay I felt for the friendship that is most likely broken beyond repair.

And it's all because of me.

"He did," I say softly.

She places her hands on her hips and then purses her lips.

"I cannot with you, Grey. Honestly, what kind of man are you? What kind of father?"

Something starts to itch deep down inside of me, and I shift on my feet. Quinn's words slowly filter up through my mind, the ones where he told me I'm a good father, that I'm worthy. I meet Karen's blazing stare, feeling suddenly fed up and defiant.

"I mean, honestly, you're all kinds of fucked up to do that to him. Your relationship was already rocky enough and then you go and fuck his best friend."

"He fucked me," I tell her, my voice low and Karen freezes. "He fucked me, Karen. I'm a bottom. Which you'd know if you bothered to *talk* to me. If you bothered to be a *friend* to me. I thought that's what we agreed upon when we split. That we'd stay friends, that things would be amiable, but you're so damn angry all the time."

She blanches and I clench my shaking hands. "I'm a damn good dad, despite you trying to make me out to be the bad guy. I am. You fucking know it too. You know I am."

Those words are but a whisper, but it's enough. The itch is vibrating within me now. I feel it pulsing through me.

"You know it and still, you chose to hurt me anyways. You did it because you could. So yeah, I fucked around with Quinn, but you've been degrading me to our son for years, Karen. Motherfucking years. So what does that make you?"

Karen hesitates, not used to me standing up for myself. I never was good at it, and I can already start to feel myself deflate. I'm done with this conversation. I just want her to go, so I can sulk and be lonely in peace.

"I'm sorry I hurt him. I didn't mean to. I know it was wrong, but at the time, it felt right..."

I sigh and run a hand down my face before meeting her flinty stare.

Her lips are pulled down into a frown, but she's silent, so I add, "Still feels like it was right."

She huffs and throws her hands up in the air.

"Goddamn you, Grey," she says, and I shake my head, cutting off whatever remark she was going to make. She's said her piece. Now we can move on.

"Can you come over and yell at me another time?" I ask, and she shakes her head as I move toward the door. "I just want to be alone."

"We aren't done talking."

"We are, for now. But you're right. We have things to discuss...like Joshua's college and the money you're going to put into it. It needs to be equal from now on, Karen. I'm tired of always shouldering the burden."

She huffs in frustration and disbelief. "I raised him. Without you. How's that for equal?"

"I would have too...if you had let me. I wanted my son in my life more than you'll ever know, and you kept him from me. You did it on purpose to be spiteful. And I always paid more than I had to because I felt guilty, but I want Joshua's college to be split between us. It's only fair."

"I can't afford it."

"You can, Karen. I know you can. You just want to punish me some more. And I'm done."

She scoffs, and I push the front door open to my house and step inside. Winter gets up, trotting after me like the loyal dog he is.

"We can discuss it more, but I'd appreciate it if you didn't spin this to Josh like I'm not going to pay for his college. I am, I just want you to help."

She rolls her eyes, and I shut the door in her face, leaning up against the wooden frame and breathing deeply.

I hadn't planned to say all that, but it felt damn good.

But now, I'm starting to shake, my entire body trembling with adrenaline and misery. I slide to the floor and press my face to my knees. Winter pushes his cold nose to my cheek and it jolts me out of my panic.

I can't believe I just did that. I can't believe I told her off.

Oh fuck, what have I done?

Chapter Twenty

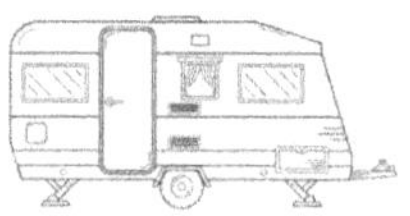

Grey

I half-expect to receive texts from Joshua about my conversation with his mother, but I don't. It's oddly silent. I'm not sure if that's because she didn't call him the moment she left or she did and he's just thrown me away with the garbage.

God, I hope it's the former. I don't want him to have given up on us because of Quinn.

Fuck.

Quinn.

My chest aches and I rub at it. Maybe I'm having a heart attack. Maybe the end is nigh.

I wouldn't put it past the Grim Reaper. Even he is probably mad at me, watching me all these years, shaking his head at all my bad decisions. Maybe it's time.

Blowing out a breath, I glance down at my phone, the unanswered text to Quinn staring up at me.

ME:

I'm home. Can we talk?

I haven't heard a thing from him. It's radio silence on his end too. I'd expected *something*. Anything. But perhaps now that he's had some time away from me, he's realized that I'm not worth it after all.

The thought drives me into a downward spiral, and I end up on my couch, watching wildlife documentaries. Nothing like watching live animals get eaten to really put things into perspective. It could be worse. I could be that water buffalo getting chomped on by a crocodile.

Though it does feel like my heart is getting chomped on as we speak. Masticated and death rolled.

Winter looks a little worse for wear too and I know he can sense how upset I've been. Maybe he misses Quinn just as much as I do. I should tell him. I am so going to use this as an excuse to get him to talk to me. Because Winter is technically *our* dog. He can ignore me all he wants, but he can't ignore his fucking dog.

In a moment of desperation, I pull my phone out and snap a picture of Winter looking forlorn and send it to Quinn with a comment that he misses him. I also ask if he'd like to take him for the weekend.

He can't ignore this, right?

The thought of being alone for days makes my heart clench. I don't want to be alone, but if this means I could see

Quinn, could talk to him, I'll be glad I did it. Even if it seems pathetic.

I just need to make sure he's okay.

I lay my phone on my thigh and my eyes drift back to the TV. Then I pick up my phone and stare at it. It's only been a few seconds, but the fact that my text still goes unread makes my heart sink. Ridiculous, I know. I'm thirty-three and yet, in this moment, I'm reduced to a fifteen-year-old boy desperately pining after his crush.

This is going to be a long-ass night if I keep this up. My phone will die soon if I keep checking it like I want to. Then what the fuck will I do?

I sit up and run a hand over my head, staring at Winter and then at the door.

I don't know much about where Quinn hangs out, but I do listen when he speaks. I know where he works and that he takes art classes at the community center. So, what the fuck do I have to lose by doing a little stealthy drive-by? Winter could do with getting out of the house, and if Quinn happens to see me, I'll have an excuse as to why I'm suddenly showing up where he is. Maybe Winter can lure him in with his sad eyeball.

Maybe I will be somewhat of an incentive, as well.

Goddammit.

Come back to me, Quinn. Or at least, answer my damn texts.

I drive around town for a bit, gathering the nerve to become a legit stalker. I need fortification, so I stop by the ice cream parlor and grab an ice cream cone. It ends up toppling onto my pants after two licks, and I don't even have a chance to salvage it because Winter lunges and gobbles it down.

I stare at the white splotch on my pants and then glance over at Winter, who looks mighty pleased with himself. I mean, I would be too if I got a free scoop of ice cream.

His tongue lolls out of his mouth and then he leans over and laps at my pants, smearing the ice cream right into my jeans.

Well, if this isn't just great. It looks like wet cum now. How the fuck am I supposed to properly stalk Quinn with dirty pants? What if he sees me and I have to get out of my truck? What will he think I've been up to? I look terrible. I look like Robert and his bird-shit shirt.

Oh fuck.

I glance at my face in the rearview mirror and see the dark circles under my eyes. I look like I just rolled out of a grave. Quinn will for sure want me now. What's not to love?

I wince and pat Winter on the head and then start up the truck, realizing I have nothing to lose now. I'm at death's door. So, I drive by his house first, and when I don't see his car out front, I drive by his place of work. His car isn't outside the pub either and I momentarily debate going inside and standing around like a real creeper, but decide against it. I have dirty pants, after all. At least my underwear is clean. I think.

I lean my head against the headrest and say to Winter, "At least you like me."

He wags his tail and blinks at me. I guess that's at least a maybe. He was probably won over by the free and unexpected ice cream.

"Guess I have nothing to lose," I say, trying to convince myself, and then drive across town to see if his car is parked outside the community center where he takes art classes. I know that he's mentioned it before and I'm hoping like hell that he's here. I just want to look at him, to fucking see that he's okay.

He left so suddenly. My broken heart just needs a peek, as a balm. Oh, who am I kidding? I need a full-on fucking body cast at this point.

But as soon as I arrive, I realize I've made a mistake of epic proportions. Because yeah, Quinn is here, but I don't know what I thought I'd find.

Quinn utterly wrecked without me? Miserable and lonely?

It's not what I find.

Not at all.

No, instead, I linger on the side of the street in my idling truck as I watch Quinn laughing and talking animatedly with another guy. A guy his age, by the looks of it.

He doesn't look nearly as upset as I feel. Nope, he looks damn good, so fucking perfect in those jeans and that loose shirt. And his hair, which is falling across his shoulders, looks like someone ran their fingers through it.

I don't know why I'm thinking it was someone else who rumpled him, but I hope like hell it wasn't. I can't...I can't fucking breathe.

I close my eyes and clutch on to the steering wheel, trying

to gain my bearings, but they're so out of control. I don't know how I'm gonna manage this. I'm a fucking wreck. I've never felt like this.

Never.

I peel my eyelids open and look at the scene in front of me—Quinn listening intently to something the other guy is saying.

Maybe it's nothing. Maybe this is all a trick of the mind. If I get out and move closer, maybe I'll see something on that face of his, something telling, something that shows me that this is nothing more than a friendly encounter.

I can totally think rationally about this. I can also behave like a logical adult. Maybe even introduce myself to this...guy. This friendly guy.

God, he's *overly* friendly—the way he's touching Quinn, the way he leans into him.

I turn off the engine and pull the keys from my truck, hopping out and walking around to the passenger-side door to let Winter out. I grab ahold of his leash, and he jumps down and sniffs at my pants, reminding me that they look god-awful.

Well, nothing to be done about it now. I'm just going to have to pretend it doesn't exist.

I am sex. I am *sexy*.

I sigh. Yeah, not working. I'm not. Not really. But I'd felt sexy when I was with Quinn. He made me feel...young and alive—like I was someone who mattered.

And I let him leave. Like a fucking coward.

"Come on, boy," I say, bending down and patting

Winter's head, and then forcing my gaze back to Quinn. I can be brave now. I know I can. I'll take what I want.

I tug on Winter's leash gently, pulling him forward. Quinn hasn't seen me yet. His gaze solely focused on the guy in front of him. I don't blame him. His ass is fantastic. I'm sure his front is even better. You don't have an ass like that and not have a nice dick.

I wonder if Quinn has seen it. Has he been with someone else? Has he really waited for me? Or has he forgotten about me already?

He couldn't have forgotten already, right? It's only been a few days.

But maybe he has. He's young and easily distracted. Although, he does have those sparrows tattooed on him. Steadfast.

There's nothing steadfast about the way he's talking to this guy and *smiling*. So much smiling. Almost like he wants him to kiss him. He's just showing off those lips, those red fucking lips. Like, *plant one on me*. I mean, he doesn't need to make them so enticing. They're already bad enough as they are.

I've stopped moving, my brain making me freeze. I stand like a statue in the middle of the parking lot, just staring at him, with Winter next to me tippy-tapping on his toes. He sees Quinn and probably wonders why he can't go straight to him. I should move, should interject, but suddenly I feel so inadequate. So damn old.

And I know that I'm not. That thirty-three isn't that bad, but fuck, in this moment, I feel like I've lived a thousand lifetimes. I can't compete with fabulous ass over there with his young face and his *energy*.

The guy leans forward and brushes his lips across Quinn's cheek and my heart pinches in my chest.

I grip Winter's leash tighter and make my decision.

I'm gonna go. I'm not going to stand in the way of something that could make him happy. And maybe that isn't me. Maybe it's this guy.

With one last look of longing, I turn on my heels and walk back to my truck.

If he wants me as much as he claims, he can come to me. I tried.

I'm tired of being burned by people who are supposed to want me but end up rejecting me.

Maybe this makes me more of a coward, but I fucking *tried*.

Chapter Twenty-One

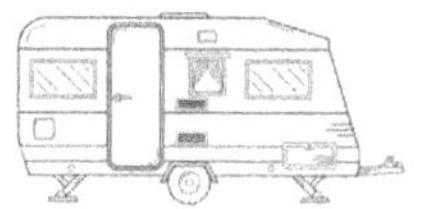

Quinn

This is misery. Four long fucking days and I've resisted texting him back by sheer willpower. Art class tonight was torture, my phone burning a hole in my pocket.

Tonight. I will answer those damn texts. I will fucking *cave*. I cannot stand it. I don't know how I managed to resist the temptation, but I did. I received some kind of divine intervention to do it. It's like my body aches without him, my heart just thumping away pathetically in my chest.

I'm only half alive.

When I left him in the UP, I needed time to process it all, but I'm *done waiting*. Enough time has passed and now I just want to know what he's thinking, what he's feeling. Obviously, he wants to meet to chat because he sent me those messages. Several, in fact.

It has to mean something, right? It has to be something *good*. He wouldn't have bothered if he wasn't interested.

I laugh at something Derek says, trying to pay attention to what he's saying. He touches my arm, and I swear to god, any other time I'd be into him, but my mind is solely focused on Grey. I miss him. I've been in a pit of depression since Becca toted me away from the campground. It took everything within me not to have her turn around and drive me back. I should have. I should have fought for him harder. I should have stayed and we could have talked about it.

Instead, I just ran—and sobbed—my way back to the Lower Peninsula. I've spent the past two days in a fog, lying under my covers, trying to figure out what the fuck I was going to do. Those pictures Becca took only cut me deeply. I stared at them for hours, *remembering*.

I knew going into this, pushing him like this, that something bad could happen. I knew there was a minute possibility that he'd reject me. But I didn't realize how bad it would feel when it actually happened. I feel like a piece of me is missing.

"You wanna come over tonight? We could just chill," Derek says, and I hold back a wince because I know that I could have him, but I don't want to spend the night with *him*. Instead, I want to drive by Grey's house and linger out on his street, staring at his darkened windows and wishing to see his face.

I've done this, I admit.

I've lingered like a stalker in the shadows outside his house. I haven't actually gotten out of my car, but I've sat there, emo music filtering through the speakers as I just communicated telepathically.

I miss you.

I almost convinced myself to go up to his porch and knock, to see if he was home, to ask him...no to *beg* him to let me inside.

To let me inside of him again.

But I resisted. God, it was hard. But I kept myself in my car and didn't fucking move. I seat-belted myself in so tight, my chest was constricted and it hurt to breathe. I got a boner and then wondered for a moment if I was into breath play.

God, maybe I am. I want to try it with Grey.

I want him to wrap those big hands around my neck and squeeze as I'm plowing into him.

It's been four long days and I don't think I can wait any longer. I'm going crazy.

Derek leans forward and presses a kiss to my cheek, and I rear back slightly, surprised that he did that. I hate the feeling of someone else's lips on me. They're not Grey's.

I only want his. Always his.

"Hey," I say with a small smile. I reach up and brush my hand against his cheek, trying to lessen the blow. Derek has been into me for ages, and I want to let him down softly.

"You know how I feel," I tell him, and Derek blushes, looking contrite. "I'm sorry."

He nods, pulling his lips between his teeth. "I had to try, you know?"

"Yeah. You gotta shoot your shot. I get that."

I do. I did this with Grey and I won. For a few days I'd had him.

Best fucking days of my life.

My hand falls to my side, and I sigh.

"But I have to go. I have places I need to be," I say and then step back.

And that's when my eyes catch on a familiar object in the background—a familiar truck. So many memories in that fucking truck.

The lights flip on, and I hear the rev of the engine.

I watch as it pulls away from the curb and onto the street, driving away with all of my hopes and dreams.

Fuck.

Oh shit.

What the hell did he just see?

Chapter Twenty-Two

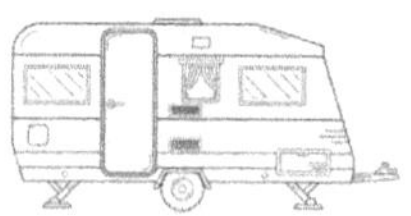

Grey

I don't go home right away. I take a nice long scenic drive across town and then park in a Walmart parking lot and people-watch. You can see a lot of weird shit go down in one of those. It distracts me from my heartache a bit.

When I finally head home, Winter is asleep on the seat, his head in my lap, and I'm exhausted—emotionally, mentally, and physically. I want to hibernate for the rest of the summer. I wonder if that would be possible. Maybe I should quit my job, pack up, and travel like Quinn suggested.

But then, the thought of traveling alone makes my heart hurt. I don't want to be alone anymore.

I pull my truck into my driveway, put it in park, and hop out. Winter clambers down after me, and before I can grab on to his leash, he bolts forward.

And then I see the shape of him. Quinn is sitting on my

porch, his head leaning back against the door, his long legs spread out before him. As soon as he hears the clang of Winter's leash, he bolts upright so quickly that he falls to the side and throws his hands out to steady himself.

"Quinn," I whisper and his eyes meet mine.

"Hey," he says, Winter jumping on him and wagging his tail excitedly.

I take a step closer, and then another, my heartbeat pounding in my chest. I can hear it in my ears, it's deafening.

Quinn starts to move his lips, trying to communicate with me, but I can't make out the words coming out of his mouth. I can't fucking hear past the white noise roaring in my head. God, I missed him. I fucking felt his absence.

"Huh?" I manage to ask, my eyes honing in on his lips. He wets them, and I feel like I'm going to combust.

Why is he so far away? Why the fuck is he all the way over there?

His breath stutters out of him and his hands clench into fists at his sides, and I want nothing more than to step into him, to crash against his chest and press my lips against his.

"You took a while to come home," he says, and I manage a small nod.

"Took a detour."

He lets out a shaky breath and uncurls his fingers. I can see the clay on them, those *fucking hands*. I want them on me.

It's all ruined anyways. What does it matter if I take what I want? What the fuck does it matter? Everything bad that could happen has already happened. I have nothing more to lose.

"I waited," he says and rolls those red lips between his teeth.

Don't take them away from me.

"I didn't know you were here. I thought..." my voice cracks and I inhale shakily, so fucking relieved he didn't go home with someone else. Someone that wasn't me.

He closes his eyes and shakes his head. "No. Never."

Our eyes lock and we move at the same time, our bodies colliding, my hands moving around his waist and pulling him into me. His hands clutch my face, dragging my lips down to his, kissing me desperately, his tongue slashing into my mouth —tasting, *owning*.

I whine as I reach down, needing him closer, needing him inside of me. I heft him into my arms and his legs wrap around my waist as we crash into the house. Winter falls in step beside us, but he goes ignored as the door slams shut behind us. I press Quinn up against the wall, grinding against him, feeling his cock swell against mine.

"Fuck," he murmurs, wrenching his lips from mine and trailing kisses down my neck, biting, licking, taking. "Fuck, I missed you."

I'm gasping and arching up against him, needing something only he can give me. And he's just as feral. He's practically clawing his nails down my skin, his teeth sinking into my neck.

"I want in you," Quinn hisses as he bites down on my shoulder so hard it stings. I arch back, and his lips leave me with an audible pop. I clutch on to him tighter and carry him to the bedroom.

When I step inside, I toss him onto the bed and shut the

door, pushing Winter to the other side so we can have some privacy. Because I need privacy for what we're about to do—for what I'm going to let him do to me.

Quinn watches me from the bed, his hair completely loose now and falling across his shoulders.

I rip my shirt off and shuck my pants as quickly as I can.

His breath comes out in short huffs, his pants tented as he watches me.

"All of it off," he says and I don't even hesitate. I just push my boxers to the floor and stumble toward him. He's propped up on his elbows, his bottom lip pulled between his teeth as I crawl up him, and then I'm ripping him out of his clothes, not able to stand another minute of not being against him, skin to skin.

It's been a miserable four days. Fucking torture. I want him around me, inside of me. Everywhere.

I hover over Quinn and he reaches down between us and pulls our dicks together, stroking them quickly, bringing me so close to the edge I almost topple over, but then he stops and lets go.

I gape, my cock bobbing out in front of me.

"Why'd you stop?" I ask, my heart thundering in my chest. "Please don't fucking stop."

"Should punish you," he says, his eyes hooded. "Should make you beg."

Well, my dick perks right up at that—doesn't seem like much of a punishment to me. More like a reward.

"Yes," I wheeze, and Quinn smirks up at me and then pushes me onto my back.

I fall back and reach for him, but he slips away.

"Lube?" he asks, and I point to the end table with a shaky finger because words have evaded me. He grabs it and the snap of the cap echoes around the room.

"Spread them," he says, looking at my legs.

I do as he says, pulling my knees up into my chest. He stares at my hole for a long fucking time before sliding two fingers into me.

My head arches back, my entire body thrumming with pleasure.

Fuck. Yes. This...this is what I needed.

I don't want to go another day without him inside of me. My eyes slam shut as I bare down, fucking myself against his hand, and when I feel his hair tickling my leg, I open my eyes and watch as he pulls my cock into his mouth.

And I lose all control.

I cry out, gasping as he bobs his head, hollowing out his cheeks as he attempts to pull my brains out through my dick.

My thighs clench around his head, holding him in place as he moans loudly, working me steadily to the edge until my balls are hard and aching, ready for release.

But before I can topple over, he pops off my cock and inhales deeply.

"Don't stop, please," I beg and he groans, running his hands up my thighs and pushing them once more onto my chest.

"You been with anyone else?" he asks, and I shake my head, nearly sobbing in frustration.

"Me neither. No one but you," he says as he slots his cock at my hole and slams into me.

The sting of it, the *ache*. I groan loudly, reaching out to grab on to him to keep me anchored. Because my soul is leaving my body.

He cants his hips back and slams into me again, and I shout, the windows nearly rattling from my cries.

"You didn't pick me," he huffs, as he fucks into me, almost violently. "You didn't make me stay."

I wrap my arms around him tightly, pulling him closer. Closer. Oh fuck, I need him. I fucking *need* him.

I can't even form the words to apologize because he's wrecking me so completely. I can't fucking *think*.

He leans down and licks his way into my mouth, biting painfully onto my bottom lip as he pummels my ass, and I just take it, like the winner I am.

I can give him this. I can always give him this.

"Don't ever fucking make me leave again," he groans as he picks up the pace, my cheeks wet from tears as he pounds into me. The bed creaks and rocks beneath us, knocking into the wall with each thrust.

My hands thread through his hair and I pull him into me, crashing our lips together once more. I don't want him to remind me of my faults. I want him present with me here. This is my apology, me begging for forgiveness.

I'm sorry, Quinn, I think as he fucks me, pushing me over the edge.

My orgasm crests as I explode across my abdomen, and Quinn lets out a strangled groan and follows me over, filling me up completely.

I twitch beneath him, coming down from the high of being fucked like that, of being pummeled so damn good. My body is so sore, wrung out, and impossibly ready to go again.

I stare up at him longingly and his gaze slams into mine, a collective shuddered breath escaping us at the same time.

"I'm sorry," I whisper, my throat hoarse from screaming.

He lowers his lips to my cheek. "I know. I am too."

We just stare at one another until he slips out of me, leaving me feeling distraught and empty.

He sits up and runs a hand through his messy hair.

"I didn't come here for that," he says, and I let out a shaky breath. "I really didn't."

"I know."

"But I saw you and I couldn't help myself. Even after what happened, I still find you sexy as fuck."

I swallow and wet my lips, wanting him to come back, to hold me.

He's silent for a minute, his hands fisting the comforter.

"Do you want me to go?" he asks, his voice cracking, and I shake my head.

"Stay."

That word. That fucking word. I should have said it before he left me in the UP. I should have said it sooner.

"Stay and shower with me," I tell him and sit up, my cum sliding down my chest and pooling on my limp dick. He watches it, his eyes darkening. Oh, he still wants me. Even after he's had me.

That's a good fucking sign. I can work with that.

"Yeah, okay," he murmurs.

I don't waste a second. I stand up on shaky legs, my ass twinging as I walk to the en suite and turn on the shower. As soon as it's warm, I pull him inside, under the spray.

We stand facing each other, our eyes locked. He reaches

out, his hands sliding up my chest, one coming to rest on my cheek, the other on my shoulder.

"You need to shave," he says, and I let out a huff.

"Guess so."

His fingers scrape through my facial hair. "Although, you do look good all rugged like this. I kind of like it."

"I can leave it, for you," I say softly, my eyelids drooping as he scours his fingers up and through the hair at the side of my head. Probably need to get a haircut too.

"I'll have to think on it," he says and then pulls my head down so his lips can settle on mine. He kisses me softly, pressing into me, pulling moans from my mouth. "You're perfect any which way."

I grasp him and hold him to me, licking my way into his mouth, desperate for him again.

But he doesn't give me relief, he just teases me until I'm whining again. Then he tortures me some more by running his hands across my body, washing me.

"Please," I nearly beg. Once wasn't enough, and I'm desperate for more.

But he doesn't give in, despite my begging. Instead, he rinses us off, turns the shower off, and steps out.

I'm just left standing, dripping wet and hard as a fucking rock as he dries off casually, like this was no big deal. Well, this might be news to you, Quinn, but my dick thinks this is a big fucking deal. It's feeling ignored.

"Come on, Grey," he says, holding out a towel to me. His eyes slip to my hard, straining cock for a second, so I know he sees it. He knows how desperate it is.

But I don't mention it. I just take the towel from him, my

words lodged in my throat, and for a moment, I wonder if he's punishing me. If he's drawing out my torture for not making him stay. I probably deserve it, if I'm being honest.

I follow him into the bedroom, holding my towel over my crotch as he throws on his pants and opens the bedroom door, letting Winter in.

Winter blinks up at us with his sad eye, and I feel guilty for leaving him outside the bedroom for so long. But then again, I couldn't have him watching—gets a little creepy at that point.

But I guess that since Quinn let him in, it means I'm not getting anything more tonight. I bite back a sigh of disappointment and pull on some boxers. But I'm not gonna complain. I'm just happy he's here. With me.

Quinn kneels down, his hands on Winter's head as he coos at the dog, and my heart just floods with yearning for him.

I want him so damn bad.

I don't know how he managed to turn me into this needy man, but he did. I need him. I *want* him. I don't want to go another day without him. I just don't know what to do about my son. I don't know how to repair what I've broken.

That's life though, right? We just fumble about, trying to make the right decisions. Sometimes we get it right and sometimes we don't. I just fucking hate it when I get it wrong. I feel like such a failure. I feel like a failure a lot.

It seems I got this thing with Quinn all fucking wrong when I let him walk away from me. I just don't know how to move forward with him. I don't know how to do this.

"He missed you," I say, and Quinn glances up at me, his wet hair sticking to his cheeks.

"Yeah, I missed him too."

I wet my lips, feeling suddenly nervous and not quite sure how to bring this up.

"You, uh, you can take him anytime you want."

Quinn's brows meet and he stands up, his arms folding across his chest.

And I just stand there with my hard dick, feeling suddenly so exposed.

"Is that so?" he asks, his words biting.

What the fuck did I say wrong? I scramble to figure it out as he narrows his gaze even further.

"Um, yes?" I ask and then blink a few times, trying to unscramble my brain. I mean, it's not really my fault. All the blood is in my groin right now. I can't be held responsible.

He lets his arms unfold and he takes a step toward me. One. Two. Until he's right in front of me.

His green eyes are stormy as he watches me—really peers right the fuck into my soul—and I start to squirm.

"Was this just a quick fuck for you?" he bites out, and I swallow.

"Wh—?"

"Was that what this was? Because if that's all this was, then I'm gonna go."

"I'm...what? I was just talking about Winter," I say, my voice cracking a bit.

He closes his eyes and lets out a sigh. "Yeah...but it's what was implied."

"What was implied?" I ask because I wanna know what I

insinuated. Someone needs to enlighten me. I'm not that smart.

"That we're gonna do this separately from here on out."

His words settle on me, and I shake my head. "I didn't mean it like that. I just...I meant that you can take him anytime you want. It doesn't mean...it doesn't mean that I'm asking you to stay away."

He almost sags in relief. "Oh."

"Yeah," I reply, and a smile quirks his lips up.

"Sorry, I read too much into that."

"Yeah, you fucking did. I'm not that sly, Quinn. I usually say what I mean."

He reaches out and pulls me into a hug, our bare chests crashing into each other.

"Fuck, I'm so relieved. I don't want to give this up, to leave. I don't fucking wanna."

I hold him against me, breathing in his unique scent.

"I don't want you to either. I want you to stay."

We hold each other for a little longer and then Quinn pulls away slightly.

"What about Josh?"

I swallow, my Adam's apple bobbing furiously. "Don't know what to do about that actually."

He rolls his lips between his teeth. "Yeah, me either."

Winter whines at our feet, and I reach down and pat his head. His tongue laps at my fingers, and I chuckle a little at his enthusiasm.

"Has he talked to you?" I ask, and Quinn shakes his head, looking suddenly sad.

"No, not that I blame him. I mean, I punched him in the

face..." I pull him back into me and he sighs against my neck. "I just lost my temper. The things he was saying about you..."

"I know."

"He'll come around. I know he will. He just needs time. And we can figure this whole thing out together," Quinn says. "But we need to do it *together*."

"Yeah, okay," I say, nervous about what the future holds, but knowing with certainty that I want to move forward with him in my life.

"Let's go to bed. I'm so fucking tired," he says, and I nod, following him underneath the covers and pressing against him, resting my head on his shoulder, my eyes slipping closed.

And for the first time in days, I feel like I'm home.

* * *

I wake up early, a throbbing between my legs sending an ache of need through me. God, I missed him when he was gone and now he's here. Quinn is fucking *here*.

Need him.

Need him.

I've been reduced to base needs right now. Getting relief is all I can think about.

I rub up against his side, my hand sliding across his chest, my lips against his shoulder. He smells so fucking good and feels like heaven. My fingers slide across his nipple and I feel it pucker at my touch.

My tongue slides up his neck as I arch against him, rubbing my hard, aching cock against his side.

"Mmm," he groans as he wakes up slowly, stretching seductively against me.

My hand has shamelessly found its way down the front of his pants, stroking his already hard dick. I want that inside of me. Now.

"Greedy in the mornings, aren't we?" he murmurs and I hump against him faster, desperate for some relief. He left me hanging last night, and I accepted my punishment. But now I'm just ready to blow.

"Hurry," I groan, my voice raspy from sleep and lust. So much fucking lust. I haven't been this horny for someone in forever.

Never, ever have I felt this way.

"Where's Winter?" Quinn asks and we collectively hold our breath, listening for his telltale snores.

We hear them across the room and Quinn lets out a relieved huff.

"He's asleep. But he'll wake up with all the noise you make. Let's go in the bathroom," he says softly.

He doesn't need to convince me. I get up so fast I'm light-headed and topple into the nightstand, knocking the lamp sideways.

"Jesus," Quinn chuckles. "Could you be any nosier?"

I whisper my apology and jog to the bathroom, just as Winter starts to get up.

"Hurry," Quinn says with a laugh as we skid into the bathroom. Winter lets out a woof just as the door is shut and locked.

"Just in case he can open doors," he says with a smile, and I just reach for him. It's dark inside the small space, the only light coming from the small window above the shower. But it doesn't matter. I don't even need to see Quinn. I just need to feel him, to sense him.

I just want him against me.

"You horny for me, Grey?" he asks, his voice low.

I swallow and nod as he backs me up against the counter and tugs my boxers off, my cock jutting up between us. His pants are hanging open, his cock pressing out from the denim, and I reach for it, but he swats my hand away.

"No," he says and I groan, my head falling back against my shoulders as I hump at the air.

"Hurry," I say again and he smirks at me as he pulls his dick out completely and pumps it a few times, watching me.

"Look at how fucking hot you are, Grey."

"Don't care about that," I murmur, feeling like I'm about to explode.

"I want you to know," he says, but I can't hear him. I'm just staring at his dick, watching the tip of his cock peek out of the foreskin with each downward thrust.

I eye it, licking my lips, wanting it in my mouth.

"Eyes up here," Quinn says, but I can't do it. I can't fucking move.

"Ah, so you wanna watch?" he says and I let out a shaky breath as he brings the tips of our cocks together. "I'm gonna dock you, Grey."

Oh my god.

"Fuuuuuck," I moan as he rolls his foreskin over the head of my dick, connecting us. Just one long dick. Goddamn. The feel of it, fuck. It's so damn *sensitive*.

"You gonna come in me? Fill me up?" he asks and I gulp,

nodding frantically as he starts to work his fist between us. It's slow at first, tentative, but he builds his pace, his hand working faster and faster.

"Oh fuck," he moans, looking down at where we're connected, his eyes hooded, his cheeks puffing out with exaggerated breaths. "Look at us."

I am. I fucking am. And I'm not going to last—just going to come in seconds. It feels so damn good. Oh hell, and seeing us connected like this makes me lose all ability to breathe. I've never done this before and now I know what I've been missing.

"Can't last," I moan as he leans forward and brings our mouths together. His tongue fucks into my mouth as he works me closer and closer to the edge. And the thought of my cum filling up his sleeve makes me nearly feral.

"Fuck. Fuck. Fuck," Quinn chants as he rips his mouth away from mine, and I dig my fingers into his shoulders so tightly I know that I'll find bruises on his skin. And I can't even fucking regret it.

I feel my balls draw up and I explode into him without warning, and Quinn gasps, his eyes wide as he finds his release as well. And then we stand there, chests heaving, his foreskin still stretched out over mine, filled and dripping with our release.

"Holy shit," he murmurs, and I swallow, my throat clicking. "Never done that before." I feel some kind of primal instinct well up within me. I was his first for something. His first for *this* and I fucking like that.

I love it.

His cock slips from mine and our mess splatters to the

floor. I release my tight grip from his shoulders one finger at a time, and Quinn smirks at me.

"Hot. So fucking hot," he says, leaning in and pressing a kiss to my lips. "Morning, Grey."

I bob my head and try to repeat it back to him, but it just ends up as gibberish. My brain is mush.

Quinn lets out a chuckle and then nods to the shower. "Let's shower and then I'll make you breakfast."

"Don't have any food," I murmur.

"Then I'll take you out to eat. Plus I need to grab some clothes from home if I'm gonna stay over here. That okay with you?"

I nod as he leans down and wipes our mess up, and then I follow him into the shower.

"We'll take this thing between us one step at a time," he says as he pulls me against him. "Baby fucking steps."

Chapter Twenty-Three

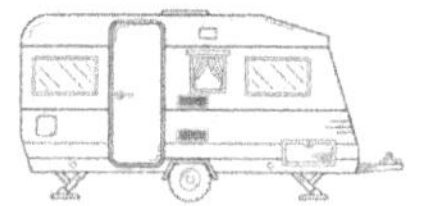

Quinn

"I'll stay in the truck," Grey says, and I eyeball him. We're outside of my parents' house, the truck idling on the street. Grey looks damn nervous and I don't know why. I mean, I guess I know why, but I don't understand it. I told him how my parents are. They won't give a shit what I do. If anything, they'll be happy I'm gone more often. They like their space.

"My parents probably aren't even home," I say as I take a large sip of my coffee. After our shower, we grabbed breakfast at a coffee shop and then headed over to my place so I could pack up a few things.

I mean, we didn't really talk about the fact that I'm planning on staying over, but I just made an executive decision and Grey hasn't stopped me so....

So I'm fucking going for it. Like I said at the beginning of all of this. I'm taking what I want and just making him accept that this is how it's going to be. I refuse to go back to being separated from him. Those days apart were torture. I'd lie awake in bed and just replay every moment with him in vivid detail. It was heart-wrenching.

"Come on," I say and shove at his shoulder a little. "Get out of the damn truck, Grey. I want to see you in my room. Maybe even give you a blow job while you sit on my bed."

"Not fucking happening."

I laugh loudly as I step out of the truck and Grey ambles over, looking nervous and so fucking hot. Can't help but reach down, link my hand with his, and tug him forward.

"Come on. Even if they're home, they won't care. You know how they are and they like you."

"I'm fucking their son," he mutters, and I waggle my eyebrows a little.

"I'm fucking you, Grey. If we're getting technical."

He blushes so prettily at that comment and I can see it so well. He shaved the scruff off his face this morning and I'm not sure which look I like more. I could take him either way. I like my man all hairy.

I pull Grey into the house and hear the TV on in one of the rooms.

"They're home," he whispers and I nod, smirking at him.

"I'm home, guys!" I call out and Grey's eyes widen in surprise.

"Fuck's sake, Quinn."

A laugh bubbles out of me, feeling so fucking happy for the first time in days. "Gotta rip the Band-Aid off."

He doesn't look convinced as my parents round the corner, their eyes flicking down to our interlocked hands.

"You're home early," my dad says, and I bob my head.

"Just grabbing some stuff. Gonna stay with Grey for a bit."

My mom's eyes widen in surprise, but then she schools her face and nods. "Of course."

I can tell they're curious, but they won't ask. Their whole premise for parenting has been to let me do my thing. I kind of wish they'd take more of an interest, to be honest. But whatever. As long as they're not giving me hell for this, I'm fine with it. Don't want any reason for Grey to pull away. I want to give him zero excuses.

"Nice to see you both again," Grey says, trying to pull his hand from mine, but I hold the fuck on. Like hell he's taking that away from me. I'm sticking.

"Likewise," my dad says and then slaps him roughly on the shoulder. "Take care of my boy, yeah?"

Grey stands a little taller and nods as I roll my eyes. Like they really care. I mean, yeah, I guess they do in their own way, but like, no need to put on a show, guys.

"Come on," I say, tugging Grey down the short hallway and into my room.

"Keep the door open," my dad calls out, trying to be funny, but Grey is wilting at the suggestion.

"Ignore him. He thinks he's a comedian," I say as I shut the bedroom door.

Grey looks unsure as I lock it.

"He was joking, for real. Relax."

Grey lets out a huff and looks around the space.

It's telling, a peek into my soul. My drawings are taped across one wall and some of my sculptures line the floor and shelves. My bed is unmade and my clothes are all stuffed into a hamper in the corner. Hmm, should probably get on that. I think my drawers are practically empty.

"Can I do some laundry at your place?" I ask and Grey nods as I grab a duffle bag from the closet and start stuffing it with stuff I need for the week.

"Yeah, of course."

As I pack he walks around the room, taking it all in, and I try like hell to focus, but my eyes are on his ass.

"I've had all sorts of fantasies about you in this room," I say suddenly, and Grey stumbles slightly.

"Shh," he says, trying to hush me, but my mouth won't be stopped. It's loose now.

"Don't shush me," I say with a smirk, and Grey flushes.

"Never did that before...sorry, just..." he sweeps his hand toward the door. "Your parents are *right outside*."

"They are not. They are back in front of the TV. They couldn't care less what we are doing in here."

He doesn't look convinced, but I'm not lying. They really don't care what I do.

"Come on, loosen up, Grey. Fulfill a fantasy for me."

He eyes me and then shoves his hands into his pockets. "What's this fantasy?" he whispers.

"Oh, now you wanna know," I tease and then let my hands fall from my duffle bag, and I run my hands up my stomach, my shirt riding up as I do it. Grey notices. He fucking sees. His eyes snap to the movement, to the exposed skin I'm showing him. His pupils dilate and his cheeks flush a little darker, and I know he wants to do it—wants to help me make my dreams come true.

"Wanna be bad with me, Grey?" I ask, and he swallows. "Remember, I have a lock on my door. I needed one for all those times I sat in here at night and jacked off to thoughts of you."

"Fuck," he murmurs, and I let my shirt drop, taking a step closer to him.

He lets out a low groan as my hands travel down his stomach and I grab on to his cock.

"You gotta be quiet though, or else my parents are gonna hear."

"Too hard," he grunts, and I smile widely, loving how unhinged he becomes. God, I missed that—missed hearing him scream my name.

I squeeze his cock gently and he huffs, wanting more, needing it. But I need to bring him so close to the edge that he's begging for my dick. I want that. I want him to think of nothing else but me.

"Wanna know what my fantasy was? I have so many, but the one that would keep me up at night, wanna know what that was?"

He nods, swallowing loudly. I move around behind him, my fingers trailing up and over his shoulder and down his back.

"I had this dream...you'd come over when my parents were gone and walk into my room and find me lying on my stomach, drawing. And you'd close the door. Lock it. And then you'd move toward me, those big fucking thighs..." I groan as I grasp them and pull him against me, his back now flush with my chest.

"You'd grab my legs, flip me over, and bring me right to the edge of the bed. Then those big hands would peel my pants off, you'd drop to your knees, and you'd suck me off. Just swallow me whole."

Grey groans as I palm his dick, rubbing it through the fabric of his jeans.

"You gonna do that, Grey. Gonna make me come?"

He nods, his head falling back against my shoulder. I stroke him a few more times, showing him how good this can be before stepping away and sitting on the edge of the bed, beckoning him toward me.

"Come here," I say and he moves, falling to his knees, his hands on my pants, tugging them down my thighs without hesitation.

"Oh god," I murmur as my cock bobs free and he leans forward and laps at it.

Then that mouth—the one that's so fucking quiet all the time, that just keeps everything inside—engulfs me and I arch up, my hands clutching his head as he takes me. Over and over until I'm moaning.

"Yes, just like that. Fuck, yes, Grey."

He's groaning around my length, his spit sliding down to my balls and leaving a wet spot on the sheets. But I don't fucking care because this feels insane, and I'm about to burst. This is all too much. This is all my fantasies come to life. I cannot believe he's on his knees for me...in my childhood bedroom. This cannot be real.

Tell me this is fucking real.

"I'm gonna come," I hiss, and Grey moans as I thrust up into his mouth, taking him hard. And then I'm coming, bursting into his mouth and watching as he swallows it down.

He sits back on his heels, his face a fucking mess, his hand down his jeans, pumping his cock.

He shudders, biting down on his swollen bottom lip as his body shakes with his release. He suddenly slumps forward, his eyes closed, his chest heaving.

"Oh fuck," he mutters. "Oh fuck."

I stare at him, my dick hanging limply out of my pants, feeling slightly dazed.

"I came in my pants, Quinn," he says, his eyes on mine. He looks slightly distraught. "In your parents' house. They're gonna know."

I bite down on my bottom lip, holding back a laugh. I know he's upset about it, but damn it's kind of funny.

He swipes at his wet chin. "I feel like a teenager, only I never acted this way when I was a teen because I was in the closet."

My hand reaches out and I touch his cheek, already feeling the stubble making a reappearance.

"You can have your chance to do all that stuff with me," I say. "We can experience it together."

He watches me intently and then sighs. "I need some tissues...for the mess I made."

A laugh bubbles out of me and I reach over, grab some, and hand them to him.

"Might need some new underwear too," he adds.

I stand up, tucking myself inside my pants, and toss him a

pair of my boxers. They'll be tight on him, but at least he won't be wet.

I watch as he changes out of his boxers, unable to peel my eyes away from that ass for long, but once it's covered back up, I resume packing. When we finally leave, Grey insists we sneak out, his underwear stuffed in his hand, trying to be discreet. Like he didn't just blow me in my bedroom with my parents down the hall.

Well, I'm glad he did that. He should experience what it's like to sneak around—to be a gay teen.

I'll be the one he does it with.

Ngh, he's so damn cute. I am even more obsessed with him now, his eyes wide and nervous as we tiptoe to the door.

When we finally make it to his truck, I throw my duffle bag into the back and beam at him.

"Ready?" I ask, my question lined with a deeper meaning.

"Yeah, Quinn. I think I am."

* * *

When we make it back to his house, it feels different. Awkward, almost. Last night and this morning were filled with lust and desperation, and now we're here alone in the house, not quite sure what to do with ourselves.

I set my duffle bag down in his room, and Grey leans against the doorframe, watching me.

"What do you want to do today?" he asks, shoving his hands into the pockets of his jeans. He looks bashful, so fucking cute. I pull my bottom lip between my teeth as I meet his stare.

"Well, you still have the week off, right?" I ask, and Grey nods. "I feel bad that your vacation was cut short."

"It's fine. Didn't want to stay up there by myself anyway."

I move toward him, my hands sliding up his chest, and Grey lets out a shaky breath.

"I'm glad you came home. I thought I was going to have to wait longer to finally see you."

His eyelids flutter as I reach up and cup his neck.

"You would have come to me?" he asks, and I nod, pressing my thumb against his bottom lip.

"I would have."

He leans forward, pulling my thumb into his mouth, and sucks on it, his cheeks hollowed out, his tongue sliding against my skin. And just like that, I'm ready to go again.

"Tease," I say, my voice husky.

I pull my thumb from his lips and smash my mouth to his. I press him back against the doorframe and kiss him until we're both breathless.

"Go on a date with me," I say, and Grey's fingers slide through the sides of my hair.

"Where?" he asks as I press my forehead to his.

"Does it matter? You have high standards or something?"

He snorts a small laugh, that mouth pulling up into a smile. "Nah, my standards are pretty low."

"Great, then I know you'll be impressed."

"I will."

My mind is already reeling, ready to knock him off his feet. Of course, I know that Grey has been on dates, but I want mine to be better than all of the others. I want his expectations to be blown out of the water. He deserves it.

"I can't believe you're just taking me back," he says, and I meet his stare.

"Of course I did. I fucking missed you. I was half a person with you gone."

"Same. But don't you think it's...that it's too fast?" he asks, looking worried.

I shake my head, wetting my lips, wanting to make him understand.

"Nah, Grey. It's been years for me. This isn't fast. This is the slowest I've ever moved."

He pulls me into his chest, holding me against him in a crushing hug.

"I'll try to be what you want," he says.

I press my lips to his ear and whisper, "You already are."

Chapter Twenty-Four

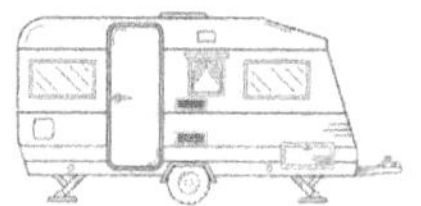

Grey

I'm nervous. You'd think I haven't been on a date before, but this seems different for some reason. Maybe it's because it's Quinn. Maybe it's because he's so much younger and we're going out where people can see us.

But despite it all, I'm kind of excited. Giddy. I feel like I'm a teen again and doing this shit for the first time.

I have no idea what he has planned, only that we spent the day in front of the TV while he scrolled through his phone. Winter was dropped off at his parents' because apparently this date is pet-free. He hasn't told me where we're going, but that I should pack an overnight bag.

This must be serious if he's planning an overnight, right?

Sounds pretty serious to me.

"So, I don't want you to guess where we're going, even if you know," he says and then bounces on his feet a little. "And when we get close, I want you to close your eyes and don't open them until I say so."

I nod my head, agreeing to whatever the fuck he wants.

"Sounds fancy," I say, and Quinn smirks at me.

"It kind of is. I mean, I'm not crazy rich or anything, but it's what I could afford."

God, this guy. I pull him into me and place a kiss on his lips.

"It's gonna be amazing."

"It so is," he says and then grabs my hand and leads me outside. "I'm gonna drive, okay? Just because I know where I'm going. And listen, there may be a chance I pull over and give you a blow job because I'm fucking horny, Grey, and I want your dick in my mouth."

My cock perks up at that. It has no reservations about that. None at all.

"Yeah, I'm down for that," I choke out.

"And I've never had road head, so if you wanna give that a go, I wouldn't stop you." He bites his bottom lip and leans toward me. "You could just lean over and suck me right down."

I can't even speak because now I'm all worked up.

"How long is the trip?" I ask, and he smiles at me.

"Oh, not gonna tell you that. Or else you'll guess."

He tosses our bags into the back of his car, and I can do nothing but let him drive me away.

We make it to a little B&B just outside of Sleeping Bear Dunes in a little under two hours, mainly because we had to stop and grab something to eat. And halfway into the trip, I did cave and bend over the console, giving Quinn road head. It was a bit uncomfortable and gave me a side cramp, but I still groaned like a whore during the whole thing. I'm so glad he didn't crash the car. They would have found me with a dick in my mouth and I'm not sure I could live that down.

Not that I'd care. I would be dead.

And I still came in my pants like a slut at the taste of him.

We had to stop and pull the car over at the next gas station so I could change my underwear. Quinn looked smug, and I just felt embarrassed. But honestly, I need to pack extra because I cannot help but explode like a volcano every time I'm near him. It's like I've reverted back to puberty again. I've traveled back in time.

"You look good blushing," Quinn said after I made my way out of the gas station bathroom, the underwear clutched in my hand.

"God," I murmured and he laughed, looking so damn happy, right before he leaned over and kissed me.

I felt that kiss all the way to the B&B, a quaint white house on the outskirts of town, with a large wraparound porch and fields of cherry trees lined up in rows. Just seeing it makes my heart swell with something I can't quite explain because he picked this just for us. For me.

"It got great reviews," he says as we trudge inside, his hand clasped in mine. He pushes the front door open and we are greeted with the sound of birds chirping loudly.

"Oh shit," I murmur, taking in the rows of bird cages

lining almost every single inch of the small living room. "There are a lot of birds here," I whisper, and Quinn bobs his head.

"This wasn't advertised in the post. It's like a motherfucking zoo," he says and then bites down on his lower lip, peeking up at me. "Are you freaked out?"

I shudder a little, not quite sure how I feel. Birds are creepy fuckers and they like to sing songs at you that no one asked to hear.

I could do without them, to be honest.

"As long as they stay in their cages," I reply, thinking about Tattletale and how he'd sit on his perch and watch as Robert fucked me.

Didn't like that so much either. Especially when he loudly proclaimed *three out of ten* after each round, like he was judging my performance. Once I got a six out of ten and felt proud. That's when I knew it had to end.

"Well, hello, you two!" an older woman says, meandering out of the back room, her hair a tuft of grey on her head, glasses sitting precariously on the end of her nose. She's wearing a long floral dress that swishes as she walks. A waft of perfume trails after her, and I feel myself start to sniffle. She really lathers it on. Probably bathes in it.

The birds flutter noisily around her when they catch sight of her, and Quinn lets out a small laugh at the sound. Well, he can laugh it up, but fuck, it's unnerving. This is straight-up Alfred Hitchcock.

"Are you Quinn and Grey?" she asks, and Quinn bobs his head.

"Yep, that's us," Quinn says with a wide smile, his hand squeezing mine.

The woman bobs her little head, her hair flopping around on top of it. It looks a bit like a nest. She probably lets birds up in there to lay eggs in her free time.

"Well, so nice to have you here. My name is Ginny. I run this place. If you need anything, you two just ask. Let me show you to your room."

We follow her up the stairs, the wood creaking beneath our feet. At one point, Ginny takes a step and her knees pop so loudly that I end up wincing. Fuck, she probably shouldn't be going up and down these stairs. She might get stuck.

"Sorry, just a bit slow," she says with a small laugh, and I can't help but smile.

"That's gonna be me in two years," I tell Quinn, and he rolls his eyes.

"Quit it, Grey. You're not as old as you think."

Ginny waddles over to a closed door and opens it, smiling widely at us. "There are towels in the bathroom and anything else you need, you just let me know. You two have fun," she says and then leaves, a small whistle leaving her lips.

"Think she was calling to her birds?" I ask, and Quinn snickers.

"Maybe. Maybe she controls them. Maybe we will wake up tonight and they'll be perched up in the rafters, watching us."

I give Quinn the biggest glower I can, but it's wiped away when he pushes me up against the wall and kisses me senseless.

"I love teasing you. You're so fucking cute."

"I am manly," I reply, and Quinn pecks me on the cheek.

"You are. And hairy. I love it." He groans, his fingers sliding down my chest before he adjusts himself in his pants. I wet my lips, thinking about that dick as he turns to take in the room. The walls are covered in a blue floral wallpaper and the queen-size bed in the middle of the room is adorned with a white comforter.

"This is cozy," I say, and Quinn grins over at me, looking so damn happy. He flops down on the bed, his legs sprawled out in front of him, and I just take him in, the lines of him, the shape. He's so damn hot.

I want to press myself down against him and *grind*.

"I mean, besides the birds, it's pretty great. Wanna just hang here tonight? There is so much I wanna do to you in this bed, and then tomorrow we can go explore. There's a trail that leads us over the dunes to Lake Michigan. Have you done it before?"

"Yeah. Once," I say as I move toward him and step between his legs. My hand runs along the top of his thigh, moving closer and closer to his hard dick, wanting so badly to touch, to feel. "But yeah. It's been a while since I've done the hike. I think that sounds great."

He arches his hips up, his breath coming out a little shaky.

"I could so go again," he whispers. "But we should probably wait until Ginny is asleep."

"And the birds," I tell him, and Quinn lets out a pained chuckle.

"Yeah, those damn birds. Fuck. I cannot believe how many she has. I swear I didn't know about those. No one mentioned them in the reviews. I mean, they said the chirping was beautiful, but I thought they were talking about the birds in the motherfucking trees," he replies, sitting up and running a hand through his hair.

Our eyes meet and he reaches out, his hand sliding across my hip.

"Hey, how are you feeling? Where's your mind at? You can be honest..."

"Oh, yeah, I'm um...I'm feeling pretty damn good."

"Not worried?" he asks, and I know what he's asking. Am I worried about Joshua? Well, fuck, I am. Just a little. Of course that's gonna be in the back of my mind. He's my son. But I feel more at peace now that Quinn is around. Now that I have him again. It's like things can finally move forward now that he's by my side.

"You sure you wanna be stuck with an old guy like me?"

He rolls his eyes exaggeratedly and stands up, pressing up against me. "*Old*. You're young, Grey. Stop being so dramatic."

I mean, has he met my knees? They're fucking fragile. But I don't say that.

"Now, come on. Let's grab a drink and sit outside. I just want to be with you for a while before we come back inside for the night and I wreck your ass."

I blush at that and let him pull me to the kitchen where Ginny makes us tea. And then we cradle our mugs and step outside into the cool summer air. All around us I hear the wind whipping through the trees and smell the scent of cherries in the air. It was evening when we arrived and now the sun is starting to make its descent in the sky. Fuck, it's romantic to just watch it set with him, to know that we are ending our day together and that tomorrow we will wake up in each other's arms.

It's simple, really. This is what I want.

We sit together on a white wooden porch swing, our hands entwined, our thighs pressed against each other's. He wraps a blanket around us and leans his head on my shoulder, and I feel so damn content.

God, I am so into him. How did this happen?

Well, I know how it happened. He captivated me—full on stole my heart. Maybe it all started years ago, when he first planted the seed—sitting with me on my birthday, bringing me cupcakes, listening to me so raptly each and every time we talked—and then it bloomed on our road trip. Just took root and blossomed.

And now I can't imagine my life without him. Which sounds insane. It's only been a few days. But has it really? Perhaps it's been years.

"I know I asked this, but is it weird that this is moving so fast?" I ask and Quinn leans up and shakes his head.

"Nah. Let me reassure you. It's just right, Grey. I couldn't wait another year for this to happen. I already waited until I was nineteen. I about died. My heart can't wait another minute to be with you."

I pull him in closer, so close he's almost straddling my legs. But that's fine. I want him on me, want him on my lap.

The swing groans and squeaks beneath us as we just cling to each other, our hearts beating in time with one another.

I bring his hand up to my lips and kiss those knuckles,

loving that they're never fully clean, that there is clay still caked on the tips.

"Love your hands," I say, my voice full of gravel. "I want to watch you work one day. Would you let me?"

Those green eyes slash up to mine. "Of course I would. I so fucking would," he says and pulls me down for a deep kiss.

I could get lost in it. I almost do but we're interrupted when a telltale squawk resounds near us. We pull apart and our eyes are drawn toward a familiar figure making his way toward us.

"For fuck's sake," Quinn grumbles as I let out a laugh. Because honestly, why the hell is Robert here? Wasn't he supposed to be in the UP? Did he return earlier than he planned? It's like he's following us or something, or perhaps the gods are conspiring against us.

"Grey?" Robert says, making his way up the front steps of the porch, Tattletale settled on his shoulder, eyeing us. "What are you doing here?"

"Could ask you the same thing?" Quinn grumbles next to me, sitting up straighter in the swing, his eyebrows pulled down in annoyance. He looks like he's ready to stand up and slap someone. Hopefully not the parrot. Don't want him in jail for animal cruelty.

"Just here on a getaway with Quinn, my boyfriend," I say, and Quinn's head swivels to mine. He blinks at me and blinks some more, obviously confused. Maybe I shouldn't have blurted that out. Maybe he doesn't want to be my boyfriend. Shit. Should have considered that. I always do this shit. I just can't help myself.

Robert frowns and Quinn turns to face him once more.

"Yeah, well, I knew you were boyfriends..." Robert says a little too snottily, and Quinn interrupts him.

"Why are you here, Robert?" he asks.

Tattletale shifts on Robert's shoulder and fluffs his tail out, probably taking a shit on that nice shirt of his.

"My aunt owns this B&B. I was traveling back and thought Tattletale could use a playdate. I'm not following you two. Don't worry."

I bite down hard on the inside of my cheek to keep myself from laughing. Because of course he is going to bring his bird for a playdate. I mean, I have to hand it to him, at least he's a devoted bird-dad.

Quinn purses his lips and then nods, obviously done with the chit-chat.

"Well, we won't keep you. Off you go. Tattletale is in need of some socialization...and so are you," Quinn quips lowly.

Robert frowns, obviously having heard Quinn, and the incredible need to laugh bubbles out of me.

I try to hold it in, I really do, but it just escapes, bursting out of me on a low wheeze.

"Fuck. Are you okay?" Quinn asks as I gasp for breath, my eyes tearing up from how ridiculous this all is. Goddamn Robert and his bird. This fucking week has been misery and now I've lost my mind; I'm completely unhinged. It cannot get any weirder.

I manage to squeak out a *yes* before bending over and laughing hysterically, my hands clenched on my stomach, my lungs searching for air. Robert hovers for a while, probably wondering if I've lost my mind, and then meanders inside, the chirps and squawks of the birds all coming together in a cacophony of sound, making me laugh even harder.

God, this is fucking crazy! How is this my life?

Minutes later, I finally calm down, swiping at my eyes and letting out a shuddering breath.

"Fuck, that felt good," I say, and Quinn smirks at me, his eyes twinkling.

"Well, I'm glad this whole getaway is providing you with some entertainment. Fucking Robert," he murmurs. "He did have shit on his shirt, by the way. Seriously detracts from those legs of his."

I pull Quinn in for a kiss, slipping my tongue into his mouth and groaning at the taste of him.

"I don't see anyone but you," I say once our lips are pried apart.

Quinn lets out a breath, his hands moving into my hair, clutching on to it.

"Love that it's longer now," he says, and I watch as his pupils dilate. "Wanna grab on to it while I fuck you. Fuck it. Let's do it now. I can't wait."

He suddenly stands up and pulls me up the stairs to our room where we lock the door, and I let him strip me out of my clothes.

I try like hell to keep it down, to muffle my cries, but I don't quite manage. I'm loud, brought to near tears, but Quinn doesn't mind. He says we should let Robert hear, let him know what Quinn can reduce me to. The birds seem to chirp louder with each of my moans.

And when we've collapsed on the bed—his hand

entwined with mine, my cheek on his chest—he lets out a slow breath.

"Boyfriends, huh? We official now, Grey?" he asks, and I smile.

"Yeah, Quinn. We are."

Chapter Twenty-Five

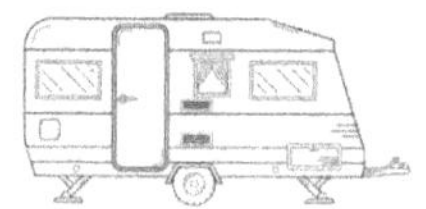

Quinn

I glance down at my phone and see a text from my best friend. Ex-best friend? I'm not sure. I'm surprised to hear from him, to be honest. My heart flutters in my chest because I've missed him and the thought of losing someone that has been by my side for so many years has kept me up at night.

But the thought of losing Grey is worse. I had a choice to make and I made it.

"What's wrong?" Grey asks, and I slide my phone into the pocket of my jeans. We trudged up the steep dune and walked down to Lake Michigan where we buried our feet in the sand and watched the waves crash against the shore. And now we're on our way back to the car to head to lunch.

"Just a text," I say, hating that I'm lying to him, but not wanting this to interfere with our date.

I just want a few more hours with him where he's not worried about Joshua. I just want him to be happy. And now that he's my boyfriend, that should be my priority, right? I am going to be the best fucking boyfriend he's ever had.

"From who?" he asks, and ugh, why does he have to look so damn curious.

"Do I have to answer that?" I reply, and Grey bites down on his bottom lip.

"It was Josh, huh?" he asks and my heart sinks in my chest because he looks so lost, like he doesn't quite know what to do.

"Maybe."

He turns his head and faces forward, and my stomach churns.

"I didn't want to tell you until later. I didn't want it to ruin things...ruin our day."

"You didn't. This was...this was really nice," he says and holds on to me a little tighter. "But I kind of want to know what the text said. Will make me worry if I don't know."

I pull my phone out and unlock it, handing it to him.

Grey takes it and glances down at the screen, his breath leaving him in a whoosh.

"He wants to talk?" he asks, and I nod.

"Guess so."

"What do you think he wants to talk about?" he asks, worrying his bottom lip. I come to a stop and reach up, touching his cheek gently.

"I'm sure it's about us. I don't know, but I promise to tell you everything."

Grey leans into my touch. "He hasn't texted me."

And there it is, the problem—the thing that sits between us so heavily—their fractured relationship.

"Yeah," I murmur, not wanting to give him false hope by saying that he surely will. Because I have no idea if he will. I'm surprised that he's reaching out to me so soon after our confrontation. I expected at least a few months to pass, for him to cool off before one of us reached out again.

Although, maybe that's Hailey. Maybe she is working some of her magic. I can only hope. Out of the two of them, she seems the most reasonable.

We trudge down to the car, our shoes in our hands, and then we sit on a bench and glance up at Sleeping Bear Dunes. I wish that Josh hadn't texted today, or that I hadn't checked my phone until later. I just wanted a day together where we weren't reminded of our fuck up.

"It will all be okay," I tell him, needing to believe it. "I know it will. It might take some time, but we did nothing wrong...well, maybe we should have told him right away, but we had our reasons for keeping it to ourselves."

"Yeah," he says and then reaches down and laces his fingers with mine. "We'll get through it. Together."

He bobs his head, his throat working, and squeezes my hand.

I have to believe it. I will believe it.

I'll do it enough for the both of us.

* * *

I meet Joshua the following day at a park outside of town. The air is muggy and hot and I'm already starting to sweat—

mostly from the weather, but partially from the fact that Joshua didn't tell me what we were meeting for. I asked, but he kept it vague. Probably his way of torturing me, of teaching me a lesson. Not that I don't deserve it, but still, help a man out. I know it has to do with our argument and the fact that I punched him, but I'm hoping that while we talk he's level-headed about it. God, I need to remain calm too.

I hope it doesn't end up like the last time.

I need to rein in my temper.

I stand under the shade of a large oak tree and pull out my phone, sending Grey a quick update. I don't wait to see his response before shoving it in my pocket, my heart already thundering nervously in my chest.

When I glance up, I see Joshua approaching with Hailey.

Thank god she's here. At least there will be a voice of reason.

"Hey," I say when they come to a stop in front of me. Joshua looks the same as he always does, a little rumpled, a little pouty, but I don't see anger stewing in the depths of his eyes. That has to be a good sign, right?

Hailey lifts her hand in a small wave and I return the gesture, trying to calm my nerves. Joshua and I have never argued like we did last week. We've never fought. I've always been the clearheaded one of the two of us, so I'm sure my outburst threw him for a loop. Punching him in the face didn't help either. Yeah, I shouldn't have done that.

I fiddle with the earrings in my ear and shift on my feet, the silence almost as thick as the humidity surrounding us.

When neither of us say anything, Hailey sighs, playing with her long braid that's draped across her shoulder.

"Well, I'll start then since you're both chatterboxes. We wanted to meet...well, Joshua wanted to meet to apologize." Joshua eyes his girlfriend, a frown on his face but he doesn't stop her from continuing on. "To make amends. He realizes he overreacted."

I don't say anything, just watch my best friend carefully.

"And we were hoping that you could tell your side of the story and perhaps offer an apology as well for blowing up and punching him in the face."

I roll my lips between my teeth and nod my head.

"I can do that."

Joshua pouts like a child and then rolls his eyes. "Fine, I'll start since I told Hailey I would. I *am* sorry. I mean, my eyes didn't need to see what you were doing to my dad..." His voice trails off and he swallows. "But I realize I overreacted."

I let those words sink in and my heart swells at the attempt he's making. It gives me so much hope.

"And I am sorry for punching you, but the things you were saying..."

Joshua narrows his eyes and Hailey holds up her hands.

"No *buts*," she says. "You are *best* friends. You need to start acting like it."

Those words hover between us, and Joshua peeks over at me and mutters, "Best friend who's sleeping with my dad."

"Josh," Hailey hisses, and he shuffles on his feet like a petulant child.

"Sorry...it's just...ugh, so gross. He had his dick in his mouth!"

I roll my eyes and say, "It's not gross to me. I like dicks in my mouth."

Joshua looks over at me and his lips quirk up. "Keep that to yourself, man. But I mean, look at it from my perspective. Do you want to see your dad getting off?"

I shudder. "Nah, I get it. Fair enough."

We stare at each other for a moment and then Josh nods his head. "Still friends?"

I don't even hesitate. "Sure."

Hailey's head swivels between us and then she sighs. "Honestly, men. I swear. It is not this easy with girls."

We both smirk at her and she rolls her eyes to the sky.

"You gonna talk to your dad?" I ask, because this is what matters the most to me. I want Grey to be happy.

Josh shrugs and Hailey huffs. "Yeah, he is. Josh texted him right when we got here. We're going to stop by his place on the way home. I think things need to be said and worked out between them."

Joshua looks like he'd rather have all his teeth pulled, but I'm so damn glad that Hailey is making him do this. Grey needs some closure. It's been eating at him. I can see it in the way he drifts off in thought, in the way he worries his bottom lip until it's raw and swollen.

"Seems my mom has been keeping some stuff from me," he mutters, and I feel my chest tighten. "You were right."

I nod my head because I want to shout that *fuck yeah I was,* but manage to contain it.

"You with him?" Joshua asks, and I nod my head. "Like are you two together?"

"Yeah, we're together."

He eyes me and then runs a hand through his hair. "You happy?"

"Yeah. We are."

He purses his lips and sighs loudly. "It's fucking weird. Really fucking weird, Quinn."

"I've been into him for ages," I explain, and Joshua's gaze slashes to mine.

"Yeah, and that's weird too."

"Can't help that your dad is a babe," I say with a smile, and Joshua slaps a hand over his face, a nervous laugh bubbling out of him.

"God, stop it, Quinn. Jesus. Like, slowly transition me into this, alright? Because it's weird as fuck and I'm trying to get my bearings. But...I realize you did nothing wrong. And Hailey helped me see that as long as you're not harming anyone, that it's fine... I just... I don't want to lose you...you know? If things go sideways with you and my dad."

"I mean, I'm pretty serious about him. I plan on sticking around forever. I mean, you'll be my best man at the wedding."

"Jesus, you're thinking about getting married? You're nineteen."

"Yeah, well, when you know, you know."

Joshua eyes me in disbelief and runs a hand through his hair, mussing it even more. "We good? I don't want to leave for college with things still weird between us."

"Yeah, we're good," I say and then add, "And please give your dad a chance. He...he loves you so much."

"Yeah, I realize that," he murmurs and then nods to Hailey. "We are gonna go meet him now. You gonna be there?"

"Can I be?" I ask, and Joshua nods.

"I mean, yeah, you probably should be. You're like boyfriends now, right?"

I bob my head. "Yeah."

"Then you should be."

Chapter Twenty-Six

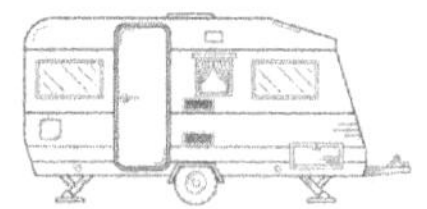

Grey

I am sweating bullets and already had to change my shirt —twice—because my son is coming over to talk to me and I feel faint.

Where is Quinn? Why hasn't he answered my panicked texts?

I gulp down some water and then gulp down some more, choking loudly when the front door opens and my son steps through.

With Quinn.

Neither are talking, but god, they're both here.

Water dribbles down my chin and I swipe at it, feeling suddenly so damn inadequate. How did I ever manage to be a father? I'm not qualified. I should have taken classes or gotten some kind of book. I should have tried harder.

"Hey," I say, and Joshua lifts his hand in greeting.

I brush the moisture from my shirt and make my way toward my boyfriend and my son.

It seems they worked things out between them because they're not fighting. That's good, right? That means they've talked, that they're friends again. God, I hope so.

"Came to talk," Joshua says and then shifts on his feet. "Came to say that I talked to Mom and she told me some stuff."

My heart pounds in my chest. "What kinds of stuff?"

Quinn moves toward me, reaching down and taking ahold of my hand. He squeezes it and Joshua's eyes dart to the entwined fingers and then back up to my eyes.

"Still weird," he murmurs, but then shakes his head. "Anyways, yeah, Mom told me all the shit you've done for me over the years. I mean, she didn't *willingly* tell me. I had to pry it out of her, but yeah...I didn't realize."

I feel my eyes start to sting and I blink them furiously. Cannot cry. Will not blubber.

"I'm sorry you were left out," he says, and I swipe at my cheeks. Well, hell. There I go. Can't stop me now.

"And yeah, Quinn and I talked. Just...I'm fine with it...or I will be. Just don't fuck when I'm around. It was...I can't unsee that shit, you know?"

"Yeah," I say, and Quinn leans over and hands me a tissue. I blow my nose, and blow it again, trying to contain my emotions, but I feel so fucking relieved.

"I'm sorry we didn't tell you," I say and my voice cracks. "I didn't plan for it to happen..."

"Yeah, well, I guess you deserve to be happy...Hailey helped me see that. After everything Mom told me...it wasn't fair to you. We weren't fair to you. I get if you don't want to help me with college—"

"I am helping you pay for college," I interject, my tone firm. "I just wanted your mom to help too."

"Yeah," he says and runs his hand through his hair. "We'll see if that happens."

We stare at each other, and I feel my shoulders sag. "Tell me if it doesn't. I can find a way."

He nods as Quinn leans into me. My hand goes around his waist, and I press my face to his temple, inhaling him.

"You want to stay and hang out? We can order food? Play some games?" Quinn asks, and Joshua shrugs.

"Um, yeah, let me get Hailey. Maybe we can stay for a bit. Don't want to see too much PDA from you two, though. Need to slowly work myself toward all that, you know?"

"Yeah, yeah," Quinn says, and Joshua smirks at him.

After Joshua moves outside, Quinn stands before me, his hands on my cheeks.

"It all worked out," he says softly. "I told you."

"Thank you. For not giving up on me."

"Never," he says softly. "I told you I'd wait. I'd wait a lifetime for you."

I blink, my eyes stinging once more, and I pull him in for a long-drawn-out kiss. When we pull apart, his lips are wet and red, and god, I want him. But we need to restrain ourselves because Joshua is going to come back inside any minute and I don't want to scare him away. Not when I've just gotten him back.

"I think things are gonna be okay," I whisper, and Quinn nods, his hands holding me tightly.

"Yeah, Grey. I think they fucking are."

Epilogue

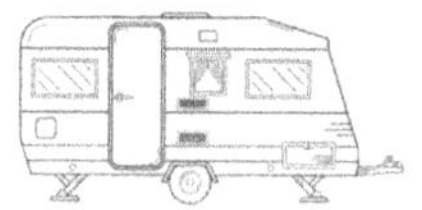

Two Months Later

Quinn

Grey is spread out on the table, completely naked except for those thin-as-fuck boxers, the outline of his dick taunting me, and it is making it hard to concentrate. I'd paid the owner of the studio a hefty fee to use the space after hours for this project, and holy hell, I am not regretting it.

What I am regretting, however, is letting Grey wear boxers while I try and sculpt him.

"Take them off," I blurt, my hands coming off the clay and pointing shakily toward his groin. "Take off the boxers."

Grey's eyebrows lift, and he blushes prettily.

"But you're in the middle—"

"Don't care," I interrupt.

"What if someone sees?"

"No one is here," I say, adjusting myself in my pants. God, they're too tight. I should have worn sweats, not these damn jeans. They're like a damn compression sleeve, but I like the way Grey looks at me in these pants, so I thought I'd suffer through. Well, I'm suffering now. "I locked the door. Take them off. I want to suck your dick."

Grey looks suddenly shy and I groan, moving toward him and grabbing on to the fabric covering the good bits. I yank it down roughly and the waistband gets caught on his delicious ass.

"Hips up," I mutter, and he does as I say. Thank god. I don't think I'm strong enough to actually rip the fabric. It would be far too embarrassing to try. Now, Grey, on the other hand, could rip shit apart. He has. He'd been so desperate at one point last month that he tore me out of my clothes, literally. Buttons had gone flying, seams ripping. I almost came on the spot with how hot it was.

I made sure he screamed that night as a thank-you.

Tossing the boxers onto the floor, I run my hands up his hairy thighs, feeling the muscle bunch underneath my palms.

"God, I wanna fuck you, right here on this table."

Grey lets out a low moan, and I lean forward and kiss him. "Yes, be as loud as you want. I want my ears to ring with your screams."

My hand moves to his straining cock, and I pump it, feeling it jump in my grip.

"I've imagined this," I say as I glance down and see my clay-caked fingers encircling his dick. "I've imagined you being here, just like this. God, Grey, you've made all my dreams come true."

He moans as I lean over and pull him into my mouth, savoring the taste of him, the feel of him on my tongue.

He's crying out now, panting and groaning, his hands clutching my hair roughly as he fucks into my mouth. And it's all too much. I reach down with a free hand and pull myself out, emptying myself onto the floor of the studio just as Grey explodes down my throat. We both just collapse, my cheek on his thigh, his hands still in my hair.

"Goddammit, Quinn," he huffs, his words shaky.

"I couldn't help it. You looked so sexy. You've been torturing me for hours."

And he has, I haven't gotten enough of him. I knew it would be like this. I knew it. I am insatiable when it comes to this man. My man.

I glance up at him, and he swipes some of the mess from my cheek. Some of *his* mess.

"I love you," he mutters, and my heart picks up in my chest. We haven't said those words yet, even though I've wanted to. I've wanted to say them for years. But I've been waiting for him to say it first.

I needed him to say it first.

"You do?" I ask, pushing myself up and leaning into him.

He nods his head, his cheeks flushing an even darker shade of red.

I run my lips across his jaw, feeling almost faint. "Since when?"

"Since...for a while. I've known for a while."

I kiss him deeply, my tongue slashing into his mouth,

feeling my cock already perking up once more. God, I just want to go home and have him ride me. Yes, that's what I want.

"I love you too," I murmur against his lips, my hands on his cheeks, holding him to me, forcing him to look into my eyes so he can see. "I have always loved you. You're mine, Grey. *Mine.*"

He moans at that declaration and then pushes me away, turning onto his hands and knees and arching his ass out toward me.

"Show me," he says lowly, and I smirk. "Show me how much you love me, Quinn."

Yeah, I'll fucking show him. I'll show him who owns him.

Me, motherfucking me.

Epilogue

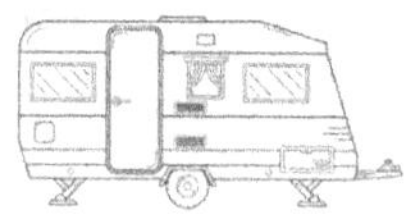

4 Years Later

Grey

"You ready?" Quinn asks, glancing up at me, his eyes full of excitement. God, he's so damn handsome. He's only gotten better with age, I swear. I don't know how I got so lucky.

I glance back at my house, the door locked for the final time, the "Sold" sign out front, signaling that this part of my life is over. It's time to start a new chapter, maybe even a new book.

It's about damn time.

I'm ready to start living, to really start living my life for me. I feel like I can now that Joshua has graduated from college and has a good job. Things are better between us, better than they've ever been. He makes a trip up with Hailey every few months and we spend the weekend together. I cherish those times. I feel like we've finally gotten the chance to really get to know each other. For the first time in my life, I feel like a real dad.

Things are back to normal with him and Quinn too, almost like nothing ever happened. The two of them hopped back into their friendship almost seamlessly. If I hadn't been there years ago to see the fallout, I never would have believed it even happened. But it did, and in a way, I'm glad that those things were said because I feel like it all gave me a fighting chance—with Joshua and with Quinn.

I glance down at my hand and see the glint of the gold ring there.

We got married at the beginning of this summer. Quinn finished up his final business class at the community college last semester, and we knew it was the right time.

Joshua was the best man, and he actually cried. He was sniffling so bad I had to stop and hand him a tissue. Not that I wasn't blubbering like a baby too. I was a wreck. I never in a million years thought I could be this happy.

And now that college is over with and Quinn has been successful at selling some of his art online, we finally have enough money set aside to do some traveling. We're gonna see the country together and I just can't wait.

"Ready for our next adventure?" Quinn asks, kissing my jaw and then nibbling up to my ear. "I can't wait to fuck across the states. When we make it to California, we are fucking on the beach."

I let out a huff, surprised that he's still into me after all this time. But he's unwavering, loyal to a fault.

And I am so in love with him.

"Yeah," I say as we move toward the truck, the trailer attached to the back. Winter trails along next to us. He's old now, in his last days. It's probably our last trip together, but he's had a good life. A happy one. "I'm ready. And we can discuss sex on the beach. Sand could get places. I don't know if my ass can handle that."

He rolls his eyes and bites down on his bottom lip. "I think I can convince you."

Yeah, he probably could. I'm a slut for it, apparently.

Quinn scrambles into the cab and buckles himself in, the rumble of the truck engine pulsing around us. Winter sits down in the back, his eye closing for a long nap. Pulling away from the curb, I turn to glance at my husband, my hand on his shoulder.

"We're starting our life together, Grey. I'm so fucking ready."

"Yeah," I say with a smile. "Me too."

Acknowledgments

First, I would like to thank my editor, Angela O'Connell, for all of your hard work on this book. You always have the best suggestions

Also, thank you to my alpha reader Lark Taylor for always being so helpful. And Nicole Dykes and Lily Mayne for encouraging me to publish this.

Thanks also to Margaret Neal for reading through this and catching all the mistakes we missed.

And last, but not least, thank you to all the readers who reached out to me with words of encouragement. They mean everything and keep me writing.

About the Author

Cora Rose loves any kind of romance and consumes way too many books each year. She currently lives in the U.S. and spends her days daydreaming about the characters inside her head.

You can reach her on her website or email her at CoraRoseRomance@gmail.com

Also by Cora Rose

The Unexpected Series

Whit

Sem

Emery

Luke

Lex

Colin

Diablo

The Inevitable Series

Until Him

Always Him

Unlucky 13

Exception